Blood Sacrifice

Books by Michael Lister

(John Jordan novels)
Power in the Blood
Blood of the Lamb
Flesh and Blood
The Body and the Blood
Blood Sacrifice

(Short Story Collections)
North Florida Noir
Florida Heat Wave
Delta Blues
Another Quiet Night in Desparation

(Remington James novels)
Double Exposure

(Merrick McKnight novels)
Thunder Beach
Spring Break

(Jimmy "Soldier" Riley novels)
The Big Goodbye
The Big Beyond

(Sam Michaels and Daniel Davis Series)
Burnt Offerings
Separation Anxiety

(The Meaning Series)
The Meaning of Jesus
Meaning Every Moment
The Meaning of Life in Movies

Blood Sacrifice
Michael Lister

a novel

2-19-14

Pulpwood Press

You buy a book. We plant a tree.

Inquiries should be addressed to:
Pulpwood Press
P.O. Box 35038
Panama City, FL 32412

Lister, Michael.
Blood Sacrifice / Michael
Lister.
-----1st ed.
p. cm.

ISBN: 978-1-888146-95-0 Hardcover

ISBN: 978-1-888146-96-7 Paperback

ISBN: 978-1-888146-97-4 Ebook

Library of Congress Control Number:

Book Design by Adam Ake

Printed in the United States

1 3 5 7 9 10 8 6 4 2

First Edition

For Jeff Moore
A true and faithful friend,
a brother in spiritual and artistic adventures.

Thank You
Linda, Jill, Amy, Adam

Chapter One

I was walking along the bay, searching for serenity, when the first body was discovered.

It was a cold December day, especially for North Florida, and the breeze blowing in off St. Ann's Bay stung my face and brought tears to my eyes. The sun was out, and though it was bright enough to make me squint, the day was dull and had a grayish quality I associated with the muted colorlessness of winter.

Taking a break from the demanding duties of prison chaplaincy at a maximum security facility, I had come to the small coastal town of Bridgeport following the second breakup of my marriage, which had come on the heels of two homicide investigations that had taken more out of me than I had realized.

Raised in a law-enforcement household and working as a cop to pay for seminary, I found myself continually getting involved in investigations. Though chaplaincy was draining enough, it was dealing with crime day after day as an investigator that had left me depleted and depressed, unable to deal with the second death of my marriage.

I had been fighting a losing battle against a powerful undertow, but rather than drown I had washed up on the shores of St. Ann's Abbey, a secluded retreat center among the ubiquitous slash pines of the Florida Panhandle. Now, it was no longer just my pride or career or even my marriage, but my very soul I was trying to save.

A crime scene was the last place I needed to go, but from the moment I saw the flashing lights near the marina, I found myself moving toward them—irresistibly drawn, like an addict, to that which threatened to destroy me.

I glanced behind me. The shoreline was nearly empty, only a few early morning walkers in the distance—senior citizens in pastel warm-up suits from the look of them. Without thinking about it, I picked up my pace and moved deliberately toward the emergency lights and the crime scene beyond them, the damp sand clinging to my tennis shoes as I did.

The first person I encountered near the entrance of the marina was a pale young police officer with a sparse beard, a round face, and an extra fifty pounds.

"Hi," he said. "Can I help you?"

Far too friendly and eager to help, he was one of the few cops I had ever encountered who erred on the side of serving.

"First crime scene?" I asked.

He glanced back beyond the emergency vehicles to the other officers, detectives, fishermen, and EMTs swarming the body.

"Not really *at* this one," he said.

"You'll be at more than you want to before you retire or resign," I said.

"I don't know," he said. "We don't get too many 'round here. You a cop?"

"Not anymore," I said.

He nodded.

Beyond him, the massive metal skeleton of Bridgeport's abandoned paper mill stood still and quiet, rising out of the fog like the rusting remnants of a former, less sophisticated civilization. Scheduled for demolition in a few days, soon the largest symbol of dying old North Florida would be no more.

"Looks like they could use some help," I said. "I better get on up there."

"I can't let you go—"

"Is Steve Taylor still the chief here?" I asked.

"You know him?"

"He was a deputy for my dad over in Potter County a lifetime or two ago."

"Your dad Jack Jordan?"

I nodded. "I'm John."

"Well, I guess it'd be all right for you to—"

"Thanks," I said, pushing past him before he realized what he was doing.

"Hey," he said.

I turned around to face him, my eyebrows shooting up.

"If your dad ever has any openings . . ."

"I'll put in a good word for you," I said. *Dad likes hiring guys who can't even keep a crime scene secure.*

"I'm datin' a girl from over there."

"Lucky her," I said, and continued walking.

"No. I mean that's why I want to move. Hey. Don't you need my name?"

"I got it from your name tag."

"Oh," he said, and looked down at his shirt.

While he studied his shirt, I hurried down the dock, its weathered and splintered planks creaking beneath me as I did, the early morning fog adding to the perpetual dampness provided by the water, and I could feel the sticky moisture on my skin and in my hair.

Past the police cars and ambulance, the small body of a young man was splayed in a spreading pool of water, his wet clothes and hair clinging to his body and the dock, the small group of officers and EMTs gathered around him. I couldn't tell for sure from this distance, but he resembled one of the troubled teens I'd seen at St. Ann's.

"The hell you think *you're* doin'?"

I looked up to see one of the officers walking toward me. He had the muscle-turned-fat build of an aging jock, but he carried himself as if he were unaware of the metamorphosis that had taken place in his unsuspecting body.

I stuck out my hand. "I'm—"

"I don't care who the fuck you are. This is a crime scene. Get outta here 'fore I arrest your ass."

"I think I know him," I said.

"The floater?" he asked.

I looked at the body again. No way he was a floater. Not only were there no signs of fixed lividity, but the body had yet to begin to decompose.

"Floater?" I asked.

Ordinarily when a person drowns, his or her body sinks to the bottom, head, hands, and feet hanging down, and stays there until decomposition causes gas to form in the tissue, making the body rise to the surface.

"The dude we found in the water," he said slowly, shaking his head. "You know him?"

"I think so," I said. "But he's not a floater."

"The fuck you talkin' about?" he asked, glancing over his shoulder at the others, who returned his look of incredulity and his laughter. "We fished his ass out of the water."

"You may have, but he wasn't floating at the time."

He turned to the others again. "Believe this guy?" Turning back to me, he said, "The hell else do you do in the water?"

"Sink."

"Sinking, floating, all I know is he sure as hell wasn't swimming," he said. "You know him or not?"

"I need a closer look?"

"Of course you do," he said. "You a reporter?"

"Prison chaplain," I said. "I'm staying at St. Ann's and I think I saw him a couple of times in chapel."

"Well, you won't be seeing him there anymore—except maybe at his funeral. Take a closer look so you can get out of here."

As I approached the body, the small group backed away from him slightly. When I reached him, I knelt down and said a prayer.

"Is it him?" Muscle-fat said.

I nodded.

"What's his name?"

"Thomas I think. They called him Tommy Boy."

"Thanks," he said, his tone dismissive. "'Preciate it."

"Where'd you find him?"

"In the water."

"But not floating," I said.

"Look, I'm sorry I called him a floater. I didn't know you knew him."

"It's not that," I said. "It's—"

"You really need to go so we can get to work."

"Where'd you find the body?" I asked.

"It was caught in the net of a shrimp boat," a thick-bodied female EMT with short, wiry hair and a large, not unattractive face said.

"Thanks," I said. "Have you already gotten a temp for the body, the water, and the air?"

She shook her head. "We just got here and were told to wait for Chief Taylor."

"You need to go ahead and take them. They're crucial in establishing time of death in a drowning."

"Listen," Muscle-fat said, "we've been patient with you, but you've got to go before the chief gets here. We've got the floater situation under control."

I'm not sure exactly why I did what I did next, but I suspect it had something to do with the deteriorated, self-destructive state I was in. Without really thinking about what I was doing, I scooped up the body and tossed it back into the bay.

"What the fuck are you doin'?" Muscle-fat said, as the others gathered around me.

The body made a splash when it went into the water, ripples moving out from the entry point, but long after the water was smooth again, the body had yet to resurface.

I took in some air through my nose, and the briny smell of the bay filled my nostrils.

We all stood there for a long moment, watching the spot where the body had entered the water.

"Guess you weren't dealing with a floater after all," I said.

"And didn't have it under control either," the female EMT said to him.

Kicking off my shoes, I dove into the cold water and retrieved Tommy Boy's body. Lifting him up as far as I could, the others took hold of him and had him lying on the dock again by the time I was out of the water.

"Arrest his ass," Muscle-fat said to the middle-aged officer standing closest to me. "And radio the chief."

I turned and held my arms behind me and Middle-aged snapped on the cuffs, led me to his car, shoved me into the backseat, and slammed the door.

Chapter Two

"The hell you thinkin'?" Steve Taylor asked.

He was leaning over, looking down at me through the partially opened window of the patrol car, his spotless, wrinkle-free uniform fitting as if it were made for him. All his clothes looked that way, and it wasn't just that he was trim and muscular. It was the way he wore them—the way he carried himself, the razor-thin line he walked between confidence and cockiness.

"That your officer's too much of an idiot to know he wasn't dealing with a floater," I said.

His pale blue eyes widened under arched brows. "And you couldn't've just told him?"

"I did," I said. "Several times."

Steve and I hadn't gotten along when we both worked as deputies for my dad. It started out as a personality conflict with an unhealthy dose of competition, but eventually escalated into dislike because of disagreements we had over cases we worked together.

"Heard you became a chaplain," he said.

I nodded.

"I'd hoped that meant you'd changed, but you haven't. Always gotta be right. Never were a team player—even when it was your dad's team. One look and I would've known that body hadn't been in the water long enough to be a floater."

He was right. I was wrong. It was obvious, but I couldn't bring myself to say it, to apologize to him for potentially destroying evidence or giving a defense attorney reasonable doubt on physical evidence alone. What I had done was yet another sign of just how badly I needed to be at St. Ann's. It didn't happen too often, but occasionally I would do something so unexpected—especially to me—act out in some erratic way, that it let me know I had far more to deal with than I wanted to believe.

Opening the door, he said, "Come on."

Without uncuffing me, he led me back over to the body. Like Tommy Boy, I was still dripping, my soaking clothes clinging to my body, but unlike him, I was feeling the bite of the breeze. He wasn't feeling much of anything at all.

The others gathered around us.

"Listen up," Steve said. "I know most of you are new and haven't had much experience, which is why I told you to wait for me to get here. We're not gonna have a lot of homicides or suicides or even accidents around here. Hell, we don't have a lot of anything— which is why we live here, right?"

"And why we'll be moving if Gulf Paper gets its way," Muscle-fat said.

The others laughed, but like the shrieks of the gliding gulls all around us, the sound was quickly carried away by the wind.

Since the paper market had softened and the paper mill had closed, Gulf Coast Paper Company, now the Gulf Coast Company, the largest landholder in the state of Florida, was in the process of developing some of its 900,000 acres of Panhandle land into resorts, golf courses, gated communities, condominiums, and other sins against the unspoiled beauty of the one part of Florida we had always naively believed was Disney and Spring Break proof.

For almost six decades, the Gulf Coast Paper Company had supervised its Panhandle acres in an unsurprising fashion, growing and harvesting pines and turning them into pulp at its mill in Bridgeport. It had quietly ruled a barely visible backwater empire of fast-growing slash pines, loggers, and paper mill workers, but times had changed, and in the new economy, the land itself and not the trees or pulp or paper had become the commodity.

Soon the Forgotten Coast of Florida would be anything but, and a way of life would become as extinct as the endangered species sacrificed in the temple of tourism to the American god of greed.

"Every time we have a suspicious death," Steve continued, "it's an opportunity for you to learn more about investigative techniques."

Each of them nodded, fully concentrating on Steve's sage-like words.

With sun-bleached blond hair and deeply tanned skin, Steve looked more like a waterlogged surfer than a respected chief of police, and I could tell by the way the women responded to him that most of them found him intensely appealing.

"Now," he continued, "someone tell me why this victim is not a floater."

"Because he didn't float," the female EMT said.

"Uh huh," Steve said, "but *why* didn't he?"

Standing there, shivering in the cold breeze, hands cuffed behind my back, I felt embarrassed, foolish, and frustrated, all of which were quickly turning to anger.

"He didn't float," Steve said, when no one was able to answer his question, "because he hasn't been in the water long enough for decomposition to begin and gas to form in his tissue causing him to float up to the surface. So, as our friend from Potter County pointed out, a body in water is not necessarily a floater."

"If he hadn't gotten caught in Eli's nets . . ." Muscle-fat said.

"It would have been a while before we found him," Steve said. "Gas forms faster in warm water and more slowly in cold water. Ours aren't as warm as they usually are, but they're not freezing either, so it would have taken days. All of this helps us establish time and ultimately *cause* of death. Speaking of which, are we dealing with a homicide, suicide, or accident?"

When no one in the group gave more than a shrug, he turned to me.

I shrugged too.

"You mean you don't know everything?" Muscle-fat said.

"I figured you were about ready to reveal the killer's identity to us by now," Steve said.

"With drownings—if that's what we're dealing with—it is extremely difficult to determine the cause," I said. "That's why it's so important to do things the right way from the very beginning."

"Like tossing the body back into the water?" Muscle-fat asked. "That's something they never taught us."

I didn't say anything. I deserved that and a lot more, and I would just have to take it.

"You guys see any signs of lividity on his face or hands?"

They all strained to look, but there was none to see, so they shook their heads.

"Why would we expect to see some?" Steve asked me.

"Because, Professor Taylor," I said with as much sarcasm as I could muster with chattering teeth, "when a body is in the water, its extremities hang down toward the bottom."

"So the fact that there aren't any signs of lividity means what?" Steve asked the others.

"He hasn't been in the water long," the female EMT said.

"Which is what we would expect to see in light of the fact that he wasn't found floating," Steve said. "There's also no signs of violence on the body, and since suicides by drowning are very rare, we're probably dealing with an accident, but let's keep an open mind while we investigate and wait for the autopsy report."

They all nodded.

"That okay with you?" Steve asked me.

I gave him a small smile and nodded, but didn't say anything.

"I think his mouth's frozen shut," Muscle-fat said.

"That's too much to hope for," Steve said, "but he does look a little blue. Better get him back in the car."

This time Muscle-fat himself escorted me to the car and shoved me into it. After slamming the door, he rejoined the others around the body, where they stayed for a long time, talking and laughing and waiting for the medical examiner to arrive.

Since I had been at St. Ann's, I had been undergoing counseling with Sister Abigail, and as I sat alone in the backseat of the patrol car, all I could think about was what she would make of all this.

Chapter Three

"You did *what?*" Sister Abigail asked.

I told her again.

"And you were arrested?"

I shook my head. "Steve said something about the embarrassment and humility doing more for me than a night in a jail cell could."

I had run into Sister Abigail on the way to my room to change into some warm, dry clothes, and she had insisted I tell her all about it first.

"Let's hope he's right," she said with a glint in her eye.

In her midfifties, Sister Abigail's pale skin, extra weight, and wispy reddish-blond hair made her look older than she was, but her wit and the wicked twinkle she often got in her eyes made her seem much younger.

"Let's," I said.

"You scaring yourself yet?" she asked.

"A little," I said. "Yeah."

"Good," she said. "If you weren't, you'd be scaring me."

Presently, St. Ann's Abbey was a cross between a spiritual retreat center, a psychiatric treatment facility, and an artists' community, but it had once been a very exclusive theological seminary and prior to that a Spanish mission.

Dedicated to art, religion, and psychology, St. Ann's was operated by Sister Abigail, a wise and witty middle-aged nun who supervised the counseling center, Father Thomas Scott, an earnest, devout middle-aged priest in charge of religious studies and spiritual growth, and the acclaimed young novelist Kathryn Kennedy, who was responsible for artistic studies and conferences.

Surrounding the small but ornate chapel at its center, St. Ann's consisted of two dormitories—one on either side—a handful of cabins down by the lake, a cafeteria, a gym, and a conference center with offices.

The natural beauty of St. Ann's was nurturing, and I found myself breathing more deeply as my eyes tried to take it all in. The small lake was rimmed with cypress trees, Spanish moss draped from their jagged branches. Enormous spreading oaks and tall, thick pines grew on the gently rising slope coming up from the lake, on the abbey grounds, and for miles and miles in every direction.

"Lucky for you, this is a slow time for us," she said. "Why don't we move our little visits to twice a day?"

Our "little visits" were actually counseling sessions to help me deal with my divorce, the death of my potential family, and the overall miserable mess I had made of my life.

It was a slow time at St. Ann's because it was early December and most everyone was already away for the holidays. Now through March was also off-season, the time when the least amount of visitors came to St. Ann's, which was what had appealed to me most.

"You sure seeing me twice a day won't be too much for you?" I asked.

"I think I can handle it, but if I have to, I can always call in backup."

Continuing past the chapel, we turned toward my dorm. As we did, I caught a glimpse of Kathryn Kennedy down near her cabin. She had her laptop out on the porch and was clicking away between sips of coffee.

She was a gifted novelist and one of the reasons I had chosen St. Ann's. Her work had entertained, enlightened, and inspired me, and I kept telling myself it was her writing and not the mysterious figure in the author photo that was the main attraction. I had yet to meet her, but hoped to soon—and to tell her what her books had meant to me.

"Why doesn't she wear a habit?" I asked.

"Kathryn?" she asked, her head still down, and it bothered me that she knew who I was referring to without looking up. "She's not a nun. She was a novice for a while, but she's never taken any vows."

I nodded and looked away, trying to seem only mildly interested.

Between our shoes and the sandy soil, fallen pine needles and the exposed roots of the giant trees made the ground slippery and treacherous for someone of Sister's age and weight, and we walked slowly, my hand lingering near her arm in case she slid or stumbled.

"She might as well have taken them, though. She lives as cloistered as I do. Such a lovely girl. Shame she's so lonely." Stopping suddenly and turning to me, she added, "You're not the type of man who would take advantage of a lonely young woman like that, are you?"

I shook my head.

"Too bad," she said.

I looked at her. "What?"

"Tell me," she said, as she started to walk again, "do you think young Tommy drowned accidentally or killed himself?"

Why had she waited so long to ask about him?

"I'm not sure," I said. "But I'll be happy to look into it for you. With drownings it's difficult to determine, but I can at least narrow it down to a likely scenario."

"Aren't you here because of how badly you've been affected by the homicide investigations you've conducted?"

"In part, yeah, but—"

"What do you think getting involved in one now would do to the therapeutic process? Why do you think I was hesitant to even ask you about it?"

The cry of a loon across the lake drew my attention in time to see Tammy Taylor and Brad Harrison emerging from the tree-covered trail at the water's edge. The narrow path cutting through the thick woods twisted around the lake and was used for meditative strolls or less lofty pursuits, as in the case of Tammy and Brad.

One of a handful of troubled teens undergoing both spiritual and psychological counseling, Tammy looked sixteen, though I was told she was at least three years older. Harrison was thirty-something and the abbey's handyman—and not the only person at St. Ann's that Tammy wandered into the woods with on a regular basis.

"What's the abbey's policy on sexual relations?" I asked.

"It's generally frowned upon," she said.

Though the libidinous couple was walking several paces apart, they were still straightening their clothes and arranging their hair—something that brought a disapproving glare from Sister Christine King, a small, boyish young nun near the chapel, and Keith Richie, the much-tattooed cook enjoying a smoke beside the dumpster at the back of the kitchen.

"I think I can handle it," I said as we started walking again.

"Sexual relations?"

"Looking into Tommy Boy's death. This isn't exactly prison. It's not someone I knew. It'd give me something to—"

"Take your mind off what you really need to be dealing with?" she asked.

"But don't you want to know what happened to him?"

"Are you the only one who can tell us?"

"No. Of course not."

Streaming down through the trees, the midday sun dappled the uneven ground, but couldn't completely remove the chill from the air.

"But you think the chances of finding the truth are better if you're involved?"

"I do. Is that arrogance or confidence?"

"Something to think about," she said.

"So much to think about."

"Father Thomas worked with Tommy for a long time," she said. "He's going to be devastated. I don't think you should work the investigation, but you *could* help me tell him what's happened."

Chapter Four

"Do you believe in the devil?" Father Thomas asked.

While waiting for him, I had begun perusing the vast library in his study, and was flipping through one of the many texts on demon possession, exorcism, and Satan when he walked in.

The question caught me off guard and I hesitated before responding, trying to come up with something to say. "Looks like *you're* the expert on that."

"Evasive, but not untrue," he said.

Father Thomas Scott was a thin man with receding gray hair, a neatly trimmed gray beard, and kind brown eyes that shone with intelligence. His body, like his voice, was soft without being effeminate, and his black suit and Roman collar hung loosely on his narrow frame.

Turning to see Sister Abigail in the corner when she cleared her throat, he said, "Why Sister, what're you doing skulking about back there?"

"We need to talk to you, Tom," she said, "and not about the devil."

Suddenly, there was a chill in the overcrowded, musty room.

"Sister would have us believe that there's no such thing as spirits," he said to me. "That everything's in our minds. All we have to do is get some counseling and we'll all be fine."

"And Father thinks the devil made us do it," she said.

"What do you think?" Father Thomas asked me.

"That I don't want to get in the middle of an argument

between the two of you."

"Evasive, but not unwise," he said.

Though there was no visible sign of it, I knew Father Thomas was a pipe smoker. Beneath the musty smell of the dusty books and the mildew odor caused by Florida humidity, the sweet ripe-raisin aroma of pipe tobacco lingered in the still air.

"But she's a nun."

"But not a sixteenth-century one," she said.

"So Christ performed exorcisms because he wasn't as enlightened as you?"

"Can we not do this right now?" she said.

"I'm afraid we've got some bad news," I said, stepping between them.

"What is it?"

"I'm very sorry, but—"

"Yeah, yeah, yeah, just give it to me," he said. "No need to soften the blow for me."

"Tommy Boy is dead," Sister said.

"What?" he asked in shock. "No."

He looked over at me and I nodded.

"Are you sure?" he asked. "I just saw him."

"We're sure, Tom," Sister said.

"When? Where did it happen? How?"

"We're not sure yet," I said. "His body was found in the bay this morning. I'm very sorry."

We were all silent for a moment, and I watched as the realization seeped into his face.

"Do you have any idea what he was doing near the marina?" I asked.

"We didn't come to ask questions," Sister said.

"No," Father Thomas said, ignoring her. "None."

"Did he strike you as suicidal?"

He shook his head. "She's the expert, but I don't think so."

"John," Sister said, and I felt as if at any minute my knuckles were going to be rapped with a ruler.

"When's the last time you saw him?" I asked.

"I thought we agreed you weren't going to do this," Sister said.

"I've got to . . ." Father Thomas began, as he made his way

over behind his desk and dropped into the chair.

Sister Abigail walked over to a credenza in the corner, opened a cabinet, and withdrew a bottle of Irish whiskey and a tumbler. Walking over to his desk, she placed the glass before him and poured a couple of fingers of Jameson.

"Here," she said.

"Thanks."

"There's no ice," she said.

"Don't need any," he said, then turned up the tumbler and took a big gulp.

I was close enough to smell the whiskey, and I could almost taste it as it went down his throat. Seized with a sudden urge to grab the bottle and take a long pull on it, I took a step back.

As if reading my mind, Sister screwed the cap back on and said, "Sorry."

Of course she didn't have to read my mind to know what was on it. I had sat for hours letting her probe its dark corners with the bright penetrative light of her insight and intellect.

"That's right, you Protestants don't like alcohol, do you?" Father Thomas said.

I wasn't sure I was any more a Protestant than anything else. In fact, I wasn't sure they had a word for what I was, but it didn't seem worth mentioning.

"Actually, this one likes it too much," I said.

He nodded and gave a small appreciative smile.

"I realize this is difficult, but do you know of anyone who would want to hurt Tommy?"

He shook his head.

"John, I must insist you stop right now," Sister said.

"Me too," Steve Taylor said from the doorway.

We all turned to see him. He was shaking his head at me.

"Wasn't it just a few minutes ago you almost got locked up for interfering in an official investigation?"

"You'd think one day I'd learn," I said.

"Why should you be any different?" Sister asked.

"Don't tell me people don't learn from their mistakes, Sister," Steve said. "That they don't change. I couldn't bear it."

"Come on, John," Sister said. "Let's leave these two to their own devices."

"I probably should stay for the questioning," I said.

Steve and Sister objected simultaneously.

As Sister and I started to leave, I turned back to Father Thomas. "I'm very sorry for what's happened."

"But not enough not to come in here and start interrogating him first thing," Steve said.

Chapter Five

When I got back to my room, Tammy Taylor was waiting for me.

The dorm rooms at St. Ann's didn't have locks. They were constructed for young seminarians who supposedly had no need for privacy. Of course, I would think few people needed as much privacy as young, isolated, testosterone-teeming seminarians.

She was sitting on the edge of my bed, her feet spread apart on the floor, a too-thin cotton dress stretched across her lithe body. Since young seminarians were entering a life of suffering, there was no heating in the dorms, and the cold room revealed that the cotton-clad Miss Taylor wasn't wearing a bra.

She gave me a sheepish smile.

The small room was just barely bigger than a six by nine prison cell, and there was no way for both of us to be in the room without being close to one another. Leaving the door open, I stepped across the bare cement floor and over to the dresser in the corner—the only other piece of furniture besides the twin bed—and began to gather some clean clothes.

When I was finished and she still hadn't said anything, I said, "Are you lost?"

Running her fire-engine-red fingernails through her bottle-blond hair, she said, "Aren't we all?" in a soft, airy voice. I was surprised to see the quality of her manicure and dye-job and wondered how and when someone like her went to the salon. "Isn't that why we're here?"

"Arguably," I said—because she was probably right and I couldn't think of anything else to say.

"Being lost can be fun, though, don't you think?"

I didn't say anything.

She wriggled her ass on the bed slightly. "Is it unsafe to be lost in your room?"

I shook my head. "Not for you."

For a moment, she looked as if she wasn't quite sure if what I had said was a compliment or a putdown, and her forehead furrowed as she tried to figure it out.

"Didn't Jesus say you've got to get lost to get found?" she asked.

"Something like that, yeah."

As if she were an actress reciting lines, her soft, airy voice, blank, wide-eyed stare, and slow, unsure movements didn't match what she was saying.

"Well?" she asked.

"Well what?"

"You wanna get lost?"

I shook my head. "But you feel free to."

"I meant *with* me, silly."

It was as if I were dealing with two different people. One showed signs of intelligence, saying things that bordered on the sublime, the other so deficient, I wasn't sure how she dressed herself.

She stood and closed the distance between us like a cat stalking its prey. Her skin was smooth and pale, and she wore colored contacts that made her eyes an unnatural too blue shade.

"You sure?" she asked, grabbing my arm with her hands.

I nodded.

"I'm a wild ride," she said, a flash of what appeared to be intelligence momentarily replacing the shallow, unfocussed glaze of her pale blue eyes.

"Well, it was nice talking to you," I said with no attempt to hide the insincerity or sarcasm, "but I really need to get back to fasting and praying."

"Some only come out by fasting and prayer," she said in a voice that didn't seem to belong to her.

I recognized the quote from the Gospels. It was something Jesus said about certain demons possessing people. They wouldn't come out except by prayer and fasting.

"What?" I asked.

"But I won't come out even then," she said in that same altered voice.

Suddenly, goose bumps were covering my body and a shiver ran the length of my spine.

"Down girl," Kathryn Kennedy said from the doorway.

Without acknowledging Kathryn, Tammy said, "If you change your mind . . . I'm not hard to find."

She then turned and strolled out of the room, forcing Kathryn to stand aside to let her through the doorway.

When she was gone, Kathryn stepped in and said, "Hey, Joe, thinking about giving it a go?"

I smiled and shook my head. "Negative."

"Too easy?" she asked.

"Too a lot of things," I said.

She smiled. "I don't think we've been introduced. I'm Kathryn—"

"Kennedy, I know," I said. "I read your books. I'm John Jordan."

Unlike Tammy, Kathryn's nails were unadorned, her long light blond hair didn't come from a bottle, and if she wore any makeup at all I couldn't detect it. In contrast to the boy-body-with-breasts so popular in our current culture, Kathryn was soft and curvaceous, a throwback to a generation or so ago when women looked and felt like women.

"Didn't Sister Abigail tell me you're a prison chaplain?"

I nodded.

"That must be exciting."

"Sometimes," I said. "And sometimes it's like Tammy."

She smiled. "*Too* exciting?"

"Too a lot of things," I said.

"Speaking of which, sorry to have interrupted. I think you were almost in there."

"You really think I had a shot?"

"I *am* sorry for just dropping in like this, but I heard about poor Tommy. Is he really dead?"

I nodded. "I'm sorry."

"So many of the at-risk kids who come here have less than

happy endings, but I really thought Tommy might defy the odds. He was so talented."

"You knew him pretty well?"

"In addition to undergoing counseling with Father and Sister, the kids are offered lessons in the artistic discipline of their choice. Most don't do anything. A few take a lesson or two and stop when it's not fun anymore. But Tommy wanted to be a writer and he had real talent. I was working with him on a short story."

"When's the last time you saw him?"

She looked up and seemed to be thinking about it, which gave me a chance to study her face in more detail. She had smooth, pale skin, delicate features, and big brown eyes that brimmed with kindness. The overall effect was gentleness and purity, which, coupled with the softly rounding curves of her body, made her well-suited for nurturing a man or his children with equal ease.

"We had our session yesterday afternoon," she said. "I saw him a few times after that, but not really to speak, just from a distance."

"How did he seem during his lesson?"

"Distracted, now that I think about it, but not enough to make me really notice it much at the time. You know how kids are."

"Limited attention span?" I asked.

"Yeah," she said. "And limited experiences. No frame of reference to process most things."

"Did he ever mention having any problems with anyone in particular or being depressed or—"

"You think someone killed him?"

I shrugged. "I have no idea," I said. "I'm just asking."

"But did you see anything that would make you think he was murdered?"

I shook my head.

"That he killed himself?"

"Most drownings are accidental," I said. "And when they're not it's extremely difficult to prove. I'm just asking."

"Because you're not just a prison chaplain, are you?"

"None of us are *just* anything."

"Someone said you used to be a cop."

"Do you think he was depressed?" I asked.

"Are you going to try to find out what happened to him?"

"Sister told me not to," I said.

"And?"

"Was he depressed?"

She smiled. "No more than reason."

I smiled. "Literate, aren't you?"

"I *am* a professional," she said. "What's your excuse?"

"Was he having conflict with anyone here—or anywhere else—that you know of?"

"Sure, who doesn't have conflict, but he never mentioned anything that would result in this."

"The smallest, most trivial things can result in this," I said.

"I guess you're right," she said. "The first one was over whose offering God liked the best, wasn't it?"

"I'm not saying this was murder. Just wondering if it might be."

She nodded. "I wasn't jumping to conclusions as much as showing off my knowledge of the Bible for you."

I smiled. "Impressive. The thing is, murder by drowning is very rare—so is suicide for that matter. So it's likely we'll never know."

"But you're gonna try to know," she said.

Sister Abigail appeared at my door and tapped on her watch, indicating it was time for our session.

"No," I said, "I'm not. I'm going to obey Sister and leave the investigating to those who are paid to do it."

Chapter Six

"Are you bent on self-destruction?" Sister Abigail asked me.

"Are you given to overstatement?" I shot back.

She smiled. "Perhaps that was a bit over the top, but not necessarily. Once you start sliding down certain slopes, you might not be able to claw your way back up again."

We were in her office, which was much cleaner if no less cluttered than Father Thomas's. I was seated on a muted floral-print love seat, she, in a well-worn cloth recliner across from me. As usual, she was not reclining, but sitting with her feet pulled back together on the floor, her hands folded in her lap.

"You think asking a few questions about Tommy is—"

"The same as taking a few drinks?" she asked.

My breath caught, my pulse quickened, and I suddenly felt very vulnerable.

Averting my eyes, I glanced around her office, which gave the illusion of extravagance but had obviously been decorated on the cheap. Pristine books—psychology and religion texts mainly—were neatly arranged on homemade shelves that sagged slightly. Holy cards of the handout variety hung in wood frames of the dollar store variety. On her walls, atop her shelves, and on her desk were a lifetime of gathered objects—gifts, mementos, collectibles—and joining her many religious icons were the framed photographs of Freud and Jung.

Seeing their pictures made me think of *The Talking Cure*, and it occurred to me that that's exactly what I was here after.

"Is it ever just a few drinks?" she asked.

I shook my head.

"Is it ever just a few questions?"

I thought back to the recent investigations I had conducted, wondering if all of them had become obsessions. Was I just a compulsive person? Merely trading one addiction for another? Maybe I lacked the objectivity and detachment needed to be an effective investigator.

"You came here because trying to be a chaplain *and* an investigator wasn't working for you," she said. "You said it had cost you your family, your serenity, and on occasion your sobriety."

She shifted in her chair, and as she moved her hands, the sweet fragrance of rose-scented hand cream tinged the cool air of the drafty old office.

"Were you serious about wanting to look at why?" she asked.

I nodded.

"Has that changed?"

I told her it hadn't, and she stared at me for a long moment, eyebrows arched, forehead furrowed, head cocked.

Though kind, her eyes were intense and penetrating, seeming to continually be searching for denial and deception, and I wondered how often she had found it in me.

"Are you sure?" she asked. "Because it looks to me like what you really want to be doing is investigating Tommy Boy's death."

Through the window to my left, I could see Father Thomas walking toward the chapel. Head down in what appeared to be avoidance of interaction more than the cold wind, he walked briskly, hands jammed into his pants pockets. Before he reached the chapel, Tammy appeared in his path, forcing him to stop and acknowledge her.

"Don't you want to know if he was—" I began.

"Yes, but I also know that we may never know, and I can accept that. Can you?"

I thought about it for a long moment before saying, "I don't know. I'm not sure I can."

"Even if it costs you your sobriety—or at a minimum your serenity?"

"I'm just not sure. I'd like to say I could, but I'm trying to be honest and I just don't know."

After what appeared to be an intense exchange, Tammy pressed her body against Father Thomas and attempted to kiss him. Grabbing her arms, he shook her angrily and shoved her backward. As she began to laugh at and taunt him, he stepped around her and all but ran for the sanctuary of the chapel.

"If it's likely that you will drink if you continue to investigate and you continue to do it, would you agree you have a problem?"

"Yes," I said, "but not in the way you think. I've got to. I can't stop. Investigating is as much a part of who I am as ministering—maybe more. May even be a form of it."

"But look what it's cost you," she said. "Was it worth losing your wife over?"

"It wasn't investigating that cost me my marriage."

"I thought it was."

Mixed in the books surrounding us on all sides were several titles—both popular and academic—about marriage, but even if she had memorized them all, what could this aging celibate know about that most difficult of human relationships?

"It coincided with an investigation, but it can hardly be blamed on what I uncovered. If we had handled it differently . . ."

"Why did you come here?" she asked.

"To St. Ann's?"

She nodded.

I thought about it. "In search of peace, perspective—I don't know. I just wanted to slow down for a little while and give myself time to heal and to see if I could figure out why I keep repeating certain patterns."

"Not to investigate what will probably turn out to be an accidental drowning?" she asked.

I laughed. "Point taken."

"Is it possible that you want to do the latter so as to be distracted from the former—from the real reason you came?"

"Anything's possible," I said with a smile she did not return.

"Do you see yourself as a controlling person?"

I shook my head. "Not at all."

"And yet you have to be the one to investigate?"

"Not always."

"Really?"

"Really."

"I mean a crime you're aware of and in close proximity to."

"So I'm controlling? *That's* my problem?"

"I'm just asking questions," she said. "*You* have to provide the answers."

"You're doing far more than just asking questions. You're leading me where you want me to go."

"Am I?"

"I don't think I'm controlling," I said. "If I were, I probably wouldn't follow your leading questions, would I?"

"Well, at least you spent a lot of time thinking about it before you answered, and that's what matters."

I laughed. "I *have* spent a lot of time thinking about it. This isn't my first experience with self-examination, you know. I know I have problems. I just don't think being controlling is one of them."

"Does it have to do with your ego?" she asked.

"Obviously."

"Is it pride? The attention? The need to know—because there are some things we never will."

"I know that," I said.

"Well?"

"What about a gift and the need to use it? A desire for justice?"

"Sounds good, but couldn't that be a way of justifying what you want to do? Giving it a sense of the sacred? And do we ever really have justice down here?"

"We approximate it sometimes."

She was silent, thinking a moment.

Was I guilty of doing what I had criticized so many others for? Had I, like so many televangelists and terrorists, become an egocentric self-righteous idolater who had created God over in my image to justify my actions?

Finally, she said, "Is Steve Taylor a capable cop?"

I nodded.

She stared at me for a long moment. "So why not just let him handle it?"

Chapter Seven

"Guess who was last seen with Tommy Boy?" Kathryn asked.

It was evening, the temperature falling with the slow diminishment of the day. I was standing at the edge of the lake where I had been for much of the afternoon, weighing Sister Abigail's words, searching myself for answers, finding few.

Though the onset of winter had muted its colors, the small lake was no less beautiful. What the brittle brown grass, straw-colored underbrush, and gray trunks of cypress trees lacked in lushness, it made up for in subtlety, and it matched my subdued, contemplative mood.

Sister was right. I had come here for healing and anything else would be a distraction—including pursuing Tommy's death or the woman who had just walked up behind me.

"Who?" I asked, turning to face her.

"Tammy. They were seen leaving here together in her Mustang late last night."

Tell her to notify the police.

"You should tell . . ."

"Huh?"

"I thought the program was for street kids?" I said. "What's she doing with professionally manicured nails, an expensive dye job, and a new Mustang?"

"How'd you know her Mustang's new?"

"There's only one Mustang here," I said.

She nodded, then rolled her eyes at herself. "Of course."

My afternoon by the lake had done me good. I felt peaceful, connected, loved, and I wondered if it was the lake, the time spent in solitude and silence, or just being away from my life. Why couldn't I ever maintain my serenity? Why was equilibrium so elusive? In the widening gyre of my life, why did things always have to fall apart? Why couldn't the center hold?

Something about the stillness of the scene was serene. It had felt so right to sit on the ground and watch a small burnt-orange butterfly flitter between tall blades of grass while hearing the splash of a fish jumping in the lake.

What I had to do was figure out how to integrate this—time for stillness, quietness, and meditation—into my life away from St. Ann's, even, or especially, when I was involved in a homicide investigation.

"Most of them are street kids," she said. "Poor. Alone. From abusive families."

"But not Tammy?"

She shook her head. "Tammy's actually the niece of the man who gave us this place."

"She's a Gulf Paper Company Taylor?"

She nodded.

"And she's here because . . ."

"Her uncle gave us this place," she said, a wry smile turning up the corners of her pretty pink lips.

"Does she come here often?"

She nodded. "When her family can no longer tolerate her, or she wants to disappear for a while."

"Which is it this time?"

"Her family didn't bring her. I'm not sure they know she's here. Rumor has it—and that's all it is—that she's hiding from an abusive boyfriend and the drug dealer they owe part of her inheritance to."

I nodded as I thought about it, then turned away from her for one last look at the lake in the soft shadow of sunset.

The reflection of the pine and cypress tress on the smooth surface of the water looked like an impressionist painting—though it was hard to imagine Monet, Renoir, or Cézanne using such a pale palette.

Across the lake, a gentle breeze blew through the trees and

onto the pond, rippling a narrow strip of the otherwise glass-like water.

"Breathtaking, isn't it?" Kathryn asked.

I nodded, and watched as a small winter wren flew across the lake and came to rest on an old weathered board nailed between two cypress trees not far from the water's edge.

"How often do you come down here?" I asked.

"Nearly every day," she said. "This is my Walden."

"No wonder you write such inspired books."

"Thank you. There *is* something to be said for the impact our environment has on us."

"Like spending most of your waking hours with convicted felons," I said.

"I can imagine that would be extremely difficult—especially on a man as sensitive and compassionate as I hear you are."

"Don't believe everything you hear," I said.

"I don't, but when it comes from a nun . . ."

"So much for confidentiality."

"Oh, she would never violate that," she said. "But it doesn't cover her trying to set us up."

"She working you too?"

"Since the moment you arrived. She lives certain things vicariously through me, which means lately she's had a boring life."

"Lately?"

She smiled. "Well, actually most of my life."

"No wonder she's so persistent," I said.

"You have no idea."

"Every man with a heartbeat that comes through the front gates?"

"Oh, no, I meant . . . She's very particular. She's just relentless about certain ex-cop, recovering alcoholic, wannabe detective prison chaplains."

"Wannabe?"

A rustling in the branches above was followed by a squirrel as gray as the surroundings scampering down the cypress tree closest to us. As we watched, he bounced across the cypress knees between the trees like a Pentecostal preacher walking pews, and scurried up another tree farther down the bank.

"And she told you all that without breaking my confidences?"

"Actually, some of that I learned on my own. You're not the only one here who can investigate. I have to hunt down information for every one of my books. Speaking of which, I want to help you investigate what happened to Tommy Boy. I'm curious, plus I might be able to use it in a story. I can be your Watson."

"As fun as that sounds," I said, "I'm going to take Sister's advice and stay out of this one."

Her deep brown eyes grew wide in surprise. "Really?"

"Really," I said.

There would always be cases, always be distractions. I couldn't keep allowing them to lure me from my path. They were becoming red herrings in my life, and like a young, untrained hound I kept losing the true scent—and my way. Since the only way to stop a destructive cycle was to stop, that's what I had decided to do. I couldn't continue to fail to live out my convictions and ideals and have any credibility as either a minister or investigator.

"Wow, so I've lived to see the day when Sister was wrong about someone," she said. "I don't know if she'll be happy you took her advice or sad she was wrong to predict you wouldn't."

"You should turn over everything you have to the chief of police."

"Steve?"

"You know him?"

She nodded. "We went out a few times."

I felt myself pull back ever so slightly, and I wondered if she noticed.

"Then you know where to find him," I said, surprised not only at my tone, but how much what she said had bothered me. It was irrational and immature, but there it was.

She nodded. "Shouldn't be hard. He'll be joining us for dinner tonight."

Chapter Eight

The tension during dinner was palpable.

For the first part of the meal everyone ate in awkward silence. At one end of the long main table, Sister Abigail sat with Ralph Reid, a trim, rigid, early graying representative of the Gulf Coast Company who had come to look over the property. She was finding it difficult to be civil to him and she didn't conceal it well.

He acted oblivious. He wasn't much of an actor.

At the opposite end, Tammy Taylor, dressed modestly in jeans and a white button-down, was seated between Brad Harrison, Keith Richie, and across from Sister Chris King. Avoiding each other's eye line, the three watched Tammy intently, but she just kept her head down, moving her food around on her plate with her fork. In fact, she was so subdued, such a different person, I found myself trying to guess if she was medicated or merely bipolar.

I was seated near the center of the table, Kathryn next to me, Steve next to her.

"Sister Abigail, where's Father Thomas?" Steve asked.

Shrugging, she said, "Am I my brother's keeper?"

"He's fasting and praying," Tammy said without looking up, her voice flat and so soft it was barely audible.

"Of course he is," Sister Abigail said. "Limiting himself to only water and whiskey."

Several people laughed, and didn't hear Tammy say, "Getting ready."

For what? I wondered, but didn't pursue it.

Everyone grew quiet again, and only the sounds of silverware clinking, ice chinking, and the loud mechanical hum of the ice machine in the back corner by the kitchen remained.

In the absence of conversation, every sound was exaggerated as it bounced from the tile floor and ricocheted off the wooden walls. The large room was plain, but not rustic. A simple cypress table surrounded by uncomfortable cypress chairs sat at its center beneath a tilting old chandelier covered with dust. Oppressively heavy and gaudy drapes covered the many windows, their appearance altered by the sun on one side and dust on the other.

Leaning over to me, Kathryn whispered, "When's the last time you had this much fun?"

"Last time I did step five."

"Which is?"

"'Admit to God, to ourselves, and to another human being the exact nature of our wrongs.'"

"That had to be better than this."

"What's going on? Hasn't been this bad before."

"Well, on one end you've got a lovers' spat and on the other, a big bad corporation wanting to close us down."

I glanced over at Tammy and her admirers.

Slumping in the uncomfortable seat made Brad Harrison's thick body seem to gather around him and made him look dumpier than he was—which along with his dark skin and eyes accentuated his difference from the light-skinned, reddish-haired Keith Richie, whose tall body and erect posture caused him to tower over his competition for Tammy's attention.

I said, "Did Tammy tell the other boys if she couldn't have me, she didn't want anyone?"

She smiled. "I think her exact words were if she couldn't have you she didn't want to live."

"If I had a dollar for every time I heard that."

I then panned to the opposite side to see the nervous Ralph Reid trying to talk to the stiff, pinched Sister.

"The Gulf Coast Company wants this land?"

"They want it back," Kathryn said.

"Why?"

"Since the mill closed, they're converting this area into resorts, golf courses, and retirement communities."

I wondered why, with so much land, Gulf Coast wanted the abbey. It didn't make sense. St. Ann's was minuscule compared to Gulf Coast's other holdings and it wasn't close enough to the Gulf to be very valuable.

"Including the abbey?"

"Everything."

"I need to say something," Tammy said, pushing her chair back from the table and standing.

Everyone stopped eating and looked at her.

"I want to apologize for how I've behaved. I've done some pretty stupid and self-destructive things, and I'm sure I've hurt some of you. I'm very sorry. I take full responsibility for what I've done, but I want you to know that some things are out of my control. That's not an excuse. It's just the truth. Anyway, I'm gonna get help and I wanted y'all to know."

She then sat down as abruptly as she had stood and began to fork through her food again.

"Well," Sister Abigail said, "thank you, Tammy. We accept your apology and offer you our forgiveness and support on your efforts to have the life you want."

"Yes," Sister Chris said, and patted Tammy on the back affectionately.

"Hear hear," Steve said.

"It wasn't a toast," I said.

Kathryn laughed. Steve glared. Everyone grew silent again.

After a few minutes, Keith Richie rose and went into the kitchen, coming out a minute later with a large chocolate sheet cake. He placed the cake in the center of the table and began to cut it into sizable slices. As he did, I noticed the pale green prison tattoos on the underneath of his forearms, and wondered if everyone here was running or hiding from something.

Eating cake seemed to lighten everyone's mood, and soon the silence was replaced by whispers and faint laughs. But not everyone had cake, and those who didn't—Sister Chris and Tammy—remained sullen.

"This is very good, Keith," Kathryn said.

"Thanks," he said, his face turning a light shade of crimson.

"Since it seems to be a night for clearing the air," Ralph Reid said, "I think I should set a few things straight."

We all turned toward him, most of us continuing to eat.

"Regardless of what you may have heard, the Gulf Coast Company is not attempting to close St. Ann's down. Obviously, things have changed since we made this generous donation to your ministry, and we have different needs now, but nothing we're proposing would cause St. Ann's to close."

"What *are* you proposing?" Kathryn asked.

"Simply to relocate St. Ann's to another parcel every bit as beautiful as this one," he said. "Just one that would enable us to go forth with our plans to be a viable company for the future."

"*Simply* relocate us," Sister Abigail said. "Relocation is never simple, and this has been our home for nearly thirty-five years."

"Anyway," Reid said, "I just wanted to expel any rumors and explain what I was doing here. I'll be staying in Daniel cabin tonight if any of you have any questions."

"You're spending the night?" Sister Abigail asked.

"Is that a problem?"

She hesitated, then said, "Absolutely not. Just unexpected."

"Y'all still keep that cabin reserved for us, don't you?"

"Of course."

"Good," he said. "I have a few more things to do out here in the morning and I'd like to get an early start."

I leaned over and whispered to Kathryn, "The paper company has its own cabin?"

"Always has had. Not only did Floyd Taylor donate everything, but he set up a trust before he died that keeps St. Ann's going. If he hadn't, we'd've closed a long time ago."

Before I could ask her anything else, Father Thomas appeared at the door. Without speaking to the rest of us, he looked at Tammy and said, "It's time. Are you ready?"

She nodded and they left together.

"Time for what?" Steve asked.

"I have no idea," Kathryn said.

"You don't think he's, ah—you know, with my little cousin, do you?"

"*No*," she said. "Ew."

"Just the same, maybe I should go see what they're doing."

As he stood, I said, "Did she tell you your little cousin was the last one to be seen with Tommy?"

"Was she?" he asked Kathryn without acknowledging me.

Kathryn nodded.

"Well," he said. "Then I'll ask her about that too."

Chapter Nine

When the banging on my door began at just before two in the morning, I hadn't been asleep long. I had returned to my room from an after-dinner walk around the lake restless and frustrated. I had hoped to run into Kathryn but she was nowhere around, and I wondered if she was with Steve.

I shouldn't have even been thinking about her, but I was finding it difficult not to, and that made me agitated and unable to sleep.

The truth was Kathryn was just a distraction. The real reason I was agitated and unable to sleep was my mental state. I felt isolated and alone, cut off from the rest of the world. I was homesick for a home I didn't have and my loneliness opened up a hole inside me that felt as bad as anything I had ever experienced. I wanted to cry but couldn't. I wanted to scream but didn't. I needed to connect but felt as though I were the only lonely soul adrift in the cosmos.

I had paced around the small room, mind wandering, bumping into the furniture, before I finally laid down and courted that which eluded me nearly as much as equanimity.

I dreamt I was floating weightlessly in a world of clear, sky-blue water, arms and legs dangling beneath me. Hearing the sound at the door, like the knock of an oar against a boat, I rose to the top, cresting the surface into consciousness.

"Get dressed, I need your help," Steve said.

In the split-second I saw his face before he spoke, I knew something was wrong, his words and tone only confirming it.

Suddenly, there was nothing between us—no competition, no unresolved conflict, no past at all, only the present, only the task at hand. Now he was just a cop, I, his best hope for help.

Without saying a word, I quickly put back on the jeans, shirt, jacket, and tennis shoes I had donned earlier to walk the lake, silently praying nothing had happened to Kathryn or Sister Abigail.

When I was dressed, he turned and began walking down the narrow corridor, his rubber-soled shoes nearly soundless on the dull tile floor. I followed a step behind him, waiting for him to tell me what had happened and what he needed from me.

"I need to know I can count on you to act like a cop and not a chaplain," he said.

I nodded.

He turned and looked at me, slowing a step so I could walk beside him, which I had to do with my shoulders at a slight angle for us to fit.

I nodded again so he could see it.

"No matter how you might feel about these people, you've got to help me preserve evidence, protect the crime scene, secure statements."

"Crime scene?" I asked.

He nodded.

"Where?"

"One of the cabins."

My heart, racing since I first heard the banging on my door, seemed now to stop completely.

"Who's the victim?" I asked.

He shrugged. "Don't know yet."

"What?"

"The cabin's empty," he said.

"Then how do you know it's a crime scene?"

"All the blood."

When we stepped out of the dorm and into the night, a cold gust of air slapped me in the face, tiny needles pricking my cheeks and nose, tears stinging my eyes, and I heard what sounded like a child screaming, but it was so faint and far away it could have been the howl of the wind.

"Did you hear that?" I asked.

"What?"

With no clouds to diffuse it, the full moon lit up the night, its bright glow casting long, dark shadows on the dew-damp ground. Like the trees surrounding them, the buildings of St. Ann's were silent, the only sound, the whistle of the wind through the woods.

The airy whine sounded lonely and eerie, and it made the abbey feel desolate, the dark woods around it disquieting, and I realized how different it seemed now from earlier in the evening when it had nurtured and inspired me.

Wordlessly, we walked past the chapel and down the hill toward the cabins and the moonlit lake beyond, our breaths visible the brief moment before we walked through them.

"Which cabin?" I asked.

"It's not Kathryn," he said.

Relief washed over me—followed immediately by gratitude, then guilt.

"How'd you discover the—what are you still doing here?"

"Fell asleep. Something woke me—a scream, I think. When I came out here, I saw the door to the last cabin open and the lights on inside. It's supposed to be empty, so I walked over to check it out."

"From where?"

"From where what?"

"You woke up and came out of where?"

"Kathryn's cabin," he said.

I nodded, but didn't say anything. I was shivering now, feeling as cold within as without as I tried unsuccessfully to still my shaking body.

As he stopped in front of the last cabin on the right, I came up beside him and waited. The door was now closed, the lights off, no sign of violence visible.

"I turned off the lights to keep from attracting any attention while I went to get you," he said.

"That was smart."

"I'm a good cop."

"I know."

He nodded, his expression one of gratitude, though he didn't say anything.

"You seen a crime scene lately?" he asked.

I nodded.

"Well, this is a bad one," he said. "So be prepared."

"I am."

"Okay," he said. "Let's do it."

Chapter Ten

The musty old cabin was cold, its damp boards smelling of mildew, its dormant fireplace of charred hardwood and ashes, but those weren't the only odors. The dank air of the small room also carried on its currents the wet-copper aroma of blood, of life and death—and it was strong enough to let me know it was most likely the latter.

I didn't need Steve to turn on the light for me to know I was witnessing—at least in an olfactory way—a scene of extreme violence and bloodletting. When the light came on my sense of sight only confirmed what my other senses had already told me, but there was something about actually seeing it that made it simultaneously more real and less believable.

The interior of the cabin was much as the exterior—simple, rustic, unvarnished—except now much of it was splattered with somebody's blood.

Beneath a bare bulb on the ceiling, a blood-soaked bed with four wooden posts extended out from the right wall to the center of the room. Leather straps like dog collars were fastened to the bedposts. What looked to be arterial spray covered the headboard and the wall above it.

Trying to locate the source of the dripping sound, I turned to look for a kitchen or bathroom, but found neither in the one-room cabin, and I realized it was blood dripping from the bed.

Beside the fireplace on the back wall, a wooden rocking chair held some clothes and books. Candles lined the hearth and circled the bed.

Nodding toward the candles, Steve said, "Looks ritualistic."

"Would make sense at a place like this."

Behind me the door slammed shut and we both jumped.

He rushed over to check outside but could see no one.

"Wind," he said, closing it back.

As we turned back around toward the room, the candles lining the hearth and circling the bed were lit, their flickering flames causing shadows to dance on the floor, walls, and ceiling.

"Wind didn't do that," I said.

"What the hell?" he said. "This shit is freaking me out. Voices in the wind, slamming doors, crazy radio static, lights flashing. I think this place might be haunted."

"Might be," I said.

"Anyway, I'm thinking maybe we interrupted the guy and he'll be back, but I need to go search the property in case the victim's still alive. If the UNSUB went to dispose of the body, he'll probably be back to clean up. I want you to wait here in case he shows."

I nodded.

"You got a gun?"

"In my truck."

He knelt down and pulled a small .22 from an ankle holster. "Here," he said, handing it to me, "use this. We don't have time for you to go get yours."

As I took the gun, something in the far corner caught my eye. Noticing my wide-eyed expression, Steve followed my gaze.

When he saw what it was, he looked back at me with a wide-eyed expression of his own.

"You gotta be fuckin' kidding me," he said.

We crossed the room, carefully avoiding the blood. There, opposite the rocker, in the dimmest corner of the room, mostly hidden behind a dresser on the left wall, was a video camera on a tripod, its lens trained on the bed.

"Got any gloves?" I asked.

He shook his head. "You?"

"In my truck."

"Well, hell," he said, and reached down and turned on the camera.

When it whirred to life, he pressed the Play button, but

nothing happened. I bent over and took a closer look.

"There's no tape," I said.

"He must've taken it."

"And not the camera?"

"Maybe he couldn't carry it and the victim, so he took the tape and is gonna come back for the camera and the other stuff."

"Maybe."

"I gotta get out there and take a look around," he said, turning to leave.

"When you gonna call for backup?" I asked.

"As soon as I figure out what I need backup for," he said. "You saw what I've got to work with. I'm not gonna have one of them fuck up my crime scene. Speaking of which, you better not either."

As he started to leave, I said, "Be careful."

"You too," he said, and quietly walked out and closed the door.

Alone in the room, I took another look around. No other camcorders. No blood-covered UNSUBs cowering in the corner. Nothing that might help me figure out what had happened in here just moments before—except maybe the things in the rocking chair.

As I walked over to the chair, I heard a light tap on the door. Figuring the UNSUB wouldn't knock before coming back in, I kept the .22 down as I crossed the room.

"Steve?" Kathryn said in a loud whisper. "John?"

I opened the door and stepped outside, closing it quickly behind me.

"Steve's taking a look around," I said. "We don't need to be out here in case—"

"Good, let's go in," she said. "I'm freezing my ass off."

"You need to wait in your cabin. You don't want to see—"

"I already have," she said.

Stepping past me, she opened the door and walked inside. I followed her, closing the door behind me.

"Sorry," she said, "but I got scared. I just couldn't sit there by myself any longer."

Unlike many people unused to crime scenes, Kathryn neither gawked nor averted her eyes. She seemed as relaxed as she could be in the circumstances.

"It's okay."

"Do you have any idea what happened in here?" she asked.

I shrugged. "A few ideas, but no. Not really."

"You think it's connected to what happened to Tommy Boy?" she asked.

"It's very different, but two deaths in one day at a place like this are more likely to be connected than not."

Turning to the back corner, she said, "Is that a video camera?"

I nodded.

"So the whole thing's on—"

"There's no tape in it," I said.

She frowned and shook her head. "That would've been too easy," she said.

"I guess so."

"You want me to put it in my cabin for safekeeping?" she asked.

I shook my head.

"I don't mind," she said. "Really."

"It'll need to be processed like everything else," I said. "We need to be very careful not to disturb anything."

She nodded, and looked around the room some more.

"Do you feel that?" she said. "There's a . . . presence here."

I nodded. "It's palpable."

"You rarely encounter this kind of concentrated evil, do you?"

"Well, I work in a maximum security prison, so I do actually, but I know what you mean."

"There's something truly wicked going on. We're all in danger. It's ancient and it's evil. Sorry, but it's so strong."

I waved off her apology and nodded my agreement.

"What's in the chair?" she asked.

"I was just about to take a look when you knocked."

"Well, don't let me stop you."

Careful to avoid the blood, I crossed the room again, this time with Kathryn in tow. Holding on to my arm, she walked right behind me, pressing herself into me when I stopped at the chair.

Slowly, I sifted through the clothes, Kathryn looking over my shoulder. Stacked on a pair of shoes with socks in them were a pair of women's jeans, a button-down white shirt, bra, and panties.

"Isn't that what Tammy was—"

"Yeah," I said, "it is."

Next to the neat stack of clothes, a Bible, a book of Catholic rites and rituals, a bottle of holy water, and a rosary looked to have been dropped unceremoniously. With the very tip of my index finger, I lifted the cover of the Bible by its edge and looked inside. Near the bottom corner of the first page an embossed logo read "Library of Father Thomas Scott," with the initials TDS in the center.

"What does it say?" Kathryn asked.

I told her.

She shook her head. "There's got to be some mistake. He could never—someone must be trying to set him up."

"Could be, but we all saw her leave the dining hall with him just a few hours ago."

"Which is probably why someone thought they could set him up."

"Possibly, but for what? We don't even know what we're dealing with here." Nodding toward the bed, I added, "That could be his blood."

If it were possible, she grew even paler. "Oh, God, please no. It can't be."

"I hope it's not," I said. "My point is, we just don't know."

"Yes we do," Steve said from behind us.

We turned. He was standing in the open door, eyes wide, hands shaking—and not just from the cold.

"Tammy's dead," he said, his voice breaking, "and Father Thomas killed her."

Chapter Eleven

The canopy covering the narrow blood-stained path blocked out much of the moonlight, and we stumbled on exposed pine, oak, and cypress roots as we slowly negotiated our way around the lake. Occasional breaks in the foliage caused intermittent patches of the path to be bathed in a pale phosphorous glow that washed out the grass and leaves and made the splatters of blood on them look black.

Steve was in front with a large black metal flashlight he had retrieved from his Explorer. I was following close behind, attempting to step where he had. Kathryn had gone to call for backup and an ambulance.

"How much farther?" I asked.

"Not far," he said. "Guess I should get my other gun back."

"I don't know," I said, "the weight of it in my jacket pocket feels pretty damn good."

"Thought you were supposed to be comforted by his rod and staff."

I let that one go and we walked along in silence for a few minutes.

The wind sounded like whispered voices warning us to turn back, and I could've sworn I heard a lonely loon across the lake.

"Was he attempting to hide her down here?" I asked.

"Not when I found him."

"Why didn't you bring him back with you?"

"I want to take pictures of the scene just the way I found it," he said.

"You didn't have cuffs, did you? How'd you subdue him?"

"Didn't have to."

"What makes you think he'll be there when you get back?"

"You'll see."

What I saw was two people unconscious and covered in blood, but it was Tammy's blood and, unlike Father Thomas, she would never regain consciousness.

They were in a small moonlit clearing next to the Intracoastal Waterway. Father Thomas was slumped against the base of an oak tree, his head hanging down, Tammy, several feet away facedown in the dirt, her naked, blood-splattered body looking black and white in the moonlight.

Though there was little doubt, I had to ask, "Are you sure she's dead?"

He nodded. "I checked."

"I'm very sorry," I said.

"Thanks. We weren't very close, but still . . ."

We were quiet for a while, the sound of our breathing joining the frogs and crickets and wind whining though the woods all around us.

After a few moments, he pulled a small camera out of his jacket pocket and began to snap pictures of the crime scene, methodically working from wide, establishing shots all the way down to close-ups. The bright flashes of light added an eerie dimension to the already horrific scene, its intermittent overexposure of the bodies as disconcerting as lightening without thunder. When he was finished taking the pictures, I said, "Can we lay him down now and take a closer look at his wounds?"

"Yeah," he said, "but what wounds?"

I carefully laid Father Thomas onto the cold, damp ground, wondering if he might not have been better in his previous position, and checked him for abrasions and contusions. Scratches covered his face, cuts and bruises, his hands, and a gash in his head left blood in his hair and a bump beneath.

"Bump on his head's pretty bad," I said. "Must be what knocked him out." Glancing back at the tree, I saw traces of blood and hair on the end of a broken branch. "Looks like he hit the tree."

Pulling out his camera again, Steve took pictures of the spot from various angles.

"Here's what I'm thinking," he said. "He binds her to the bed and starts to do stuff to her. At some point, something happens—he goes too far, she changes her mind—something, and they begin to struggle. In the process, she gets beaten and cut up pretty bad and loses a lot of blood, but somehow she fights back and gets free. She runs out of the cabin, down the trail, bleeding all the way. He follows her. She makes it here to the clearing, they fight some more, and either he hurts her some more and accidentally stumbles and hits the tree or she pushes him into it."

"It's a theory," I said, "but why run down here instead of to another cabin or a dorm for help?"

"Disoriented, dazed, confused—being half-dead and several quarts low'll do that to you."

"You sure you're okay to work this one?" I asked. "Maybe you should—"

"I'm fine," he said. "I've got to work it. No way I'm turning family over to someone else. Why be a cop?"

"I know, but the case needs someone with some objectivity."

"Like you?"

"No. Didn't mean me."

"Well, whoever you meant, just forget it," he said. "I appreciate your help so far and I know what you're saying's right, but it's not gonna happen, so just drop it."

I dropped it.

"Father Thomas is not a young man," I said, "and he's spent many years living a very sedentary life. You really think he could catch her if she were running away from him?"

"She had to be weak from all the blood loss."

"Still."

"You know how these things work," he said. "Never an answer for everything."

"Doesn't mean we shouldn't try to find one."

He looked over at Tammy again and shook his head. "Still can't believe she's dead."

"I'm very sorry."

"Fuckin' raped and beaten and stabbed—"

I thought about that.

"What?" he asked.

"If this is rape or sexually motivated—"

"*If?*" he asked. "He had her strapped to the fuckin' bed. She's not wearing any clothes."

"But he's wearing all of his," I said. "Think about it."

"Maybe he got dressed before he came out here to throw her body in the waterway."

"Doesn't fit with your other theory of her escaping somehow and running out here and him following her."

"So?"

"So if she was already dead, who knocked him out?"

"Maybe he tripped, dropped her, and hit his head on the tree."

"Look how far away she is."

"So he put her down and was going back for something and tripped and hit the tree."

"With the back of his head?"

"Maybe he turned around to look at her body again and that's what made him trip. We'll ask him when he comes to."

"What about a murder weapon?"

"What about it?"

"Where is it?" I said. "It's not in the cabin. I didn't see it on the path. It's not here in the clearing."

"He could've thrown it in the waterway already."

"I'm just saying there's a lot that doesn't add up."

"Always is," he said.

"So you keep saying."

Sister Abigail appeared at the edge of the clearing and I turned to face her.

"Is he . . ." she began.

"He's unconscious," I said.

She knelt down beside him. "Why aren't you helping him?"

"Please don't touch him, Sister," Steve said. "We don't want to contaminate any of the evidence."

She looked up at us in a shame-producing shock. "He's hurt. He needs help."

"Which is on the way," Steve said. "Don't you think I want to cover Tammy up?"

She glanced over at Tammy, then back up at Steve. "But there's nothing you can do for her. *Tom's* still alive."

"And not withstanding the fact that he killed my cousin,"

Steve said, "I want him to stay that way."

Her eyes widened. "Is that it? You're not helping him because you think he killed her?"

"That has nothing to do with it. I'm gonna process the crime scene and conduct the investigation by the book."

"Because he didn't kill her. He couldn't have and you know it. It's obvious they've both been attacked."

"With all due respect, Sister," Steve said, "Tammy's been murdered, not attacked. And all he's got is a bump on the head and a few scratches."

"I'm telling you," she said, "he didn't kill her."

"I know it's hard for you to accept," Steve said, his voice patronizing, "but I'm telling you what the facts say."

"The facts?"

"The evidence, the crime scene," he said. "I've been doing this a while and—"

"I'm telling you he didn't do it," she said. "And it's not just that he wouldn't, but that he *couldn't*. He's not capable."

"That's what everyone always believes about people they know, but—"

She shook her head in frustration. "Listen to me, please, and be quiet. I'm not talking about morally. I'm saying physically. Physically he couldn't do it. This is supposed to be a secret so please don't tell anyone, but Father Thomas is very sick. He doesn't have long to live. He doesn't have the strength to do what has been done to this poor girl."

Steve shook his head in disbelief. "What're you saying?"

"That you better come up with a different theory to fit your facts, because Tom couldn't have done this and his doctor will testify to it."

Chapter Twelve

"Don't say a word," Ralph Reid said to Father Thomas.

Father Thomas had just regained consciousness a moment before and was about to respond to Steve Taylor's first question when Reid intervened.

"What the hell do you think you're doing?" Steve said.

The crime scene techs from FDLE taking measurements and collecting evidence all around us stopped momentarily to listen. There were six of them, wearing white jumpsuits, latex gloves, and vinyl slip-on booties over their shoes with the identifying "Police" pattern in the print. They worked quickly and quietly, seemingly oblivious to us until now.

"As counsel, I'm advising him not to talk to you yet," Reid said.

"You're an attorney?"

"Among other things."

"I don't need an attorney," Father Thomas mumbled.

He was lying on a stretcher being examined by the same female EMT I had seen on the pier the previous morning. We were all standing around him. Across the clearing Tammy's body, still facedown on the damp ground, had been covered with a white sheet.

"Oh, yes you do," Reid said. "They think you killed Tammy."

Father Thomas's eyes widened. "No," he said, shaking his head. "I—"

"Need to talk with me before you talk with them. Do you want me to represent you or not?"

Father Thomas looked up at Sister Abigail, his eyes searching hers for reassurance.

"Let him, Tom," she said.

"Is that the way you want it?" Steve asked. "'Cause I can't help you if you lawyer up—and doing it so quickly only makes you look guilty."

"See what I mean?" Reid said. "That's the mentality you're up against."

The night air was cold and moist, clumps of fog clinging to the bare branches above us. Beyond the clearing the woods were loud, as if to remind us we were trespassing into a living, largely unseen world we no longer belonged to.

"He works for Tammy's family's company," Steve said.

"And *he's* part of the family," Reid said, jerking his head toward Steve, "but for now, we're the only players in this little drama. You can get another attorney later if you want to, but at least let me help you through these crucial first hours."

Father Thomas nodded. "Okay," he said, "but I didn't kill her."

"Then just tell us what happened," Steve said.

Father Thomas opened his mouth to speak, but Reid said, "Later. At the station. Let him get checked out at the medical center and give me a chance to confer with him, then we'll cooperate fully."

Father Thomas closed his mouth and nodded his head.

Steve let out a frustrated sigh and simply said, "Okay."

FDLE had set up several large halogen lights, and the entire clearing was lit up like a rescue operation, which made the woods beyond seem even darker, and cast eerie, elongated shadows onto the now trampled ground.

"And I'd like Chaplain Jordan there," Sister Abigail said.

"*What?*" Steve and I both asked in surprise.

"You're the one who asked for his help," she said to Steve. "I'm just saying since he's been involved from the start and since the victim is your cousin, let him continue at least through your initial interview with Tom."

I looked at her, my face a question.

"You can handle that, can't you?" she asked.

"Of course, but I thought you—"

"I asked for his help because there was no one else," Steve

said. "Now I have all the help I need."

"You don't question his ability to be objective, do you Steve?" she asked, leveling her gaze onto him.

"Any professional can be objective," he said, "but he's no longer a professional."

"Sure he is, and you know it."

"But—"

"To avoid even the appearance of impropriety," she said. "Why are you so resistant to just having him present? I would think you'd want to have every possible—"

"Okay, okay, he can observe, but that's all."

While the EMTs finished examining Father Thomas and FDLE finished processing the scene, Sister Abigail, Ralph Reid, and I stepped away from the others.

"I thought you wanted me to avoid things like this for a while?"

"Mitigating circumstances," she said.

"There always are," I said. "That's sort of the point."

Her eyes narrowed and her expression hardened. "Can you handle it or not?" she said, a new edge accompanying her curt voice.

"I'm just curious about why you changed your mind?"

"There's no way he killed her," she said, "and I was afraid they would trick him into saying he did. Not even consider that someone else could've done it."

"You really an attorney?" I asked Reid.

He nodded. "Haven't practiced in a while, but I'm the real deal."

"How'd you even know what had happened or where to find us?" I asked.

"Kathryn told me," he said.

"Where *is* Kathryn?" I asked.

He shrugged. "I don't know. She just told me to get out here and take care of Father Thomas."

"She's probably seen enough for one night," Sister said.

"Speaking of taking care of Father Thomas," I said to Sister, "as a defense attorney, that's his job, but I'm not a defense attorney and I won't even be acting as one."

"What're you saying?"

"I'll be looking at the evidence, following it wherever it

leads."

"Which is what I want you to do."

"Even if it points to Father Thomas?"

"Yes, but it won't."

"Well," I said, as the EMTs began to roll Father Thomas out of the clearing and down the path, "we're about to find out."

Chapter Thirteen

Cuffed so he couldn't alter evidence, Father Thomas had been briefly examined at the Bridgeport Medical Center then released back into police custody. He was now being led down the florescent-lit corridor of the police station to the small interview room in the back. When he stepped inside the room, two FDLE techs were waiting for him.

Steve, Ralph, and I, who had been following behind him, stopped at the doorway and waited.

With practiced formality, Steve presented Father Thomas with a document and said, "This is a search warrant."

"For what?" Father Thomas asked.

"You," Steve said. "These two lab techs from FDLE are going to gather any physical evidence you have on you."

Father Thomas looked at Ralph Reid, who nodded.

"I'd like to be present," Reid said to Steve.

"Sure," he said. "John and I'll wait out here."

Reid joined the others in the small room and Steve closed the door.

"Shouldn't take too long," he said to me. "Want some coffee?"

I nodded.

I followed him back up to the small squad room and the coffee maker just outside his office door.

"It's bad," he said, handing me a large paper cup full of the steaming black liquid, "but it's hot and strong."

He waved to the tired-looking middle-aged dispatcher through the glass of her communications room and we walked back down the flatly lit hallway toward the interview room.

"You're not gonna do anything in there to hinder me or help him, are you?" he asked.

I shook my head. "Just observe."

A flash of light filled the room and shone at the bottom of the door, and I knew the techs were taking pictures of Father Thomas.

"I like the old guy," he said. "I'll give him a fair shake, but we can't forget what he did."

"If he did it."

"You seriously believe it's even possible he didn't?"

"If you don't you shouldn't be heading the investigation."

"Yeah, yeah, yeah, keep an open mind and all that, but it's just the two of us talking here."

"I'm not saying it because it sounds right."

"Okay," he said, "but just from what we know, what we've seen, statistically—"

"It's likely he did it," I said.

"All I'm saying."

"Is it?"

He started to say something else, but hesitated.

Without seeing or hearing anything from inside the small room, I knew what was happening. The techs were scraping flecks of blood and tissue from beneath Father Thomas's nails, snipping a sample of his hair, and combing his pubic region.

"Are you really going to pursue other possibilities?" I asked.

"No," he said with a smile, "but only because I know *you* will."

"I'm out of it after tonight," I said.

He laughed. "Even if I charge him and you think he's innocent?"

"Innocent people're convicted all the time."

"Not while John Jordan's around," he said, his voice taking on a bitter edge that hadn't been there before.

The door to the interview room opened and the two techs came out. They were carrying various-sized plastic and paper evidence bags.

"He's all yours."

They walked away and we walked inside.

The small room was simple and, to my surprise, not cluttered. Rather than the outdated sterile, austere interrogation room, it was a warm and comfortable interview room. Cushioned chairs surrounded a wooden table, and pastel pictures of beach scenes hung on the walls.

Everything about Steve and his department impressed me.

"Father Thomas," Steve said, his voice kind and respectful, "would you like a cup of coffee?"

He shook his head.

Steve and I were on one side of the table, Ralph Reid and Father Thomas on the other. His clothes long since placed in plastic evidence bags and taken to be processed, Father Thomas was wearing a pale blue county uniform that transformed his appearance so completely as to make him look like an old-time recidivist.

"I know you've been through a lot tonight so I'll try to make this as brief as possible."

Joining the fine network of cuts and scratches webbing Father's face, blue and purplish bruises were slowly developing on his right cheek and around his throat.

"Thank you."

"Do you mind if I record this? My handwriting is atrocious."

Father Thomas looked at Reid, who shook his head.

"Is that a 'no' or a 'no we don't mind'?" Steve asked.

"You may record the interrogation," Reid said, his tone flat and impatient.

Steve pulled a small recorder out of his pocket and placed it in the center of the table. Clicking it on, he rattled off the date, time, and who was in the room.

"Father Thomas," Steve began, "we think we know what happened. The physical evidence and crime scenes tell a certain story, and, unlike people, their testimony is objective and accurate."

"Subject to interpretation, of course," Reid added.

Ignoring him, Steve continued. "What physical evidence can't do is tell us how things felt, why things happened. It can't really explain these things. And scientific facts can be cold and make things seem much more . . . ah . . . cold-blooded than they really were."

Steve paused for a moment, but Father Thomas didn't say

anything.

"I've been doing this long enough to know that there's always a context—you know, circumstances—that gives greater insight than the proof provided by cold, hard facts. So we're here as friends to let you explain to us not so much what happened, but *why*."

"We're not friends," Reid said.

"Father Thomas and I are," Steve said, never taking his eyes off Father Thomas.

"Not in this room."

"Tammy can't tell us what happened," Steve said. "She can't explain to us why things turned out the way they did. Only you can. You get the final word. You can explain your side of it and no one can contradict you."

When Steve stopped talking, we all waited, but Father Thomas didn't say anything.

"Go ahead," Steve said, "tell us why you did what you did."

"Because she asked me to," Father Thomas said, his voice small, dry, weak.

"She asked you to?"

"You know how she was."

"Yes, I do," Steve said, his voice full of enthusiastic empathy. "She was out of control. A real mess."

"Far more miserable than most people knew. She wanted to change."

"But she couldn't, could she?"

"Exactly," Father said.

"So she asked you to tie her up and—"

"Actually, she did that herself. I went to my office to get my things and by the time I arrived, she had undressed and strapped herself to the bed—well, all but one hand."

"Father, I know this is difficult, but I need you to tell me exactly what she asked you to do to her."

Father Thomas looked at him in impatient disbelief, as if Steve had not been listening. "What I've been talking about," he said. "She asked me to perform an exorcism on her."

"What?" Steve asked in shock.

"She asked me to drive out the demon inside her."

"So what went wrong?"

"Nothing went wrong," Father Thomas said. "He simply refused to go."

"So you killed her?"

"Of course not," Father Thomas said. "I didn't kill her. He did."

"Who's he?"

"The demon."

Chapter Fourteen

"You're saying you didn't kill her and a demon did?" Steve said.

Father Thomas nodded, his tired face somber and sincere.

"Father, come on. You can't expect me to believe that. You're a few centuries late for that defense to work."

Father looked offended. "It's not a defense. It's what happened."

Steve turned to Reid. "You gonna let him hang himself with this?"

Reid said, "Father, tell them the whole story from the beginning like you did me."

He took a deep breath, sighed heavily, then hesitated a moment. "I still can't believe she's dead."

He paused again, and in the intervening silence I had to keep reminding myself not to ask any questions of my own.

"Tammy was tormented. Out of control. Doing things she not only didn't want to do, but found revolting—and that's the things she even remembered. More and more she was losing time. Waking up with no memory of what she'd done. Later, when people would describe her actions, she was sure they were talking about someone else."

"And this made you think she was possessed?"

He shook his head and gave Steve a look of frustration. "Made *her* believe it. She heard I was an exorcist and began coming to see me. At first, I refused to even talk to her, but she persisted and eventually convinced me—"

"That she was possessed?"

"That she was sincere," he said impatiently, "that she really was asking for help."

Reid patted him on the back, and I could tell he was trying to get him to relax and be more tolerant of Steve's questions.

"So at this point you didn't believe she had a demon?" Steve asked.

"Of course not, but I could tell *she* did, that she genuinely wanted and needed help."

"So you began to help her?"

"I began to meet with her on a semi-regular basis, and the more we talked, the more I realized just how deeply disturbed she really was. Her promiscuity and drug use had opened her up to all sorts of . . ."

"Demons?" Steve asked, his flat tone unable to completely mask its underlying ridicule.

"As it turns out, yes," Father Thomas said, "but at the time I wasn't sure. I thought it could be psychological trauma. Often the two go hand in hand."

"What?"

"Possession and mental illness. I just wasn't prepared. Not like I should've been. God forgive me for my arrogance and blindness."

"When did you change your mind about what her real problem was?"

"I didn't," he said. "At least not until tonight. That's what I'm saying. I was unprepared for what I faced tonight because I thought she was . . ."

"Faking?" Steve offered.

"Well, to be more precise, that it was in her mind. I honestly felt that Sister Abigail could do her more good than I, but I didn't think she would even be open to that kind of counseling until we went through the ritual."

"Of exorcism?"

He nodded. "The thing about possession is—and you can ask any exorcist about this—most manifestations of the demonic don't occur until the ritual is performed. If there's any question, it's best to go ahead and perform the ritual. No one without a demon was ever hurt by an exorcism."

"And tell me, Father, is that usually done by strapping the person naked to a bed?"

Father Thomas let out a frustrated sigh and Reid shook his head, his eyes narrowing angrily as he glared at Steve.

"I told you," he said, "*she* did that. I had mentioned to her that I usually used restraints because you never knew what the demons might make a person do, so naturally she wanted to use them, but she's the one who put them on the bed, undressed, and strapped herself in. She said she didn't want to hide anything from me or God and that she wanted to be physically uncomfortable, but I saw it as yet another sign that she was suffering from mental illness, if not demon possession."

I wanted to ask how he discerned between the two, but refrained. Sister Abigail would appreciate my restraint.

"I thought being naked was the state Tammy was most comfortable in?" Steve asked.

"Because of the cold," Father Thomas said, shaking his head. "Are you trying to be—"

"So you went in that cabin last night not believing you were dealing with a demon?"

"Right."

"So you can understand why we're having such a difficult time with it," Steve said.

"Sure," he said. "But I'm telling you that's what it was. I'll swear to it in court. I'll take a lie detector test. I'm telling the truth."

"You've done exorcisms before?"

"Lots of them."

"Anything like this ever happen?"

"I've had people hurt themselves," he said. "Manifestations of the demons torturing their souls showing up on their bodies, but never to this degree. I've never seen them kill."

"Have you ever even heard of it happening?" Steve asked. "In recorded history?"

"Most exorcisms aren't recorded. They embarrass the church."

"Is that a no?"

"It's a 'not that I'm aware of.'"

"So what we're dealing with is unprecedented?"

"In my experience," he said. "Yes."

"And that doesn't worry you?"

"Worry me?"

"Yeah, you know, risking your life on something no jury will have a frame of reference for?"

"I have evidence. Well, if not of her actual death, at least of how bad it was torturing her."

"What evidence?" Steve asked.

"I videotaped the whole thing. It'll prove I'm telling the truth. You'll be forced to confront your own unbelief when you see it, and will have to let me go."

"Well, maybe you should let us see it. Where's the tape?"

"In the camera. Corner of the cabin. It may still be recording. I left it running when I ran after Tammy."

"It's not there. We checked."

"Someone took my camera? Why would—"

"Not your camera, just the tape."

"I don't understand. Why would someone take my tape? It proves I'm telling the truth."

"Maybe the devil did it," Steve said.

"That's not funny," Father said. "You shouldn't tease about powerful things you don't understand."

"Maybe it was taken precisely *because* it proves you're telling the truth," Reid said. "Maybe the murderer took it in an attempt to set you up."

Chapter Fifteen

"Whatta you know about exorcisms?" Steve asked.

We were standing next to the coffee maker again, taking a short break before we wrapped up the interview, allowing Father Thomas and Ralph Reid to have a little privileged conversation.

"Not a lot. Studied it a little in seminary—even wrote a paper on it, but have forgotten most of it. Read a few books since then. Seen a documentary."

"Well, all I know is what I've seen in movies. And I'm not much of a reader. You think you could brush up a little on the subject and give me a Cliff's Notes version?"

I nodded.

"Is what he's saying even possible?"

I shrugged. "I'm in the 'anything's possible' business."

"You believe in angels and demons and all that shit?"

"Used to. When I was a kid I believed in them in very literal and concrete ways. As I grew up and learned more, I saw them more as metaphors."

"Metaphor didn't do what was done to my cousin."

"I know. And I do believe in a spiritual realm. It's just far more mysterious and subtle than most religious people seem to think—and that's especially true of its influence and impact on this realm. I try to remain open, but I'm pretty skeptical."

"Could it be mental illness?" he asked.

I nodded. "And we've got to consider drug use as well. Depending on how many drugs she's really done, and what kind, and if she was under the influence at the time . . . Toxicology should tell us a lot."

He nodded.

We were silent a moment, sipping our coffee, looking around the dim, empty station. It was neat and orderly, obviously well run, and surprisingly modern and technologically sophisticated.

"What about the tape?" he asked. "Why would someone take it?"

"Could be what Reid said."

"Or Father Thomas could have taken it because what it really shows contradicts what he's telling us."

"Either way," I said, "you need to search St. Ann's."

He nodded. "That should be fun."

We grew quiet again, each of us stretching and yawning. Steve looked as tired as I felt, the stubbly skin of his washed-out face drawn, dark circles under bloodshot eyes, and stiff, unruly hair in need of washing. I was sure I looked worse.

"He was covered in her blood," he said.

"Yeah?"

"His hands are bruised and swollen and I guarantee the blood and tissue removed from his nails are hers and vice versa, and he has nicks and scratches on his hands and face that look like she was fighting him off."

"Yeah."

"He probably did it," he said. "Probably killed her and all the rest of this hocus pocus shit's just clouding the issue."

"Probably," I said, "but not necessarily, not definitely, not absolutely, not yet."

He frowned and nodded his begrudging agreement. "Come on. Let's go see if we can turn probably into unequivocally."

Walking back down the narrow hall, I said, "Pretty good vocabulary not to be a reader."

He laughed. "My mom gave me Word Smart vocabulary-building tapes for Christmas last year. I keep them in my Explorer. Listen to them as I drive around. Tell anybody and I'll shoot you."

"Since for the moment we don't have the tape, why don't you tell us exactly what happened inside that cabin and how you both wound up in the clearing." Father Thomas nodded, his eyes looking up and off into the distance, his face wincing with the first images of memory.

"I've been doing this a long time," he said, "and I've never seen anything like it. She started out doing all the vile stuff you'd expect—stuff she would've seen in movies. She spit out obscenities at me, touched herself sexually, and—"

"I thought she was strapped to the bed?" Steve said.

"All but one hand," he said. "She couldn't do it. She asked me to, but I told her one hand was enough."

"So her hand was free to do sexual stuff to herself?"

If talking about sexual matters embarrassed Father Thomas, he gave no indication. On the contrary, he seemed quite comfortable with the subject. He didn't blush or grow tentative, nor did he become aggressive in an attempt to overcompensate. I was reminded how much I disliked people making assumptions about me in general or my sexuality in particular because I was a minister, and realized I had done the same thing to him—though in my defense he had taken a vow of celibacy.

"And violence—to herself and to me," he said. "I should have strapped her free hand down, but by the time I knew what was going on, I couldn't."

"Whatta you mean you couldn't?"

"It was too strong. I tried, but with both my hands and all my weight I couldn't hold it down."

As tired and frayed as the rest of us looked, Father Thomas looked worse—and it wasn't just fatigue or the result of enduring an event as obviously traumatic as he had. It was how frail and feeble he was. Maybe what Sister Abigail had said about his condition was more than an attempt at making him seem innocent. Maybe he really was physically incapable of the brutality done to Tammy.

"Which hand?"

Father Thomas thought about it for a moment, looking up in the other direction this time.

"Her left," he said.

"Father, Tammy was right-handed."

"It doesn't matter," he said. "It wasn't her strength I was dealing with anyway."

"No, if she really strapped herself to the bed like you said, wouldn't she have used her right hand to do it?"

He nodded. "I would think she would."

"Sure you don't want to change your story now? Before it's too late?"

"I'm telling the truth, Steve. I'm sure the medical examiner can tell you which of her wrists was bound."

I wasn't sure if Father Thomas was telling the truth—I was inclined to doubt it—but the longer we talked, the more thoroughly convinced I became that he was telling what he believed to be the truth.

"I'm sure she'll be telling us a lot of things," Steve said.

"And every one of them will confirm what I'm saying's the truth," Father said.

"We'll talk about that some more when I get the autopsy report back," Steve said, "but for now I need you to explain to me why you carried her outside."

"I didn't."

"You carried her down the path to the clearing close to the Intracoastal Waterway. Don't tell me you don't remember. We found both of you in the clearing."

"I didn't carry her. I followed her. She ran out of the cabin. I thought she was going to hurt herself so I ran after her."

"Was the exorcism over?"

"No."

"Why did you unstrap her?"

"I didn't."

"Then why'd you let her do it?"

"I didn't *let* her do anything. Besides, she didn't unstrap herself."

"Father," Steve said in a weary, incredulous voice, "if you didn't unstrap her and she didn't unstrap herself, who—wait, let me guess."

"Be careful, Steve. Don't play around and poke fun at evil. All I did was underestimate it, and look what's happened. Take it too lightly and you'll wish you hadn't."

Steve let out a heavy sigh. "How did Tammy get out of the straps?"

"All throughout the rite, her body contorted into a variety of forms," he said. "Things would appear on her skin, her face would change into someone else's, her skin would rip and tear, and this time, her body elongated. She became taller and thinner and just pulled her hand and feet through the straps."

Suddenly, Steve's eye's widened and he sat up. "I get it," he said. "Now I see what you're doing." Turning to Reid, he added, "Did you put him up to this?"

"What?" Reid asked.

"You guys are trying to set up an insanity plea, aren't you?"

"Steve," Father Thomas said sternly, "I know how all this sounds. Believe me, I wouldn't be saying it if I hadn't experienced it. You may think it's crazy or I am, but I do not, and I will not plead insanity or anything else except not guilty, even if I face the chair."

"Sorry," Steve said, though it hardly sounded sincere. "So she got free and ran down the path and you followed her. Then what?"

"Before she ran from the cabin she flung me across the room, so I wasn't right behind her. In fact, I never saw her again. Not really. When I ran out of the cabin, she was gone. And the truth is, I can't run. I was barely walking fast."

"How'd you know to follow her down the path?" Steve asked. "Wasn't it far more likely that she would run up to the chapel or to the dorms?"

"I followed the blood."

"You followed the blood," Steve said patronizingly.

"It led me to the right, away from the lake and down toward the clearing. When I reached the edge of the clearing, I could hear her breathing, but I couldn't see her. While I was looking around, I heard a rustling in the leaves behind me and I turned to see what it was. That's when someone grabbed my head and bashed it into the tree."

"Someone?" Steve asked.

"The person's hand was covering my eyes where he grabbed my head," Father Thomas said, "so I couldn't see who it was. At the time I thought it was Tammy."

"And now?"

"Now I don't know," he said. "Mr. Reid thinks it might not have been."

"Please enlighten us, Mr. Reid," Steve said.

"My client was unconscious when Ms. Taylor was murdered. Obviously, his first assumption was she was killed by whatever was inside her that had caused her to do all the things to herself she had already done—be it drugs, mental illness, or demons—and maybe it was. Honestly, we don't know, and frankly, the burden's not ours to prove, but we now also believe it's just as likely that Tammy was murdered and that the person who did it is the same person who knocked Father Thomas out."

"So this discriminating murderer kills Tammy, but just knocks *him* out?" Steve said.

"Maybe," Reid said. "Maybe he or she couldn't kill a priest or only wanted to kill Tammy or maybe they thought they *had* killed him. That was a powerful blow. Whatever the case, the implication is clear."

"Not to me," Steve said. "So maybe you'll be kind enough to break it down for me."

"Not only could my unconscious client *not* have killed Ms. Taylor," he said, "but his very injury provides the possible evidence of the real murderer's presence—be it the demon or disease that made Ms. Taylor strong enough to deliver the blow or an as yet unknown assailant. And in the likelihood that it's the latter and it's the same person who killed Tommy, I suggest you begin interviewing the other residents at St. Ann's."

Chapter Sixteen

"It's dismissive and dangerous to call the incarnation of all that's evil mere mental illness," Father Thomas said.

I glanced over at him in the passenger seat, then into the rearview mirror at Ralph Reid in the back. Both men looked like I felt. Beyond tired. Bone-weary.

I was driving us back to St. Ann's in the seemingly sourceless soft light just before dawn, feeling fatigue in every stiff joint, every sore muscle.

"Mental illness can't do what was done last night," he added.

Breaking our long stretch of silence, Father Thomas seemed to be talking to no one in particular, but Ralph Reid responded.

"You're right, Father," Reid said. "I'm sorry. I was just making it clear to them that we could offer more than one case for reasonable doubt."

"It's the truth I'm concerned about. Not reasonable doubt."

"But we don't know what the truth is, do we?"

"*I* do."

We were riding along the coast, the Gulf to our left, pale in the low light, the horizon closer than usual, beyond which appeared to be nothingness. The scenic road was mostly empty, only the occasional serious fishermen easing by, their beer-loaded boats bouncing along behind their rusted pickups. No one else was out. What few tourists there were and the numerous snowbirds who had flocked here were fast asleep in their warm rented beds.

"Well, the rest of us are trying to figure it out," Reid said.

"We weren't there. And the truth is, neither were you when Tammy was killed."

"I was there," he said, his voice flat, detached.

"But unconscious."

"I know in my heart she was killed by what was possessing her."

"All I'm saying is it could've been someone who—"

"No. No one at St. Ann's could do something like that."

"Is *that* what you're doing?" Reid asked. "Trying to protect the rest of us?"

He shook his head, but didn't say anything.

Neither he nor Reid had looked at each other during their entire conversation. Father Thomas was looking out his window, though it was opposite the Gulf and offered only a dim view of beach cottages, and Ralph Reid, who had insisted on sitting on the small jump seat in the back, was talking to the center of the truck he was forced to face.

"Someone could have come from the outside," Reid said. "Not easily, but it's at least a possibility."

"Without being seen? And at exactly the right moment?"

"It's possible," Reid said.

"The gate was locked."

"It was open when we left this morning," I said.

"Only because Brad had opened it for the police and ambulance earlier," Father said.

I wondered how, being unconscious at the time, he could know that, but decided not to pursue it at the moment.

"The murderer could have walked in," Reid said. "It'd be a good hike, but it could be done."

Father Thomas shook his head and let out a long sigh.

Glancing at him again, I wondered if I was looking at the murderer. Could this kindly old man kill? It didn't seem likely—at least in one sense. In another, it fit—acting out on repressed sexual frustration, fear of discovery, escalating violence, a final fatal blow he couldn't take back.

"Father, his job is just to think in terms of possible defenses," I said. "Scenarios that will raise a reasonable doubt."

"If you're going to continue to represent me," he said to Reid, "know that I would rather go to jail than deny the truth or have the finger of suspicion pointed at innocent people."

"You're going to represent him?" I said, looking into the rearview mirror.

Reid nodded.

Father Thomas said, "If he does what I tell him and doesn't profane sacred things."

"You don't think I should?" Reid asked me.

"Are you a criminal attorney?"

"I've done criminal work," he said.

"I'm not talking about your job with Gulf Paper."

He didn't respond.

"Don't you think Father needs someone who specializes in it?" I said. "Someone who's not one of a very few possible suspects?"

"Being a possible suspect isn't going to keep you or Steve from investigating, but if Father wants another attorney, I'll help him find one."

"I can't afford another attorney."

"How can you afford him?"

"Apparently I'm charity," he said.

"I'd never dream of charging Father a penny. He's been as much a priest to me as anyone ever has. We've been friends for many years now."

"You could be called as a witness," I said.

"So could Steve," he said.

"Steve shouldn't be working this case."

"But it's okay for you?"

"I'm not going to do much," I said, "but no matter what I do, it's not official."

"You really don't think he should represent me, John?" Father asked.

"I don't. I think it'd be better for both of you if he didn't."

"Why?"

"Because," Reid said, rushing to say what I was thinking before I did, "if I committed the murder, I won't try very hard to keep you from being convicted for it."

Chapter Seventeen

"Whatta you think really happened?" Kathryn asked.

Before going to my room and attempting to fall asleep—something that probably wouldn't be as difficult as it usually was—I wanted to have one more look at the crime scene in the light of day.

I was standing at the edge of the clearing when she walked up behind me.

"I have no idea," I said, turning toward her. "But I have a really hard time believing the devil did it."

She looked out at the circle of trees in a kind of childlike wonderment.

"'There are more things in heaven and earth, Horatio, than are dreamed of in your philosophy,'" she said.

Her eyes were red, their lids heavy, purplish half-moon shapes beneath them. Otherwise her face had very little color.

"Well, whether his father's ghost was real or imagined," I said, "it didn't turn out too well for the Prince of Denmark, did it?"

"No, it didn't. Still, one must play the part one's assigned."

The early morning sun had yet to climb above the treetops, but there was more than enough light to see the violent scene.

"Pretty fatalistic," I said.

She shrugged, continuing to look around. "Still can't believe she's dead."

I nodded.

She opened her mouth wide and yawned, slowly lifting her hand to cover it—a gesture that seemed an afterthought, a nod to a social nicety she really didn't have the energy or the conviction for.

After a moment, she looked directly at me for the first time. "Are you closed to the solution to this mystery being a supernatural one?"

I thought about it. "I try not to be closed to anything, but I must confess that to even consider it requires a willing suspension of disbelief on my part."

"But you're willing?"

I gave a half shrug and a small nod, but I wasn't even that sure I really was.

"You think he did it, don't you?" she asked.

"I think it the most likely scenario so far, but the investigation is just beginning."

"Like you, I'm not sure if I believe in demons or if it's even possible for one to inhabit a human being or if they can, if it's possible for them to kill the person. In fact, I find the whole notion highly unlikely, if not out and out impossible, but I can tell you this—the devil's more likely to have done it than Father Thomas."

"How long you known him?"

"My whole life," she said. "He and Sister Abigail raised me."

"You grew up here?"

She nodded. "My mother dumped me on their doorstep when I was just a few days old," she said. "They raised me like their own."

"Which could cloud your objectivity."

"There's no such thing. Surely you know that."

I nodded. "You're right. But there are degrees of subjectivity."

"Sure. I admit to little or no objectivity, but I'm telling you after a lifetime of living with the man that he could no more murder a person than you could."

"Bad example," I said. "You just proved my point."

"I stick by what I said. I'm not saying you've never been capable of murder, just that you aren't now, but even if I'm wrong about you, which I'm not, I've just met you. I've known Father for over three decades."

I nodded.

As if oblivious to the blood-covered leaves and broken branches, the birds in the trees whistled and sang enthusiastically, creating the background music of the forest soundtrack, their sweet songs soothing on a nearly subconscious level.

"And I meant what I said earlier," she added. "There are a lot of things we don't understand—about both good and evil. Living in a place like this teaches you that."

"How?"

She sighed and gave me a wide-eyed expression. "That's a long conversation for another time, but trust me. It's true."

"Give me the short version," I said.

"There's something so safe and artificial about civilization. It insulates you from nature, from Goddess, and from evil. Everything is so domesticated and homogenized. Most people live apart from reality. Being out here, living this kind of wild lifestyle, we're close enough to the raw, natural universe to know how little we understand, how little we know, how little control we have over very ancient powers—including evils."

"That's an interesting perspective, and one I share. I don't exactly live in a city."

"Even a rural area like Pottersville is not the same as being here."

I nodded.

We were quiet a moment, then she said, "Well, I'll let you get back to what you were doing."

She turned to leave, but I stopped her. "One question before you go."

"Sure."

"Steve said the two of you spent the night together last night, what time did—"

"We most certainly did not," she said.

My eyebrows shot up. "He wasn't with you just prior to discovering the crime scene in the cabin?"

"Well, yeah," she said, hesitantly, her brow furrowing, "he was in my cabin, but only because he fell asleep. He asked if he could talk to me after dinner last night. He seemed lonely, so I let him. We talked for a while. He didn't seem to have much to say, which confirmed my suspicion that he just needed company. After we ran out of things to say, we sat there in silence a while, until we both drifted off."

"Did either of you leave the cabin while you were together?"

She shook her head.

"Who fell asleep first?"

She shrugged. "I guess I did, but I'm not sure. Why?"

"And when did you wake up?"

"He woke me up because he thought he heard a scream," she said.

"So he could've left while you were asleep?" I asked.

She nodded. "I guess he could have, but do you realize what that means?"

I did, but wanted her say it. "What?"

"That if he really was asleep like he claims," she said, "I could have been the one to sneak out of the cabin."

Chapter Eighteen

When I got back to my room, I found a leather rose-colored journal lying on my unmade bed. A small gold key tied to a short length of burgundy ribbon sat atop the small book. Carefully placing the key into the lock on the side, I popped open the latch and lifted the top cover. A name was scrawled in black ink across the first page. Tammy Taylor.

Gently placing the journal on the floor, I fell into the bed, clothes, including my jacket, and shoes still on, and thought about what I should do.

If I really wasn't going to investigate, I didn't need to read even one of the entries. Before I could think about it long, my eyelids fell shut and I drifted off. I woke a moment later and looked down at the little leather volume on the cold tile floor.

One must play the part one's assigned, I heard Kathryn say as clearly as if she were in the room with me.

I reached over and pulled the book into bed with me and began to read. As I did, the bulb above me began to flicker and emit an electrical hum.

Why do I keep doing the same stupid things over and over again? What's wrong with me? I don't set out to fuck up, but that seems to be what I always do. Why? What's in me that's so weak or wicked? I try to be good, I really do. And I am for a while, but it never lasts for very long. I want to get better for real this time. Not just come off the shit I'm on, but stay off it. And that includes Clyde. I've got to stay away from him if I'm going to make it. I love him so much, but we're no good together. It's like we're self-destructive soul mates. Why does it have to be so damn hard? We should be able to be together without hurting each other so much. Why can't we just be in love? Just spend our whole lives loving each other, making each other happy? Why does he have to be so restless? Why do I have to be so weak? I can't think about that now. Maybe we can be together one day, but for now I've got to take care of me, work on me, get me better. Maybe Clyde will do the same thing. I begged him to. Told him if he loved me he would. Well, we'll see, won't we? Says he'll die for me, die without me. I told him if he wants to be with me he's got to be clean and sober and sweet. He can be so sweet sometimes, and not just when he wants to bone me, but mainly then. I wish he was here to make love to me right now. I've got to stop thinking about that, about him. I've got to really concentrate on getting better. It's our only hope. I can do it. Can he?

I fell asleep feeling sorry for Tammy Taylor, and thinking how much all of us addicts sound the same. When I woke a few hours later and read another entry, I felt less sympathetic.

At St. Ann's. God, could this place be any more boring? Not many people here, but more losers per capita than anywhere in the world. It's a beautiful piece of property. Shame to waste it on a few frigid bitches and dickless pricks. Going out of my mind, biding my time until I can get back to living. Think I'll fuck with these assholes for some fun. Seduce every last one of them, then make fun of their limp little dicks or the dykes for wanting but not having one. Scoring a couple of priests and nuns should be fun. Find out what they won't do and figure out a way to get them to do it. Show them what real power is. The power of me. I've got more power between my legs than all their pathetic little prayers put together. This whole place will be pussy-whipped inside a week. And then I can get on with my real plan.

Was someone trying to supply me with other suspects, or helping to build a case against Father Thomas? Was he one of her conquests? What was Tammy's plan? I thought about it, but not for long. Soon I was asleep again and dreaming, but not for long. Soon I was awake again and reading.

I don't think Father Fuckup thinks I have a demon. He thinks I'm out of my mind. Mad as a hatter. Still wants to fuck me, though. I can tell. Well, we'll see who's mind is more warped when I get finished with him. Don't see any real challenges. Maybe old Sister Abigail, but I couldn't do her anyway 'cause that's just gross. I'm committed to my mission, but I'm not that committed. I'm crazy, but not that crazy.

"John," Tammy said from the hallway.

I jumped up and ran to the door.

Just as I put my hand on the knob, it turned.

"John, let me in. Now. Help me. Please."

I tried to open the door, but couldn't.

Then someone began banging on the door so hard it shook, but a moment later when I was able to open it, no one was there.

I stepped out into the hallway and looked up and down. It was empty and quiet and I was alone.

Had I imagined all that? Was I still asleep? Was I so creeped out by all that had happened, so freaked out by Tammy's diary, so bone-weary that I was hallucinating? Or was it something else entirely?

I returned to bed and to the journal, Tammy's voice from the hallway still in my head.

I'm so sorry. Oh God. What's wrong with me?

I don't know why I wrote those things. I don't mean them. Sometimes I think mean things. Sometimes I feel so bad inside I want to hurt someone, but I'm not a bad person. I'm not. God, please forgive me. And help me. I'm so sick of this shit. I don't want to live like this any longer. Help me. And be with Clyde wherever he is. Please protect him and let him get clean and bring him back to me. I miss him so much. Especially his cock. I wish he was inside me right now. God, I'm so fucking horny. Father Fuckup isn't much of a substitute, but he'll do. Kill two birds with one stone. Get off and knock him off his goddamn high horse. Of course, he's probably got a pussy in his pants. Good thing I know what to do with one of those too.

I was disturbed and a little uneasy, but more than anything else, I was so lonely I could hardly breathe—and reading Tammy's diary only made me more so. Weary and sad, confused and adrift, I was in limbo between a restless sleep and a dreary waking world, my isolation an ice pick puncturing and deflating a lung.

Chapter Nineteen

"Were you having a sexual relationship with Tammy?" I asked.

"I was about the only one who wasn't."

Father Thomas and I were seated on the first pew of the chapel, dark figures amidst candlelight and weak illumination from the overcast morning streaming through the stained glass. He had been kneeling at the altar when I came in, dozing I suspected, his weary eyes falling shut as he had begun to pray. I had taken a seat on the first pew and when he awoke or finished he joined me.

"I shouldn't've said that," he added. "It was childish and judgmental. You'll have to forgive me. I've yet to grow accustomed to being thought of as a murderer."

I nodded.

"You do think of me as a murderer, don't you?"

I shook my head. "No," I said, "I really don't. I *do* think of you as a suspect."

"You don't really know me," he said. "If you did, and you could think I was capable of doing what was done to her, I don't know what I'd do."

We fell silent a moment, and I let my eyes wander around the small sanctuary as I thought about what I'd read and what he'd said.

The deep colors of the stained glass along the sides and behind the pulpit in the front were far darker than usual, their rich burgundies and blues looking more like a tapestry than a window, and in the flickering candlelight the hand-carved furniture and statues looked not modern but medieval.

"I've spent my entire life helping people," he said. "Or trying to. It may be in small ways, but I've done some real good. Given my life to easing the suffering of others. But this is what I'll be remembered for."

If possible, he looked even more feeble this morning than he had last night, his wrinkled skin thinner, paler, his small, watery eyes more sunken and unfocused.

"Do I look like someone she would have sex with?" he said. "Do I look like I am able?"

His last comment made me wonder if he was trying to appear more feeble than he really was.

"Her diary says she intended you to be one of her conquests."

"Oh, she propositioned me. Sure. But I didn't take it seriously, and I certainly made no attempt to take her up on it. Does her diary say otherwise?"

"Not through with it yet. Just got it. Someone left it in my room. Any idea who?"

"None. No locks in this place. Be easy enough to take it from her room and put it in yours, but why would they?"

"Because of what's in it," I said. "But are they trying to help or hinder the search for the truth?"

"If it's truly her journal, it can only help with the investigation, even if not everything she wrote in it is true."

"You don't fear anything in it?"

Hesitating a moment, he glanced at the confessional in the back. Following his gaze, I studied the large handmade wooden box. It was ornate and antique and I wondered how it had wound up here.

"It's good for the soul," I said.

"Can it stay between us?"

"I'm not a priest," I said. "I can't absolve you."

"If it has nothing to do with her death, can it stay between us? If it's not relevant to your investigation, will you hear my confession as a minister?"

I nodded.

He looked over his shoulder, then all around the chapel, before lowering his voice and saying, "I was attracted to her. She was so . . . There was something about her. I knew it was wrong—I think that was part of the appeal. I could tell she knew. She looked at me as if I was like every other man she had met and it infuriated me. She knew she had power over people and she enjoyed it. When I walked into the cabin last night and found her strapped to the bed without any clothes on I was more aroused than I've ever been. It was hard for me to concentrate. I think maybe that's part of why things got so out of hand. I was distracted . . . I just needed to tell someone. I never did anything about the way I felt. Never broke any of my vows—except in my heart."

"And you're sure nothing ever happened?"

"The only place we ever had sex was in my mind. I swear it."

In the silence that followed, I thought about what he had said and how he had said it, running it through the filters in my head, sifting for lies, hoping for truth.

"Don't you want to chastise me?"

"For having sexual thoughts about a highly sexualized girl?" I asked in surprise.

"I know it sounds silly," he said, "but I feel so guilty—especially in light of what happened."

"If you're looking for condemnation, you confessed to the wrong sinner."

The back doors swung open loudly and we both turned to see who it was.

"What's this?" Ralph Reid said, walking down the aisle toward us. "I thought I made it clear I didn't want my client questioned unless I was present."

"It's okay, Ralph," Father Thomas said. "We're just talking."

"*He* wasn't. He was interrogating you and the fact that you think it was just talking shows how good he is at it."

I laughed and shook my head. He was either one overzealous lawyer or he had something to hide. My money was on the latter. I doubted he was capable of looking out for anyone but himself and, because it was in his interest, the Gulf Coast Company, and his reaction was not commensurate with the threat I posed to his client.

"What prompted this little chat?" Reid asked. "I thought Father had answered all your questions."

"Actually, he answered all Steve's," I said, "but what prompted our discussion was Tammy's journal."

"Her journal?" he asked in surprise. "She kept one?"

"I suggested that she did," Father said. "It's helpful in the healing process."

"Do we know where it is?" Reid said.

"I have it," I said.

"How did you—"

"Someone left it in my room."

"What does it say?"

"I just started it."

"I need to see it as soon as possible. It could point to other possible suspects."

"I'm going to turn it over to Steve. I'm sure you'll get to see it if there's a trial."

"I want to see it *now*."

"Well, then," I said, "you're being given an opportunity to practice patience."

Chapter Twenty

"I really like Father Thomas," I said.

"But you think he killed Tammy?" Sister Abigail said.

Did I? I wasn't sure. I just didn't know enough yet, but for the moment he was still the prime suspect.

I was in her office again. As if our previous session had never ended, we were in nearly the exact same positions, she sitting upright in her recliner, I in the center of the love seat in front of her. On her desk, a single large candle burned, its gardenia fragrance filling the room.

"What does that mean?" she asked.

"What does what mean?"

"Your expression."

"Wasn't aware I was making one."

"Well, what were you thinking?"

"That I don't want to think he could've done it, but at the moment I have little choice."

"But you're still investigating?" she asked.

"Just beginning really."

"Good," she said.

"You don't mind me looking into it?"

"No. And not just because it suits my purposes. I've been thinking a lot about the things you've shared with me, and I think the key is not to choose between chaplaincy and criminology, but to figure out a way to do both."

I was sure her change of heart had more to do with helping

Father Thomas than me finding balance between my disparate vocations. Regardless of her motives, the result was the same. I could be involved in the investigation with her blessings instead of her constant protests.

"And have you?" I asked.

"Have I what?"

"Figured out a way to do both."

"I'm not the one who has to. And don't be fooled into thinking you've got it figured out if things go well while you're here. You're on retreat. You'll only really be tested when you're back in prison and under pressure."

I laughed.

"What is it?"

"I tell inmates that all the time," I said. "Doing well inside doesn't ensure they will when they get out."

"Tell me about Susan."

"Who?" I asked in surprise, the sudden change in subject jolting.

"Your two-time ex-wife," she said, adding with a smile, "You do remember her, don't you?"

"She neglected to file the papers the first time. We've only really been divorced once."

"But how many times in your heart?"

"Two."

"So what happened?"

"The usual," I said. "Dependency, co-dependency, anger, resentment, bitterness, faithlessness, recovery, breaking cycles, changing at different paces—and that was just the first time."

"And the second?"

"Her dad and I had a falling out. She sided with him."

"You do a lot of counseling," she said.

I nodded.

"What does it usually mean when someone becomes flippant over significant experiences in their lives?"

I smiled and nodded.

"I'm just saying there's more to it than you had a falling out and she sided with her dad."

"He's the inspector general for the department of corrections. We were working a case together at my institution. It didn't turn out well. It's a long story. The short version is, a line was drawn in the sand and she chose to stand on his side of it."

She nodded and looked up as she considered what I had said, her eyes narrowing, her lips twisting. Very little of her face was visible through her habit, but when she looked up it covered more of her forehead and less of her neck. The part that had pulled up off her chin showed a faint sepia stain from a patina of makeup powder and perspiration.

"Any chance of reconciliation?"

"She didn't fail to file the papers this time, but even if she had . . ."

"Even if she had what?"

"I'm in no condition for a rematch."

"So even if she wanted to be together, you do not?"

I pretended to think about it for a moment, though I knew the answer, then nodded.

"Then there's something you're not telling me," she said.

I smiled. "Lots."

"What's her name?"

"Who?"

"*The* woman. The one you're not telling me about."

I shook my head and sighed heavily, the familiar mixture of guilt-tinged desire and joy, like a river, rising inside of me. "Anna."

"And I take it she's unavailable?"

"Married."

"So were you," she said.

"I used to work with her. It was difficult, but good. Sweet torture. I've loved her my whole life. When Susan and I got back together, I told Anna I needed to stay away from her if it was going to work with Susan."

"What happened?"

"She transferred to Central Office and I haven't talked to her since."

She nodded.

We were quiet a long moment, everything receding as I tried to see myself clearly, honestly, objectively.

"I think maybe my marriage failed in part because I always held a part of myself back—and not just for Anna. I don't know. It probably wouldn't've made a difference in the final outcome. It's not what ultimately caused our demise, but I feel guilty for it."

"What do you mean not just for Anna? Why else did you hold back?"

"I'm not sure."

"But I bet you've thought about it."

"I'm not sure I was even doing it. If I was, it's not on purpose. I don't know. I just feel so fuckin' isolated. So alone. Always have. Don't know if it's something I'm doing or just the way I am— or the way most people are—but if I can change it I want to."

She nodded.

"It's not all the time, but it's too much of the time. And it's particularly acute right now."

"So you suffer from acute loneliness?"

"I do."

"I want us to come back to that. It's something we need to explore. There are probably lots of reasons you feel that way, and we'll look at them all, but just know this: Part of the reason you experience the isolation you do is your desire for true connection—to have authentic interactions and real intimacy. Small talk and surface distractions are never gonna do it for you, but we'll come back to that. For now, let's stick with your divorce."

"Okay."

"Maybe your holding back—or the way you are versus the way she is—*did* contribute to your breakup. Perhaps Susan sided with her dad as a way to get back at you. If she felt you were holding back—and I'm sure she did, even if on a subconscious level— perhaps she decided to do the same. Or maybe she really didn't think she had a choice. She might have felt she couldn't make the leap required to be with you because she knew you weren't really there and her father was."

I thought about it. She was probably right.

When Susan ended our relationship the last time, she refused to even take my calls. Eventually, I stopped calling, stopped all attempts at making contact. Now I wondered how hard I had really tried. Was I guilty of just making a few half-hearted attempts and then quickly giving up, relieved she was so unresponsive? Maybe Sister was right. Maybe Susan only held back because she knew I had been—knew I always would. I needed to call her, not in an attempt to reconcile our marriage, but our relationship, to accept responsibility, ask for forgiveness, seek peace, give healing a chance to begin.

"You may be right," I said. "Probably are. But I honestly felt at the time I had gone all in, given her everything, given our marriage every chance. Saying goodbye to Anna was a big part of that. So maybe you're right or maybe she had a sick dynamic with her dad."

"Or," she said, "possibly both."

"Who do you think killed Tammy?" I asked, attempting to turn her abrupt transition ploy on her.

Her eyes grew wide and her head snapped back slightly. "What?"

"You said you're convinced it's not Father Thomas. And I take it you don't believe the devil did it."

"No," she said, "I don't think the devil did it. I'm not sure I even believe in the devil."

I nodded. "But is that just a product of misguided modern thinking?"

"Well, obviously, if I thought it was, I wouldn't think it," she said.

"Kathryn said something to that effect to me earlier and I've been thinking about it. I've always seen myself as a postmodern thinker. I certainly don't think science has or will ever have an answer for everything. I know existence is profoundly mysterious and there are forces we can't even fathom, but . . ."

"You can't really believe the devil did it."

"Is that just ignorance or arrogance? It'd be ironic for someone who hates dogma as much as I do to be just as dogmatic as the religious right—just about different things."

"Something else for you to think about."

"I wonder if that's part of the problem," I said. "I spend so much time in my head. I think things through, even though I know the limitations of reason and logic. Maybe Kathryn's right and I need to be more intuitive in my approach to both types of work I do—and to life."

"Something for you to feel your way around," she said with a wry smile.

I nodded.

"Just remain open. Question everything. Including yourself, your beliefs and assumptions."

"If you don't think it was a demon, you've probably got

someone in mind."

She shrugged. "Not really. Apart from the fact that it has to be one of us."

"Someone at St. Ann's last night?"

She nodded.

"Of those of us who were here, who's most likely?"

"Under the right circumstances, we're all capable," she said. "I'd be very hesitant to point the finger at one person over another."

"What about those having a sexual relationship with the victim? Wouldn't you agree they're more likely than—"

"Those who weren't, but wanted to?" she asked. "Hardly."

"Who wasn't, but wanted to?" I asked.

She leaned forward slightly and lowered her voice. "Rumor has it, Ralph Reid—who not coincidentally works for her family—has always carried a torch for her."

"And they've never . . . I didn't get that she was discriminating."

"That's what added insult to the injury," she said. "Which, of course, is why she did it. It was a game. Her way of torturing him."

"Did you put her diary in my room?" I asked.

"Her what?" she asked, sitting back in her chair again.

"Father asked her to keep a journal while she was here," I said. "Apparently she did, and someone left it in my room last night—or this morning."

"I wasn't aware of its existence. Is it helpful?"

"I think it will be," I said. "I haven't finished it yet. Who besides Reid?"

"Is a frontrunner?" she asked. "I'm not sure. As you say, perhaps her harem."

"What about Keith Richie?" I asked.

"Why him more than the others?"

"He's an ex-offender for starters," I said.

"How did you—" she began, "but of course you'd know."

"What did he do time for?"

"I don't know. Even if I did I doubt I'd tell you. He's paid his debt. He's come here for healing—same as you."

"I'm not talking about a previous debt," I said. "I'm looking for a pattern."

"Well, I don't know," she said, "I really don't. If you want to know, you'll have to ask him."

"Thanks," I said. "I think I will."

Chapter Twenty-one

On my way to interview Keith Richie, I called the institution. The coverage was poor, the reception filled with static, and I could barely hear when the control room officer said, "Good morning, Potter Correctional Institution."

"Hey, Officer Williams, it's Chaplain Jordan. How are you?"

"Where are you? You sick?"

"On vacation."

Shrouded by thick gray clouds, the diffused light of the sun had yet to burn off the low-lying fog or dry up the dew, and the moist air felt wet on my face and caused bits of damp sand and grass blades to cling to my shoes.

"Well, we miss you," she said. "Hurry on back."

"Thanks. Merrill working today?"

"Yeah, but he's on a transport to Liberty CI."

"Okay. If you see him, would you ask him to call me? And can I have Classification?"

"Sure, sugar. Hold on one minute for me."

I was on hold for maybe ten seconds before the familiar but unexpected voice answered the phone. "Classification, Anna Rodden."

I stopped walking. For a moment, I couldn't speak.

"Hello?" she said.

"Anna?"

She hesitated, then softly said, "John."

Several things ran through my mind and I wasn't sure which

one to say.

"I'm surprised to find you there," I said.

"I was surprised to find you gone."

"Had to get away for a while," I said. "What're you doing there?"

"I work here."

"You do?"

"For a little while longer anyway," she said. "I'm still toying with the idea of going back to school full-time. I'm never gonna finish at this rate."

I nodded, though she couldn't see me. I was walking again, though I couldn't recall making a conscious decision to do so.

"John?" she asked. "You still there?"

"I'm here."

"You broke up. What'd you say?"

"I can't remember," I said.

"'Let me stand here till thou remember it.'"

I was surprised—not that she knew the quote, but that she said it given our estrangement.

"Sorry," she said. "Instinct."

"'I shall forget, to have thee still stand there, remembering how I love thy company.'"

"'And I'll stay, to have thee still forget, forgetting any other home but this.'"

Suddenly the world was warm again and I felt less lonely.

"Wow," she said.

"Yeah."

We were silent a long moment. Around me, St. Ann's seemed to grow more green, more lush, more vivid.

"Well," she said finally, "who were you calling?"

I felt dizzy and disoriented, as if my world were rotating on the wrong axis.

"I'm not sure," I said.

"What?"

"Anna, I'm sorry for what I did," I said.

She didn't say anything, and we just listened to static for a long moment.

Walking around the chapel and toward the dining hall, the cold, stiff grass crunched beneath my feet. I took in as much of St.

Ann's as I could, but saw no one. It was as if the abbey were empty, and maybe it was.

"I was just trying to—"

"I know what you were trying to do," she said. "Maybe we should talk about it when you get back."

"Okay."

"You remember why you called yet?" she asked.

"Yeah," I said, but didn't elaborate. I didn't want our conversation, awkward and painful though it were, to end.

"John?"

"Sorry. I need some information on an ex-inmate named Keith Richie."

"Why?"

"I'm investigating a suspicious death and he's one of the suspects."

"I thought you were on a spiritual retreat?"

"I am."

"So how are your vacations different from work?"

"I'm not surrounded by a few thousand felons," I said. *And you're not here.*

"I'll see what I can find out about him and let you know."

"Thanks."

"John."

"Yeah?"

"Be careful."

Pressing the tiny button that severed our connection, I walked through the dim dining hall to the brightly lit kitchen in the back.

Above the hums of ice machines and refrigerators, the mechanical sprinkler-system sound of the dishwasher, and the distorted music of a small radio, the loud banging, scraping, and chopping of Keith Richie's food preparation seemed violent.

Deciding to try to knock him off balance first thing, I turned off his radio and said, "How long you been out?"

"What?" he asked.

"Where'd you do your time? You ever at PCI?"

"You done time?" he asked, dropping his large knife on the stainless steel table and wiping his hands on his soiled apron.

"Still doing it," I said. "I'm the chaplain at PCI."

"Well, you may want to think about doing something else," he said.

"Why's that?"

"You're treating me like an inmate."

He was right. I was doing something I swore I never would—treating a person differently because he had been incarcerated.

"Bet you won't question any of the others so rudely," he said. "Didn't say hey or anything, just began to ask me invasive questions about my past. Only way you can do that is if you don't see me like everybody else. I'm not a person. I'm a convict. You said you're a chaplain?"

"I'm sorry," I said. "You're right. I shouldn't've done that."

Keith Richie was so tall I had to tilt my head back to look him in the eye. Freckles flecked the pale skin of his face and his thick reddish hair was long and straight. Tattoos of vastly varying quality peaked out from beneath his clothes.

"You gonna offer an explanation or an excuse or something?" he asked.

I shook my head. "Just an apology," I said. "Again, I'm sorry."

"Well, you're right. Congratulations, you win the prize. I am what you think I am—a convict, a menace to society, state property."

"State property?" I asked. "You got paper following you?"

He nodded. "And I'm clean. I've got this good job in this quiet place and I'm putting my life back together. Growing spiritually. Getting my head together. I didn't kill that girl and I don't know who did. Know nothing about it."

"Were you two involved?" I asked.

He let out a little laugh, cold and ironic. "You know the funny thing? I was told PCI had a good chaplain. Guys said he was different. Really cared. Treated you with respect. Like a human being. You don't get a reputation like that inside without it being true."

I didn't say anything, just waited.

He considered me intently, his eyes squinting, brow furrowing.

"Don't be offended by it. I'm asking everyone, even Father Thomas. Were you and Tammy involved?"

"She wasn't *involved* with anyone," he said. "You're asking if we were fuckin'."

"Am I?"

"Yes, you are."

"Were you?"

"No," he said. "We were not. She was far too into Brad."

Chapter Twenty-two

I found Brad Harrison installing sensor lights on the main gate. He was on a ladder screwing a lightbulb into one of the sockets. His large body was covered by faded jeans and a camouflage jacket, both of which were flecked with primer and paint, and spotless work boots that appeared new.

"Little late for this," he said, nodding toward the lights, "but Sister Abigail said it was better late than never."

"These wouldn't've made a difference," I said, "but they make people feel safer."

"It's not this kind of light that drives out Satan," he said.

I waited for him to smile, but he didn't.

His movements flexed his upper body muscles and they pressed against his tight clothes. He was thick and muscular with the quiet confidence of a man who knew he could figure out a way to build or repair anything.

"It's the darkness in our hearts that's the problem," he continued. "And stringing up lights along the perimeter and putting locks on the doors ain't gonna deal with that."

He finished tightening the bulb and flipped on the switch behind it. When he ran his hand in front of the sensor, the lights came on. Snatching up a screwdriver and a pair of pliers from the top rung, he shoved them in his jacket pocket and climbed back down the ladder.

Standing in front of me, he cocked his head and studied me intently. "You a preacher *and* a detective?"

The pungent smells emanating off him were a sour mixture of sweat, testosterone-tinged body odor, cheap cologne, a bland, ineffectual deodorant, dirty hair, and the greasy metallic scent of tools and labor, of screwing and unscrewing, tightening and loosening, of repairing and installing.

"Prison chaplain. I was a cop for a while. Still help with investigations occasionally."

"With all the souls that need to be saved?"

The only responses I could come up with were smartass ones, so I didn't respond.

Shaking his head slightly to himself, he turned, grabbed the ladder, and dragged it to the other side of the massive wrought iron gate.

"You close and lock this every night?" I asked.

He nodded. "Nine o'clock."

"Every night?"

"Haven't missed one in five years," he said.

"And last night?"

"*Every* night," he said.

He pulled a box with another light fixture in it off the ground and carried it up the ladder with him. Placing it on the top rung, he withdrew the pliers and screwdriver and began fastening a bracket to the top bar of the gate.

"How did the police cars and ambulance get in?" I asked.

"I let them in."

"How'd you know to?"

"Sister Kathryn."

"I thought she wasn't a nun?" I asked.

He stopped what he was doing and looked down at me with a perplexed look on his face. "She's still our sister in Christ," he said. "Right *brother*?"

"Did she call you?"

"We don't have phones in our rooms," he said. "She sent Brother Keith to tell me."

"Who all has a key to it?"

"The gate? Myself, Father Thomas, Sister Abigail, Sister Kathryn, and there's a few in the front office of the counseling center."

"If someone needs to get in or out after nine, what do they

do?" I asked.

"They don't," he said.

"You're saying the chief of police was trapped in here?"

"If he was inside he was."

My next question was for personal and not investigatory purposes, but he didn't know that.

"Had he ever been locked in before?" I asked.

"Not that I know of."

"Someone said the night before Tommy Boy was found, he was seen leaving with Tammy," I said. "Did you see them leave together?"

He nodded. "Yeah."

"Our best guess is that he didn't die until late that night or early the next morning," I said. "If Tammy was with him, I'm wondering how her car got back into St. Ann's."

"She must not've been with him," he said. "I locked the gate at nine."

"Did you see her return?"

He shook his head. "No. I didn't."

Having finished mounting the sensor light, he descended the ladder, exchanged the empty fixture box for one holding lightbulbs, and ascended the ladder again.

"Look like what Jacob must've seen," he said.

I knew he was talking about the story in Genesis in which, on the run and sleeping on the ground with a rock for a pillow, Jacob dreamed of a ladder with angels ascending and descending, but from what I could tell he was no angel.

After a moment of silence, he said, "You think a demon killed Tommy Boy too?"

"I don't."

"Then why all the—"

"You had a relationship with Tammy, didn't you? I base that not only on my observations, but witness testimony—and I have her diary."

He finished screwing in the lightbulbs and descended the ladder before answering.

"Brother John, let me tell you something. I'm saved, sanctified, and filled with the Holy Ghost, but no matter how willing my spirit is, my flesh is weak. I have feet of clay and a tendency to backslide often."

"I'll take that as a yes."

"It wasn't a relationship," he said. "It was just occasional sins of the flesh."

"It wasn't occasional for her, was it?"

"It wasn't her. She was possessed."

"Even if you believe that, it had to make you jealous," I said.

"I cared for her."

"As a sister in Christ?" I asked, unable to help myself.

"That and more," he said, his expression and tone sincere. "I would've married her once she had been set free and was really right with God."

"Who was she fornicating with beside you?" I asked.

He shrugged. "I don't know."

It was the first time during our conversation that I thought he was lying to me.

"You didn't just backslide again, did you?"

"What?"

"You're lying," I said. "I've seen and done it enough to recognize it."

He grinned as if caught doing something cute. "Pray for me, brother," he said. "I need strength."

"Where were you last night after dinner?" I asked.

"In my room praying."

"Like the rest of us, you saw Tammy leave the table with Father Thomas," I said. "Did you know what they were doing?"

"Why you think I was praying? She was gonna come to my room afterwards to let me see the new her, but she never did."

"Did you go out looking for her?" I asked.

He hung his head. "I fell asleep."

"Because the spirit is willing but the flesh is weak," I said. "So you didn't go out of your room at all?"

"Not until I had to open the gate."

"Did Kathryn tell you what had happened?"

"Just said to open the gate."

"What'd you think?"

"Honestly? That something had happened to Father Thomas."

"Why?"

"It was just a feeling I had," he said. "And it was right. Just wasn't the only thing that happened."

"You really believe a demon is responsible for Tammy's death?" I asked.

"You don't?" he said, looking at me with a mixture of surprise and disgust.

"If it wasn't a demon, who do you think did it?"

"No one," he said, "because it was a demon. 'We wrestle not against flesh and blood, but against powers and principalities.' How can you know so little about our adversary who roams about like an angry lion seeking whom he may devour?"

He then began speaking in tongues—the Glossolalia of Pentecostalism, that speech-like vocalization of nonsense syllables—throwing his head up, arms out, his eyes rolling back in his head.

Chapter Twenty-three

Father Thomas was slumped in the chair behind his desk. He looked old and weary and guilty. A gold banker's lamp with a green shade provided the only illumination in the room apart from the sunlight streaming in the narrow strip of window that wasn't covered by a bookshelf. Light jazz played softly in the background.

"How long you been doing exorcisms?" I asked.

"Over thirty years."

He had pulled several books on the subject from his shelves for me to borrow and they were in a stack in the pool of light on his desk. Both hardback and softcover, with simple to elaborate artwork, the books claimed to plumb the depths of the dark side.

"That's a long time," I said. "How'd you get started?"

He shrugged. "Saw a need."

"How many have you done?"

"Hundreds."

"There aren't many exorcists, are there?"

"More than you'd think," he said. "Most avoid the inevitable circus that accompanies notoriety." Touching the books gently, he added, "Some of the most renown are featured in these volumes."

I glanced at the books again. He hadn't arranged them by size, so smaller books were beneath larger ones, and the stack looked like it could topple over at any moment. Their titles left little doubt as to their subject: *An Exorcist Tell His Story, Possessed, Hostage to the Devil, American Exorcism, Speaking with the Devil, Deliverance from Evil Spirits, Beware of the Night.*

"A couple of my cases are written about in this one," he said, withdrawing *Cast Out* from the center of the pile and placing it on top. "The names have been changed—including mine."

"There has to be more to it than you saw a need," I said.

"Why're you a minister? Why're you an investigator? No simple answers to those questions I bet. We're complicated beings with complex motives."

"Last night at the police station you mentioned knowing the difference between someone who's possessed and someone with mental illness."

"You just know," he said. "Especially after doing this for so long. I know evil when I sense it, and no matter how demented a person becomes, no matter how bizarre their behavior, there's a difference."

"But are there specific signs you look for to confirm someone's possessed?"

"The *Ritual* mentions three symptoms," he said. "Talking in unknown languages, exhibiting superhuman strength, and knowing what's hidden."

I nodded.

"And," he added, "in my considerable experience, and that of the countless exorcists I've spoken to, these always surface *during* an exorcism, *never* before."

"Did Tammy exhibit any of them?"

He nodded. "All three."

"Really?"

"You don't believe, do you. Not just about Tammy, but in general. You don't believe in possession."

"I don't disbelieve. I'm just not as certain as some people— and that's about most things, not just possession."

"I can understand that for an investigator, but for a man of faith?"

I frowned and nodded slowly. "I really go back and forth between belief and skepticism," I said. "But most of the time it's not that I don't believe, it's that I'm not sure what I believe. Practice is more important to me than belief. I'm open. Seeking. I attempt to be faithful even as my knowledge and beliefs are fluid."

"We live in cynical times," he said. "It's the age of the brain, and I'm afraid the soul is what suffers the most."

I wasn't sure I agreed with him exactly. There seemed to be more religiosity than cynicism in the world—especially in our culture. Fundamentalism was on the rise. There was a revival of conservatism and literalism. The religious right was enjoying political power like never before. Maybe what he was saying accurately reflected one segment of the population, but for another significant part nearly the opposite was true. Perhaps more than anything else what we had was a great divide. On one side the post-Enlightenment, scientific-oriented skeptics and on the other the faith-filled, dogmatic fundamentalists. Religion was just one of many ways the world was deeply divided these days—and like politics, education, technology, environmental protection, and wealth, the gulf seemed to be growing wider by the minute. We seemed to be heading toward a revolution that would not only see a battle between the haves and have-nots, but between the fundamentalists and the progressives—actually that war had already begun, and it did so long before September 11.

"If we only had the tape, you could—'course that's not the same as believing, is it? These really are matters of faith. Plenty of people see and still don't believe."

I nodded and thought about it.

"'Blessed are those who have not seen and still believe,'" he said. "Speaking of which," he added, "what about all the exorcisms Jesus performed? Are they just legends that grew up around the Christian tradition?"

"I don't know," I said. "I think—"

"But isn't that part of the problem? All your thinking. What about feeling, discerning, intuiting?"

The jazz stopped and we sat in silence for a long moment.

"I'm not judging you," he said, "just asking questions."

"They're good questions, and I'm fine with you asking them. I do all the time. I have faith, just not certainty. I'm a devout agnostic. And I think I have to be to do what I do, but you're right. I live in my head way too much."

Compassion filled his face and he sat up in his chair a little. "When I was a teenager, I underwent an exorcism that not only saved, but changed my life."

Frederick Buechner was right. All theology really was autobiographical.

"There's not a doubt in my mind about possession," he

continued, "because I've experienced it firsthand. I had an uncle—
step-uncle really—who systematically abused me sexually and in
other ways. In fact, it was more like torture. He also got me strung
out on drugs. I was vulnerable and angry and the dark place deep
inside me became the home of a truly evil presence."

"I'm so sorry."

He waved off my apology. "I didn't tell you for sympathy.
That angry young man seems like another person to me—a stranger
now. I just wanted you to know that I'm not crazy or making all this
up, and, now that I've had time to think about it, I think Tammy's
experiences with sex and drugs were far closer to mine than I
realized."

"You think she'd been abused?"

"I think you should find a solitary place on this sacred ground
and read these books. Then read the rest of her diary and see for
yourself."

Chapter Twenty-four

The afternoon sun made it warm enough to take Father Thomas's advice. Sitting in a wooden swing between two cypress trees near the lake, Tammy's journal and the exorcism books beside me, I was working my way through the stack, the desultory sounds of the day far more distracting than I could've imagined they'd be.

The first book, *Psychiatry and Possession*, was by a psychiatrist, Dr. Samuel Peters, who after years of private practice had come to believe in something beyond human evil and mental illness—demonic possession. He was a respected doctor and best-selling author, and seemed to have academic clout and clinical credibility. During his later years of practice he worked with a patient he believed to be possessed, ultimately performing an exorcism on her, attempting to find empirical evidence of demonic possession.

In making his case for the reality of possession, Dr. Peters reported that during the ritual the following happened: The patient's face altered extremely and dramatically into what he called "satanic facial expressions" during the manifestations of each of her demons, which a video camera was unable to capture onto tape; the emergence of four separate demonic personalities, which he believed to be impossible for the patient to create herself; the exhibiting of negative responses to holy water and the Book of Common Prayer; her inexplicable snake-like appearance, which was apparent to everyone present, but not captured on the video recording; and her display of superhuman strength in spite of being severely underweight, malnourished, and sleep deprived.

This singular experience led Peters to assert that he had answered four complex questions with a degree of scientific certainty: Yes, the devil or a demonic world exists; the phenomenon of the demonic possessions of human individuals also exists; the process of exorcism can, in certain seriously possessed patients, be either curative or strikingly beneficial beyond any other known remedies; and that it is only during the process of exorcism that the demonic possession is fully revealed.

Peters concluded the following: Possession is not an accident. In becoming possessed, the victim must cooperate with the devil in some way. Such cooperation can range from a conscious and deliberate pact with the devil to a child's seemingly innocent denial of reality, choosing lies over the truth. He also believes that the initial cooperation is often made under great duress, and that thereafter possession is a gradually growing process. He defines an exorcism as a massive therapeutic intervention to liberate and support the victim to be able to choose to renounce the possession and reject the devil. Often the victim will not offer an explanation of why he or she became possessed until after the exorcism is concluded. The more recent the time of the onset of the possession, the more the exorcism is likely to be successful. Exorcisms of genuinely possessed people should be expected to be combative—some physical restraints are almost always necessary. Exorcisms should be conducted by a team, never an individual. He also highly recommends all exorcisms be videotaped—both for legal and educational purposes.

Though a non-denominational Protestant, Peters argues that the Catholic Church, through its rigorous hierarchical and authoritarian control, was a guardian of "correct" theology and practice for all of Christianity on several issues, including possession and exorcism. According to him, it has been the only church to have maintained over several centuries formal instructions concerning the diagnosis of possession and the ritual of exorcism.

I looked up and thought about what I'd read. Here was a doctor, a respected man of science, who had taken a scientific approach to the subject. He was rational, reasonable, and credible. I couldn't easily dismiss him or what he was reporting. Much of what he described was similar to what Father Thomas was claiming happened with Tammy. Of course, Father Thomas had no doubt read this account. I remained skeptical, but not as incredulous. I could feel myself becoming more open to all possibilities—and not just as a commitment to the concept, but truly more curious and open. Putting aside the book on exorcism, I picked up Tammy's journal and began to read.

Depressed. So down last night I felt like I couldn't breathe. Up until three in the morning thinking about how different my life is than what I thought it would be.

Everything I've ever attempted has failed. Everyone around me seems to be succeeding at what they're doing—their careers and businesses are not only going well, but bringing them fulfillment. Unlike me, most of the people I know are satisfied with their lives.

How can they be so damn content? They seem to be good at life—the little things of life that I abhor. I'm no good at living. At finding meaning in the mundane, at doing what needs to be done. I resent it.

I've never found a job completely satisfying, never not longed for something else. Maybe my restlessness is merely faithlessness, my avoidance of pain, of discomfort. Or maybe it's just delusions of grandeur. I'm living a little life—obscure, anonymous, on the fringes, making no significant contribution to the world—and I loathe it.

Countless people have told me I'm special, beautiful, can do anything. They've said I'll do great things, go places, succeed, and I've believed them. But so far I've done nothing, been nowhere to speak of, made no contribution, and I wonder whether I ever will.

Looking up from the page, I saw a young woman with badly cut short black hair coming toward me with a small brown paper bag. She was dressed plainly in worn, inexpensive clothes and walked like someone trying not to offend the ground she was stepping on.

When she reached me, she looked at me briefly, gave me a hesitant smile, then ducked her head and looked away.

"Keith said to bring this to you," she said, holding up the bag. "It's lunch."

"Thank you," I said. "And him."

"It's a couple of sandwiches, an apple, and a soda."

"I don't think we've met," I said. "I'm John Jordan. I'm here for a visit."

"I'm Amber," she said. "I help out around here. I've been visiting my folks."

"So you live here at the abbey?"

She nodded.

"When'd you get back?" I asked.

"Last night," she said.

"What time?"

She shrugged. "I'm not sure. 'Round eleven."

"How'd you get in?"

She looked perplexed. "Nothing's locked. I just walked in. This is a very open place. People come and go all the time. All of the homeless in the area know they can come out here any time of the day or night and find shelter and something to eat—same for teens."

I realized how little we knew about who was actually at St. Ann's last night, and how their reputation for openness would make it virtually impossible to ever know for sure. Could Tammy have been murdered by an opportunistic killer, someone who was just passing through? It was possible, but improbable, and it certainly didn't feel like that type of murder to me.

"The front gate wasn't locked?" I asked.

"Oh," she said, "yeah, it was. I just had him drop me off at the gate and walked the rest of the way."

"Him?"

"My boyfriend."

"You've heard what happened?"

She nodded. "It's so awful."

"You see or hear anything?"

She shook her head. "No, I swear. I'd tell you if I knew anything."

"How well'd you know Tammy?"

She glanced down at the book I was holding. "Is that her diary?"

I nodded.

"Then I'm sure you know," she said.

"Actually, I'm just starting it. Haven't read anything about you yet."

"Well, let's talk when you do. I need to get back to the kitchen right now."

"Okay," I said. "Thanks for the sandwiches."

When she had gone, I withdrew one of the sandwiches and ate it as I read another entry.

Sometimes I really like the people here. Sometimes I think they're all right. A little strange, but good people. Well-meaning. Sincere. Simple and honest.

Dull as debutantes, but not out to take advantage of you like most everybody else you meet. But other times all I can think about is how they stole my land. How I'd be set for life if they weren't here. That's taking advantage of people—even if they don't know it, but somebody here does. I know it. Someone here orchestrated the whole thing. Why else would Uncle Floyd give them all this land? Of course, when he did it, it wasn't nearly as valuable, but it was still one hell of a generous gift, though. And he wasn't like that. He didn't just give stuff away. Hell, his motto was 'You can't spend it and have it.' And he wasn't religious. Someone tricked him or bribed him into giving all this land and the old buildings and so many donations over the years. They may've fooled old Floyd, but they're not gonna fool me.

So far I couldn't see any reason to believe that Tammy Taylor was extremely disturbed, let alone possessed, and then I read an entry that gave me chills.

I fell like lightening. Cast down. Thrown out. Expelled. Now I wander the dry places looking for a new home. And I've found one in this hollow space inside this stupid bitch. She thinks she's just tripping, but she's not the only one living here anymore. And soon Tammy won't live here at all. She'll just be a shell—the body. I'll be the soul. It feels good to be incarnated again. I so enjoy the corporeal. And oh the things I'm gonna do with this body. Fuckin' wear this cunt out. Take my revenge. Blood will spill. Death will come. They won't know what hit them until they're dead. I AM GOD. I AM POWER. I AM FIRE. I AM HELL. Wait now. Be patient. Don't get carried away just yet. The best attack is a surprise one. And boy is Father Fuckup and his little band of buttfucks in for the surprise of their pathetic little lives.

An icy wind blew in off the lake and right through me, the sound of a thousand whispered voices in it—taunting, mocking, harassing.

"Why didn't you help me, John?" Tammy said softly.

It was as if her lips were at my left ear—nearly touching but not. Had I not seen that no one was there, I would've sworn there was.

In my right ear, the playfully demented voice of a wicked child said, "You're going to die soon too. Ring-a-ring-a-roses. A pocket full of posies. Ashes. Ashes. John is a dead man."

The laugh that followed was worse than anything said by the child, and Tammy began to cry.

"Shut up bitch or I'll hurt you some more."

She stopped.

I did too.

Refusing to give in to fear, I returned my attention to the journal, this time reading aloud.

I found myself wondering if what I was reading had even been written by Tammy. What if someone else had written it after her death and left it for me? I'd be more persuaded to believe it if there were more consistency—and if I weren't hearing voices. The abrupt transition from Satan-like speak to typical teenage angst was jarring.

Will I ever find the right guy? Everyone says he's out there, but . . . I don't know. I thought it was Clyde. I guess it still could be, but he's such a jerk. Sometimes I don't think he even loves me at all. Others I think he does, but he just doesn't know how to treat a woman. I am a woman. I have needs. I have desires. I need him to think about me for once. Consider what I want, what makes me happy. Maybe I should just dump Clyde and get busy finding Mr. Right. Can't do it in here. I've got to finish up and get back out there. Of course, when I've finished what I'm doing, I bet I'll have many more prospects. I'll be able to take my pick. They'll probably just want me for my money (and my honey hole, they always want that), but they won't get much of either unless they convince me that they really love me. They're gonna have to prove their love for me. Do what I tell them. Tommy Boy'll do anything for me, and he doesn't even know I'm about to be a very rich girl, but he's too . . . I don't know, he's just not Mr. Right, but that doesn't mean he can't help me do what I need to do to get in a position to attract Mr. Right. And it's not like I'm just using him. He gets what he wants. What every man wants. I'll keep giving him pussy payments and he'll think he's been well rewarded. And he has. Mine's no ordinary pussy. Sometimes I feel like I've got hell itself between my legs, sucking not just semen, but life out of the pricks that keep poking in there.

"What're you reading?" Kathryn asked.

"You don't want to know."

"I've probably written much worse in my novels."

"Did you write this?" I said.

"What?" she asked, sitting down on the swing beside me.

"To help Father Thomas."

"John," she said with a wry smile, "we can't go on with suspicious minds."

I smiled back at her.

"But seriously, there's a few things I need to tell you, and I've got a few questions about the case."

"Good," I said, "because I have some for you too."

Chapter Twenty-five

"I stopped by your room before coming out here," she said.

"Yeah?"

"Not the neatest person in the world, are you?" she said.

"Either that, or it's been ransacked."

"*Ransacked?* Who uses the word *ransacked* anymore?"

"I do. Actually, I don't think I've ever really gotten to use it before. I'm grateful for the opportunity."

"Well, I'm pretty neat," I said, "so evidently it *was . . .*"

"Ransacked?" she said.

"Yeah," I said. "I was giving you another opportunity to say it."

"You don't seem too worried about your room."

"Didn't have much in it. Nothing of value. I'm sure they were looking for this," I said, holding up Tammy's journal.

"Who all'd you tell about it?" she asked.

We were still sitting on the swing, facing the small, bouncing waves on the surface of the lake. Even in the wind, I could smell a hint of her perfume—something I hadn't smelled in our previous encounters, and I couldn't help but wonder if she was wearing it for me.

"I'm sure most everybody knows by now," I said. "But I think I only mentioned it to Father Thomas, Ralph Reid, Sister Abigail, Keith Richie, Brad Harrison, and Amber. Plus, there's the person who put it there in the first place, but it'd be hard to see why they'd give it to me and then take it back."

Her hair was like that of a little girl, thick and a light blond the color of straw. The brisk breeze blowing through it whipped it, giving it that sexy, just-out-of-bed look, and I couldn't help but wonder what it would be like to wake up beside her.

"Wonder what they're so anxious to keep hidden?" she said.

"Won't know until I finish. May not then."

Glancing down at the exorcism books between us, she said, "You reconsidering what happened?"

I thought about what I had read and its impact on me. I couldn't easily dismiss the experiences and conclusions of Dr. Samuel Peters. A lot of people viewed much of what people claimed to be spiritual phenomenon—everything from hearing God's voice to demonic possession—as mental illness, but surely Peters would know the difference.

"Your boyfriend asked me to brush up on the subject and break it down for him," I said.

"He's not my boyfriend," she said.

"Who?"

"Steve. I'm practically a nun."

She pushed her hair out of her face with the fingers of her cream-colored hands, the nails of which were painted a soft pink. Like the perfume, I didn't recall her nails being painted on our previous encounters and wondered if I had just been distracted. Her hands looked cold and I wanted to take them in mine to warm them.

"Speaking of which," I said, "I wanted to ask you about the abbey. Is it owned by the Catholic Church?"

She shook her head. "It's an autonomous non-profit organization. It's far more interfaith than it seems right now because so many of the other teachers and workers are away for the holidays."

"I got the sense while talking to Brad that he's Pentecostal."

She nodded. "We have a Jewish teacher on staff who's away for Hanukkah, and a Buddhist monk who works as a counselor in our drug rehab program. Then you got me. I don't know what the hell I am. A Judeo-Christian Buddhist Pagan artist."

"How has the church allowed Father Thomas and Sister Abigail to be here so long?"

"They started it. I think they have a special dispensation from the bishop, but the truth is everyone knows they wouldn't go anywhere else and I'm not sure anybody else would put up with them. They're used to doing things their own way. They fuss like siblings, but they have a lot of respect for one another. I'm not sure what Sister's gonna do without him."

"What's wrong with him?"

"Cancer. Treatment would've given him a little more time, but he opted for quality not quantity. I really don't think he could stand the thought of leaving this place. He wants to die here."

"You realize that having nothing to lose makes him more likely to have committed the crime."

"I realize it might seem that way, but it's not. He's been working hard to prepare himself for the life to come. He's too close to it to . . . I'm telling you he wouldn't—*couldn't* do it."

"I hope you're right," I said. "If Gulf Coast wants this land back, can it just take it?"

She shrugged. "I'm not sure. I don't think so."

"What if St. Ann's closes?"

"I'm really not sure, but that's exactly what would happen if they stopped their support, so as usual, the big greedy corporation has all the power."

We were silent a moment, during which she seemed to be trying to work out something in her mind, chewing on her top lip as she did. As I waited for her, I scanned the windswept world around us—the light chop on the surface of the lake, the twisting and turning Spanish moss on the waving branches. Everything was movement, like a sacred dance to a silent orchestra, more felt than heard.

When she turned and looked at me from the depths of her dark brown eyes, neither of us spoke for a long moment, and I had to resist the urge to lean in and kiss her full, soft pink lips.

"I wish we had the tape," she said. "I guarantee it'd show he's telling the truth."

"Maybe."

"The fact that it was there shows he didn't plan on killing anyone."

"Not planning to do it and not doing it are two different things."

Chapter Twenty-six

We were in the clearing when we were attacked.

Tired of sitting, we had decided to take a walk around the lake, but as if being pulled back to the crime scene, we found ourselves drifting down the path in that direction.

Beneath the ancient oak canopy, the shaded path was colder than the water's edge from which we'd come and we walked close to one another for warmth.

She was wearing a gray FSU sweatshirt, jeans, and a jacket, the pockets of which held her ice-white hands.

We walked slowly, enjoying one another's company, as the sun began to sink behind the pines.

"Hard to believe something so profane happened in such a holy place," she said.

"Not if you believe the devil did it. What better to profane than the holy—in fact, what can you profane *except* the holy?"

"The world's such an enchanted place," she said, glancing up the slope to our right at the sunlit tops of oaks and pines ablaze with the fading brilliance of the day. "Don't you feel far more connected to the Mystery when you're out here?"

"Actually," I said, an involuntary shudder running through me, "I do."

"We can't rush past the sacred so easily out here. We're not so insulated from her. What is it the Kabbalah teaches?"

"That all of creation is within God," I said.

"I love that. The universe hasn't even been born yet. We're

still inside the womb of God."

Caught up in the moment, or using it as an excuse, I stopped abruptly, took her by the arms of her jacket, pulled her to me, and kissed the mouth that had just said such beautiful things. And the beautiful mouth kissed back.

"That took you long enough," she said.

"Yeah?"

"Yeah. Why you think I'm saying all this Kabbalah shit? Figured it's an aphrodisiac for a man like you."

She then withdrew her cold hands from her pockets, pulled my face back to hers, and kissed me again.

"Yeah," I said as we began walking again, "I definitely feel God out here."

She smiled. "Goddess."

"Of course."

We walked a little way longer in silent rapture over the moment we had just shared, and I began to worry about what I had done.

"I just went through a bad breakup and divorce," I said.

She nodded.

"And at least some part of the reason is I'm still, and probably always will be, in love with a woman I can never have."

"Jesus. It was just a kiss," she said.

I smiled. "Just wanted you to know."

"Newsflash, I know you're damaged goods," she said. "Who the hell isn't? I'm a big girl. I won't break. We can kiss, do some heavy petting—hell even fornicate a little. I won't stalk you. I won't try to replace . . ."

"Anna," I said.

"I won't try to replace Anna, okay?"

"I'm stupid," I said. "I'm sorry. I shouldn't have . . ."

"No, you're sweet, but my guess is you try to take care of everyone, and not everyone needs taking care of."

"You're right," I said. "Maybe I should kiss you again to show you I can do it without trying to take care of you."

"Well, if you think you should," she said, stopping at the point where the path became the clearing.

"I do," I said, and I did.

It was a nice kiss—even better than the first two—or it was right up until the guy with the knife cut in.

He grabbed her from behind, putting his arm around her body and pulling her away from me, as he put the knife to her throat.

I tried to remain calm, not react until I had a better handle on what was going on. He was just holding her, not cutting, not dragging her away.

He was a shortish, thick, muscular man with an acne-scarred face and a buzz cut.

"Old jealous boyfriend you forgot to tell me about?" I asked her.

She didn't respond, and I could see the fear in her eyes quickly approaching frenzy.

"Just stay where you are and be cool," he said to me. "Nobody's gonna get hurt."

"Oh, that's where you're mistaken," I said.

"We just want the book," he said.

"We?" I asked, wondering if he was referring to voices inside his head or if he had an accomplice.

"Hand me the book," he said.

"Hand it to him, John," Kathryn said.

"This?" I asked him, holding up the journal. "This is just some love poems I've been working on. You want me to read a couple to you?"

"I ain't playin'," he said. "Hand me the fuckin' book now."

"Or what?" I asked. "See, that's the second time you've given me an order without a threat. I know. I know. You'll argue that the threat is implied. And I'm not saying you're wrong, but don't you think it'd be far more effective if you said exactly what it is? You might even try growling a little when you say it."

"Give me the fuckin' book or I'll fuckin' slit her fuckin' throat," he said, his voice angry and menacing.

"That's it," I said. "Much better."

I considered my options. The distance between us was too great for me to rush him. He could cut her before I could even reach them. I wasn't sure what he'd do if I didn't give him the journal, and I wasn't sure he did either. He was probably working for someone else, and they probably just told him to get the book, not what to do if I wouldn't give it to him. Still, Kathryn was too upset to be any help and I couldn't let this go on much longer. My best bet was to give him the book, get Kathryn back, then take the book from him.

"Last chance, funny man," he said.

Kathryn screamed as the tip of the blade pierced her skin and a small dot of bright red blood appeared on her neck.

"Okay, okay," I said. "We'll trade. Take the knife away from her neck and I'll put the book on the ground. Then I'll back away from it and you let her walk over to me. Then you get the book and run for your life."

"Yeah, okay," he said, pulling the knife away from her neck, "but don't you try anything slick."

I placed the journal on the ground and took two steps back from it.

"Back up some more," he said.

"Let her go first," I said.

He released her and I took another step back.

"Now, let her walk to me and I'll continue to back away from the book."

He did.

She took a few steps away from him, panicked, and began to run. He tried once to grab her, but missed and decided to go for the book instead.

By the time Kathryn had reached me, he had snatched the book and was running toward the opposite side of the clearing.

I smiled. Only water beyond the trees over there. He was trapped. The Intracoastal was too wide for him to swim across and he was too big for me not to catch him if he tried.

"You okay?" I asked Kathryn.

I had my arm around her and she was holding on to me, her body trembling with the wash of adrenaline.

She nodded.

"Can you run back to the abbey and let me go after him?" I asked.

She started to nod, but her eyes grew wide, then she flinched.

A sudden jolt from an unseen object swung with force connected with the back of my neck and I fell down face-first, the oak limb that had hit me landing beside me on the ground.

I tried to get up, but couldn't. I just laid there, watching as the second man joined the first and disappeared into the trees on the other side. A minute later, I heard a boat motor crank, grow louder as it passed by close to us, and then fade into the distance.

"Are you all right?" Kathryn asked.

I nodded slowly, but even that hurt.

"You recognize either of them?" I asked.

She shook her head. "What could be in Tammy's diary to make them do that?"

"Good question. Wish I'd've finished it."

"Sorry I freaked out," she said.

"You did fine."

"Remind me to tell you sometime why I did."

"Not now?" I asked, sitting up.

"Not now," she said.

"Okay."

We stood, still staring toward the unseen waterway where they had escaped.

"I can't believe they have the diary," she said. "You think they're the ones who ransacked your room?"

I shook my head. "My guess is they were his or her backup. When the ransacking didn't work, he or she called them in, but that could have revealed far more to us than the diary will to them."

"How's that?"

"Two ways. First, who here would even know how to hire guys like that? But more importantly, the way they did it. Coming in by boat, attacking us, and escaping by boat down the waterway."

"Why?"

"Because," I said, "the killer could have done it the exact same way."

Chapter Twenty-seven

"So you think maybe the killer came and left by boat?" Steve asked.

"I think it's a possibility. We need to check with the landings to see if anyone remembers someone launching late last night."

Steve nodded. "We also need to check with the houses and camps along the waterway. Boat may not have been launched because it was already in the water."

I nodded. "It could've been stolen or borrowed or the killer could be the owner."

Kathryn, Steve, and I were standing at the far edge of the clearing looking down into the Intracoastal in the last light of the day. The waterway resembled a small river, only too straight, too square, too symmetrical for the meanderings of Mother Earth.

"You realize if you had turned the diary over to me like you should have, we'd still have it," he said.

"Yeah, but then we wouldn't have this clue."

"This clue? I'd much rather—"

"I'm kidding. Sorry I didn't turn it over to you sooner."

"It *was* left for him," Kathryn said.

"Doesn't matter," he said, "it's evidence."

"He's right," I told her. "I should have."

In the darkening day, the water in the Intracoastal looked black, its surface flat as slate.

"What were you thinking?" he asked.

"That I'd read it first."

"Well, what'd it say?"

"I had just started it."

He shook his head. "I could arrest you for obstruction."

I nodded.

"Were you ever going to give it to me?"

"The moment I finished it," I said.

"I thought you were out of it after last night?"

"I did say that, didn't I?"

"Yeah, but it doesn't count. I didn't believe you."

"Steve, he saved my life," Kathryn said.

"You gonna arrest me?" I asked.

"Our search of the abbey didn't turn up anything and I should have the prelim in the morning."

"Yeah?"

"If you're gonna work this thing, you might as well work it with me."

"Do I get a badge and a gun?"

"No," he said. "You get bossed around and the privilege of making me look good."

"In other words," I said, "my dream job."

Chapter Twenty-eight

"There's a beautiful woman at the abbey looking for you," Sister Chris said as Kathryn and I emerged from the path near the cabins.

Long after Steve had left, we had lingered in the woods together.

"Of course there is," Kathryn said. "Happens everywhere he goes."

I laughed. "Yeah, it's a real problem. Actually came here to hide from them."

"Will you just toss me aside now," Kathryn said, "after all we've shared?"

"What all have y'all shared?" Chris asked.

"Depends on who it is," I said.

"Who is it?" Kathryn asked Chris.

"I think she said her name was Anna."

"Uh oh," Kathryn said.

"What 'uh oh'?" Chris asked.

"Where is she?" I asked.

Chris's eyes widened at my tone. "In the chapel."

"It's a sign," Kathryn said.

As I began to walk away, she started singing, "He's going to the chapel and he's gonna get married."

Turning, but continuing to walk, I said, "You're not a nice person."

"You have no idea," she said. "But you're gonna find out."

"I can't wait," I said, adding to Chris, "Pray for her, would you?"

Growing up, Anna had been my older sister Nancy's best friend. In high school, when our attraction began to blossom, the two years that separated us seemed insurmountable. After graduation when Nancy fled our family, Anna left for college. Four years passed before I saw her again and, by that time, she was married.

Several years later, following the breakup of my life and the first breakup of my marriage, I came home, began rebuilding, and not coincidentally became the chaplain at the same prison where Anna was a classification officer. Since then we had been a big part of each other's lives, until I had told her that if I were going to make my marriage work a second time, I would need to see less of her.

My marriage had not worked the second time despite my best efforts, and I was now without Susan or Anna.

The last time I had seen Anna, she told me she was leaving the institution for a job in Central Office. Only a few months had passed, but it seemed a lot longer.

The chapel was dim and cold, the creaks of the pews and beams above them the only sounds. I looked around to make sure we were alone, and though I saw no one, I got the feeling we weren't. Was this place and all the talk of the supernatural making me more sensitive to an unseen realm, or just more imaginative? And then it occurred to me that the two could be far closer than most people think. Maybe it's primarily through creativity and the use of the imagination that we access the spiritual.

Anna was on the far end of the back pew to my right, kneeling in prayer, backlit by the votive candles behind her. She looked like a dark-haired angel, and I was sure I had seen something like this before in my dreams.

Seeming to sense my presence, she turned her head and looked up at me, her humble posture and tentative expression childlike in its beauty, and it broke my heart.

When she smiled, I walked along the pew toward her. Standing, she took a few steps toward me, and hesitantly we embraced.

She felt familiar in the best possible way and I held the embrace longer than I should have, but she didn't pull away until I did.

"It's good to see you," she whispered.

"I'm sorry," I said.

Without responding, she eased down onto the pew and I sat beside her.

"I really am," I said.

She shrugged. "You had to try to save your marriage. Besides, maybe it *is* best we don't see each other."

As if continuing where we had left off, I could tell we were both still vulnerable, raw from emotional exposure and the pain we had inflicted upon one another.

"I was dead wrong," I said.

"I'm not so sure."

"And yet here you are," I said, "and you're back at PCI where you know we'll see each other every day."

"It doesn't take a lot of insight to see that my words and actions don't match," she said. "Doesn't mean they always won't."

I looked up at the large wood-carved crucifix hanging above the altar and wondered why life had to hurt so much. Art, religion, and philosophy had tried to explain suffering for as long as they had existed, nearly as long as there had been suffering, but ultimately every explanation fell short. The best they could do was offer companionship, the consolation, such as it was, that none of us were alone in our suffering. To me, that's what the mystery of Christ's crucifixion did most profoundly—vividly conveyed God's intimate understanding of our pain and his mysterious presence within it.

"I can't help the way I feel about you," she said, "that unquantifiable thing we share."

"Any more than I can you."

"But . . ."

"But what?"

"I don't know. I'm not even sure what I was going to say."

I didn't know what to say either, and we both fell silent a moment.

"Merrill said to tell you to get your narrow white ass out of the woods and back to the prison."

"You think my ass is narrow?" I asked.

She smiled.

"I love you, Anna," I said. "I love to make you smile. I love being with you—even if it hurts."

"It's just not fair to Chris," she said. "My heart is so unfaithful."

Just hearing her husband's name on her tongue made me feel guilty and ashamed, yet, in a warped way, it also felt like she was betraying me.

"You're right," I said. "I'm asking you to do something I wasn't willing to do. It's unfair of me and . . ."

"And?" she asked.

"And I'm not about to stop doing it," I said. "I can't help but feel like I have the prior claim—that I'm the one being cheated on."

"I'm not cheating on you, John," she said, her tone taking on an edge. "I'm not cheating on anyone. You left me, remember? You got out of Pottersville the moment you could. You didn't ask me to go with you to Atlanta. You didn't even say good-bye."

Just that quickly she had changed, and there was nothing I could say or do now to change her back. I had seen her like this many times before. Her strong will and mental discipline made her as stubborn as anyone I had ever met.

"I thought I was coming right back. I'm sorry."

"I've heard," she said. "You know what, I'm not gonna feel bad for you or guilty anymore. You left me—twice." She shook her head. "That's all I have to do—just think about that. That gives me enough anger to see more clearly."

She stood up abruptly. "I've got to go," she said. She grabbed a file folder from the pew beside her and handed it to me. "I shouldn't've come. I could've just told you this on the phone."

"It wouldn't've hurt as much on the phone."

She shook her head and frowned at me. "I'm talking about this," she said, nodding toward the folder. "It's copies of Keith Richie's file. After you read it, you'll probably want to move him to the top of your suspect list."

Chapter Twenty-nine

The pounding I did on Kathryn's door matched the heavy thump of my heart.

"I knew you'd be back," she said with a self-satisfied smile. "They always come back."

I pushed her in, closed the door behind me, and began to kiss her, spinning her around and pressing her against the door. She kissed me back, though not as passionately as I was kissing her.

"Anna get you going?" she asked, her words gasps.

"Yes," I said breathlessly. "That okay?"

"Depends," she said.

"She made me angry and aroused."

We kissed some more, our hands beginning to explore each other's bodies.

"On what?" I asked.

"Huh?" she said.

"Depends on what?"

"If you're with me right now or pretending I'm her," she said.

I stopped. "I'm with you. I'm not pretending anything, but this isn't right."

"Feels right," she said. "God, I can't believe I just said that."

I took a step back. "I really am sorry."

"Don't be."

"I find you very attractive and I guess I was just out of control enough to do something about it."

"Hey," she said, pulling me toward her. "I like it. I don't mind if you're in love with her as long as I'm the one you're making love to. Did I really just say that *making love* part out loud? I'm really not very good at this."

She then kissed me hard on the mouth and I kissed back. We did that for a while, both of us feeling the other's bodies through our clothes, until finally we began to take them off.

After a few minutes of awkward but fun fumbling, our clothes were in a pile by the door and we were walking toward her bed.

Her body was full, round, and soft, and I liked the way it moved when she walked. Her small white belly sloped outward as if showing the first signs of motherhood, and I rubbed it gently.

The cabin was cold and before I even touched her large white breasts, her nipples were erect. On the bed, she cupped my head with her hand and pulled me to them, but before I lost all control, I stopped.

"You're sure you want to do this?" I asked.

She looked down at her nakedness. "Don't get much more sure than this."

"I feel like I'm cheating," I said.

"You can only cheat on a married woman if *you're* the one who's married to her," she said with a wry smile. "Now, shut up. Get out of your head. And fuck me."

I did, and then a little later I did again.

Easing out of the bed where Kathryn was still sleeping, I dressed and carried the stack of exorcism books over in front of the fireplace. I had only taken Tammy's journal when Kathryn and I had walked down to the clearing, leaving the other books on the swing. With all that had happened—the journal being stolen, the whack on the back of the head, and seeing Anna—I had forgotten about them. Fortunately, Kathryn had not. She had retrieved them while I was meeting with Anna. After adding a log to the fire, I opened the next book, *Exorcism Nation* by Howard Reese, and began to read.

Exorcism Nation is an exploration of popular culture's influence on exorcism in America. More social study than theological treatise, the book takes a journalistic approach to the proliferation of exorcisms in contemporary American culture.

According to Reese, exorcism is more readily available today in the United States than at any other time in history. And though Jesus regularly performed exorcisms and the Roman Catholic Church has always conceded the possibility of demonic possession, it's clear that the practice of exorcism in contemporary American culture has been more deeply influenced by the entertainment industry than anything else. During the mid-seventies, after decades of neglect and near invisibility, exorcism suddenly became all the rage. This not coincidentally followed the release of the novel and film *The Exorcist*.

While conducting research for his book, Reese witnessed over sixty exorcisms, yet was still unable to say for sure if he believed in demonic possession, though he was quick to add that several people he met during the process claimed to have experienced significant improvement in their personal lives as a result of undergoing an exorcism. After reading Reese's accounts, I realized that what he had witnessed were not Catholic exorcisms but Pentecostal deliverances, which are different enough to be noteworthy. Not only is there a difference in theology—Catholicism has developed its over two thousand years, Pentecostalism just over one hundred—but whereas the Catholic Church is extremely slow to even entertain the possibility that an individual might be possessed, and this only after the person has undergone extensive psychiatric evaluation, the Pentecostal faith is quick to pronounce someone possessed and as a general rule doesn't trust psychiatry or psychology.

Refuting the claim that exorcisms and deliverances are harmless rituals performed by superstitious simpletons, Reese chronicles some of the fatalities that have resulted from them. In 1995, a group of overzealous Pentecostal ministers from a sect in the San Francisco Bay Area pummeled a woman to death while trying to drive out her demons. In 1997, a Korean Christian woman was stomped to death by a deacon and two missionaries operating out of a church in Glendale, California. The three men had gotten carried away trying to expel a demon they believed was lodged in the woman's chest. A five-year-old Bronx girl died after her mother and grandmother forced her to drink a lethal cocktail containing ammonia, vinegar, and olive oil and then bound and gagged her with duct tape. The two women claimed that they were merely trying to poison a demon that had inhabited the little girl several days earlier.

In 1998, Charity Miranda, a seventeen-year-old cheerleader, spent her final hours undergoing an exorcism at the hands of her mother, Vivian, and her sister, Serena, as her other sister, Elizabeth looked on, at their home in Sayville, Long Island. After Vivian put her mouth to Charity's and told her to blow the demon into her and she would try to kill it, she concluded that it didn't work, that it wasn't Charity at all but the demon who had taken over, and tried to destroy the demon by smothering the teenager with pillows and a plastic bag.

Reese concludes that the prevalence of exorcism in modern America is the result of many forces, including traditional religious symbolism, current notions of psycho-spiritual healing, and perhaps especially pop culture iconography.

I thought back to the other exorcism book I had read earlier in the afternoon. It was as different from this one as two books on the same subject could be, yet I found them both persuasive. After reading them, I knew a lot more about the modern phenomenon of exorcism in contemporary culture, but the increased information had done nothing to change the mixture of faith and skepticism that seemed my norm these days, nor demystify the events of last night. Perhaps nothing would, but I wasn't about to give up.

Chapter Thirty

It had rained overnight, and the fresh, clean air of the morning was warmer—still thin and crisp, but not nearly as biting as it had been—and the bright sun glinted off the beads of water on the blades of grass.

The whole world was glistening and sparkling.

I felt numinous, as if pure energy instead of blood was flowing through my veins. My mind was clear, except for a twinge of guilt over Kathryn, and I was focused on the case. As I walked up the hill toward the kitchen, I reread Keith Richie's file, thoughts of Anna gnawing at the edges, which was followed by more guilt.

It was still early, the empty grounds of the abbey struggling to wake up, and I found Richie alone cooking breakfast. The moist air of the kitchen was thick with the smell of bacon and coffee and eggs, beneath all of which was the pungent odor of old grease.

"You here to harass the ex-con some more?" he asked.

"That won't work this time," I said, holding up the file. "I have your records."

The transformation was as instant as it was complete, and I saw it as well as felt it. Keith Richie was no longer a cook at a religious retreat, but a man of the mean streets, an ex-con, whose time inside had served to hone his hardness.

"Yeah, so?"

"So I know," I said.

"Whatta you *think* you know?"

"What you're capable of."

"No, you don't," he said, "and you don't want to. Promise you that."

"Now's not the time to be convincing me how menacing you are."

He shook his head and dropped the ladle he was holding onto the stainless steel table. It clanged loudly then bounced onto the floor where it made an even louder noise.

Something about the violent noise seemed to set him off and he turned quickly to face me, puffing out his chest, his eyes just inches from mine.

"I ain't takin' no shit off you or anyone else. Just 'cause I done time don't mean I'm gonna bend over and take it up the ass the rest of my life."

His breath smelled of cigarettes and coffee and it was all I could do not to wince.

"This isn't harassment," I said. "I'm questioning everyone."

"By shoving their past up their ass?"

"No," I said, "but only because it doesn't pertain to the case or I don't know it yet."

"I don't have to answer a single goddamn question."

"That's true. For the moment anyway, but eventually you will. So why wait? Why make things harder than they have to be? Unless you killed her."

"Fuck you," he said.

I shook my head. "No thanks."

"I ain't a fag, if that's what you're tryin' to say. Some awful big fuckin' niggers tried, but nobody was able to turn me out."

He was clenching and unclenching his fists at his sides.

"You get in a lot of fights?" I asked.

"Enough."

"It's usually a lot harder on rapists," I said. "Not as much as child-molesters, but—"

He relaxed, took a step back, and smiled. "You must have the wrong file. I went down for assault not rape."

I stepped toward him, leaning in as he had. "I'm talking about what you are, not what you did time for."

Anger twitched in his face and he drew in a breath, but he didn't say anything.

I waited.

"Got nothin' else to say."

"Okay," I said, "you can talk to Chief Taylor and Sister Abigail."

He gave no indication he even heard me mention Steve, but his eyes widened momentarily at the mention of Sister Abigail.

"You were honest on your job application, weren't you?"

Chapter Thirty-one

"What are you most afraid of?" Sister Abigail asked me.

I thought about it for a moment. "I'm not sure."

"Come on."

"Being alone. Not—"

"Aren't you alone much of the time?"

"Too much. And I hate it."

"Really?"

"Yes, but it's complicated. I need a certain amount of time alone and I'm always comfortable with it, but too much and I'm miserable. Maybe finding a balance is impossible, but . . . what I want, what I need, is to belong, and in the state of belonging I need to be alone some—just not too much. It really is impossible. But what I meant was ultimately. I don't want to wind up alone."

"Do you think you will?"

"I think I might."

"Why?"

"It's where I find myself at the moment, where I always seem to wind up."

"Ah."

"Ah?"

"Ah."

We were quiet a moment.

"The thing is . . . I feel lonely when I'm not connected—I mean really connected. I seem to have this deep need to connect on a deep level. I'm talking intense and intimate connections on a soul level."

"And right now you don't have that with anyone?"

I nodded. "I guess. Partly because of what happened with me and Susan and Anna. Partly because I'm here, cut off from my life, but yeah. I mean, I'm experiencing some of that with you, but it's one-sided. And there might be potential for it with Kathryn, but we just met, so . . ."

"Do you feel like you cut people off, shut them out?"

I took a moment to really consider the question. "Not knowingly, but I must. I wish I knew what I was doing."

"We can explore that, but it may not be anything you're doing. Some of us are just called to solitude. What else were you going to say when I interrupted?"

"When?"

"What else are you afraid of?"

"Meaninglessness. Even more than loneliness, though they're related. I'm afraid of not mattering. Of not meaning to—well, anyone. Of not making a difference. Not fulfilling my purpose."

"Being afraid of not fulfilling your purpose means you're convinced you have one," she said.

"Guess it does."

"What is it?"

"I'm not sure I can define it—or that I even understand it enough to verbalize it, but I do live with a sense of it at least some of the time."

"Tell me about your calling," she said. "You do feel as though you have one?"

I shrugged. "I'm not sure I'd call it that anymore, but yeah, I feel I'm meant to do certain things."

"Which includes what?"

I thought about it some more. "Helping people. At its most basic. Whether it's counseling or interviewing, teaching or investigating, I've got a nearly naive idealism about helping people."

"Nearly?"

I laughed.

"But you're certainly not naive," she said.

"I feel like I'm pretty realistic about the limits of what I'm able to do," I said. "I have no illusions that I'm doing much good, but don't think I'm any less committed."

"Would you say you're from the social gospel school?"

"Not exactly," I said, "but I can see why you'd say that. I feel like there's a spiritual, ministerial component involved that differentiates me from a social worker, but I'm probably closer to a social worker than most ministers."

"Could you ever be fulfilled, to use your word, exclusively ministering or exclusively investigating?"

I shook my head. "Don't think so. It'd be a hell of a lot easier, but . . . I don't think it would be satisfying."

"You're sure?"

I nodded. "I've tried both exclusively before at different times in my life."

"What's your greatest concern about doing both simultaneously?"

I took a moment to really think about it, though I had gone over and over it in my mind countless times. "I don't have just one. I'm concerned about being ineffective, doing a half-ass job at one or both of them. Of losing balance, surrendering my serenity and sobriety. Of how violent I become, particularly working cases inside. And the costs involved to me personally and those I love."

"Speaking of Susan . . ." she said.

I took in a deep breath, let it out slowly, and paused for a long moment before I began.

"When Susan and I were married the first time," I said eventually, "we talked about but never got around to having children."

She nodded, her expression encouraging me to continue.

"We actually tried a couple of times, but never got pregnant."

"You just tried a couple of times?"

I smiled. "We had a lot of sex, Dr. Freud. What I meant was, a few different times throughout the course of our relationship we went off birth control in an attempt to get pregnant."

"Gotcha," she said, smiling, but holding up her hand as if she wanted no further details.

"I've always wanted kids," I said.

"Why?"

"I guess I believe I'll make a good dad. Mine is, and I wanted the opportunity to try and be even better. And, of course, there's all the normal selfish reasons too—unconditional love, adoration, belonging, redemption, a shot at immortality."

As with my comments about being alone, I felt uncomfortable talking to a celibate about children, but she seemed fine, so I continued to press past my discomfort.

"But it was not to be," she said.

I nodded slowly, unable to keep from frowning as I did. "When we got back together recently, the subject didn't come up. I assumed we would try again someday soon. We weren't getting any younger and we wanted to have three, but we were together such a short period of time and our union seemed so fragile."

She nodded again, still urging me onward. She was attentive and nonjudgmental, willing to hear anything I had to say. I felt safe. I knew I could reveal my deepest darkest secret and it would be okay. And that's what I was about to do.

"Shortly before we split up again, she told me she was pregnant," I said.

"Oh, John."

"When she gave me her ultimatum—asked me to do something I just couldn't do, she said if I didn't do it not only could she not be with me, but she could not have my child."

She nodded, her face full of kindness, her eyes brimming with compassion, and we sat in silence for a long moment.

"Which do you regret most?" she said. "Getting together again or making the decision you did that caused her to abort?"

I shrugged. "I regret everything. But I also don't see how things could've been any different given the circumstances. And the truth is, it was more her decision than mine that ended us again. Someone very close to her forced her to choose a side."

"How does that make you feel?"

I didn't respond. I couldn't.

"Hurt? Rejected? Sad? Angry? What?"

I shook my head.

"Say it," she said. "Say it out loud."

"I can't."

"You can. Tell me. Say it."

"I . . . feel . . . I just can't."

"You need to. Come on. Just say it. I promise it won't be as bad as you think."

"Guilty. I feel guilty. Okay?"

"For . . ."

I didn't say anything.

"For what exactly?"

"For . . . Because . . . For . . . For what else I felt."

"Which was?"

I swallowed hard, my dry throat constricting further.

"Relieved. I feel guilty because of how relieved I felt that there would be nothing keeping us in each other's lives. She used her pregnancy to try to manipulate me into doing something illegal, something I couldn't do, and she used terminating it as a threat. She thought it would make me do what she wanted me to." Tears filled my eyes and my voice broke. Clearing my throat and blinking several tears, I added, "And at first it was, but soon, the very fact that she was trying to exhort me with it made me glad she wasn't gonna go through with it."

"It's a pretty normal reaction I think," she said.

I narrowed my eyes in disbelief. "To want the potential for your own child to be wiped out just to be free of his mother?"

"I think you're being too hard on yourself," she said. "You didn't ask her to do it. You didn't encourage her to do it. You were just secretly relieved she did."

"But still—"

"Your parents divorced when you were young, didn't they?" she asked.

I nodded.

"You know what it's like for the children involved," she said. "Couldn't part of what you wanted was to spare your child of that?"

I thought about it, then shook my head. "I wish I could say it was, but I just don't—"

"Perhaps on a subconscious level," she offered.

I shook my head. "But wouldn't it be pretty if I could think so?"

Chapter Thirty-two

My heart beat just a little faster as I pressed the distantly familiar numbers. As I waited for a connection, my throat tightened a bit and my mouth became dry.

I had retrieved my cell phone from my room where it had been charging, and brought it with me down to the lake.

The connection was poor, and I didn't have any idea what I was going to say, but I was determined. Chances were she wouldn't answer anyway. I had called her cell, which meant my number would be displayed on her phone. Usually when I called her home line, which didn't have caller ID, she'd answer but immediately hang up when she heard it was me, but because her cell phone displayed my number she often just didn't answer. Maybe I'd get her voice mail and be able to say whatever it was I was going to say to it.

"Hello."

There had only been two rings and I wasn't prepared—of course there could have been two hundred and I'd have felt the same way.

"Susan?"

"Yes," she said, her voice sounding hesitant, unsure.

"It's John."

She didn't say anything, and I waited a moment for her to hang up, but she didn't.

"I'm surprised you answered," I said.

"I didn't realize it was you."

"Oh."

"Not that I wouldn't have answered if I did."

"Really?"

"What can I do for you?" she asked, her voice flat and emotionless—cold, not angry.

"Accept my apology," I said.

"Why? So you can feel better about yourself? So you can complete a step? It doesn't change anything. Nothing's ever going to change between us."

"I just needed to tell you I'm sorry again," I said. "And that I think I have a better understanding of your decisions and why you made them."

"You think so, do you? Well, I still don't know why the hell *you did* what you did to me, to my family, to *our* family, but as long as John Jordan has insight, can apologize and feel good about himself again, that's all that matters, right?"

I didn't say anything. I couldn't.

We were silent for a long moment.

After a while, I thought she might have ended the call, but then I heard her sigh heavily.

"I wish we had never met," she said. "And I'm trying to pretend we never did, so if you're really as sorry as you say you are, you can prove it by never calling me again."

"Okay," I said, but I was saying it to myself.

Shutting the phone, I slipped it into my pocket.

"She's not wrong," I said aloud.

Looking across the lake, breathing more deeply, I tried to take in as much of the beauty and serenity as I could, allowing the power of this sacred place to help heal me.

For a long moment, I just stood there, praying for forgiveness, for insight and wisdom, for Susan and her family, for Anna and Merrill, for my mom and Father Thomas and St. Ann's, and for all the people I had wronged or hurt—even unintentionally.

Eventually, the healing began, and I felt connected and nurtured by my surroundings, as if they were a direct conduit to what I needed most.

As I continued to stand there, I tried to open myself to the sacred, to everything, to let down my guard that seemed so necessary for survival at the prison, to wake up and become fully alive to everything—every positive and negative experience, every feeling, every person, every thing.

As I did, I was reminded of the Buddha and the way people came to him in his later years and asked him what he was. Are you a god or an angel or a saint? they would ask. No, he would respond. Then what? they would ask. Merely a man who woke up, he would say.

I wanted to wake up—to be as fully conscious, fully aware of myself, others, the world, God. To awaken from my slumber and become an open receptacle, taking in the fullness of all that life had to offer. I had spent too much of my life avoiding certain experiences, whether through alcohol, violence, religion, another person, investigating. I had continually anesthetized myself against what I thought would be painful or unpleasant, but in doing so, I had been sleeping through some of the most important experiences of my very limited existence.

Before the peace and beauty of the lake and the sacred presence within it, I committed to awaken—awaken to the beauty, to the truth, to the sacred—to more fully experience and embrace every opportunity I was given.

Chapter Thirty-three

     Eventually Kathryn joined me by the lake with a blanket and picnic basket and entreated me to come away with her into the woods. Through her words and desire I could feel the pull of the divine and hear in her words the echo of the *Song of Songs*: "Arise, my love, my beautiful one, and come away with me. The winter is past; the spring has come. Flowers appear on the earth; the season of singing has come. Arise, come, my love, my beautiful one, come with me."

     It wasn't spring, of course, but it might as well have been, for something was resurrecting in me. I felt more alive, more aware, more open than I had in a long time.

     I was waking up to all the possibilities. I was seeing beyond what I could see, perceiving what was beyond. The veil was parting and I was being granted a glimpse of something extraordinary.

     I wasn't so far gone that I didn't realize that part of my experience was simply, perhaps profoundly, infatuation with Kathryn, but it didn't make the experience any less powerful or persuasive.

     I knew too that I was grasping for Kathryn out of loneliness and pain, that at least part of what I was doing was diversion and distraction, but that was something I would investigate later. For as true as that was, it was also true that what I was experiencing, this erotic euphoria, was also an epiphany.

     Perhaps it was being at St. Ann's, so close to the raw enchantment of the earth, or just being away from the prison and the normal demands of life, or maybe it was confessing my secret to

Sister Abigail, but something inside me had broken loose. I felt more free, more fully me than I had in many, many years.

As Kathryn and I made love, it was as if she had become an incarnation of the divine, as if God were loving me through her. It was an amazing, even mystical experience that seemed to encompass the enchanted world around us, and I was far more grateful than I could express to her. Many people would live their entire lives without ever having such an encounter—and others, like Tommy and Tammy, would never again be given the opportunity.

"Was that like the best sex you've ever had?" Kathryn asked.

We were lying on the blanket beneath a magnolia tree, only partially undressed, becoming cognizant for the first time of how cold it was.

"It was okay," I said, unable to suppress the silly grin spreading across my face.

She punched me in the arm.

"What?" I said. "You want me to be honest with you, don't you?"

"I'm not even saying it had anything to do with me."

"Well, it had *something* to do with you."

"You were possessed," she said.

I thought about it. It was an interesting way to put it—especially in light of everything that had happened—but it fit. Maybe I was. Maybe we were. Maybe in another way Tammy had been. Was it so different? So hard to accept? This place was enchanted. Could it not also be haunted?

"It was a religious experience."

"I knew I was good," she said. "I didn't realize I was a revelation."

Chapter Thirty-four

When I walked out of my room after having showered and changed, Steve was waiting for me. He was leaning against the hallway wall holding two Styrofoam cups, a small, white wax-coated bag, and a file folder.

"I got the prelim and doughnuts," he said.

We walked over to the counseling center and into one of the empty classrooms where we sat in desks beside each other. Taking the lid off the cup he handed me, I blew the hot, dark liquid and felt the steam rise. The unused classroom was cold and the heat felt good against my face.

"They're still warm," he said, handing me the bag. "The bakery in town makes them fresh twice a day. They don't have one of those Hot Now signs, but I usually time it just right."

I set my coffee down and took the bag.

"Always said you were a hell of a detective," I said.

I withdrew a warm, soft doughnut, its glaze sticking to my fingers, and passed the bag back to him. I then took a big bite that seemed to melt on my tongue before I could chew it.

"You in love?" he asked.

Choking, I coughed and took a sip of coffee. "What?"

"With Kathryn?" he said. "I always had in the back of my mind I'd marry her one day."

He looked like a man trying not to look sad, and I felt ashamed of my insensitivity and impetuousness.

"We just met," I said.

"But there's a spark?"

"There's something, yeah," I said. "I didn't realize you—"

"She's not interested in having anything serious with me. I'm just carrying a torch for her."

Few things in life were as pathetic and painful as unrequited love, and the hopelessness of it hit me anew as I thought about it. The person not in love could no more control her feelings than the person who was. I shook my head at the helplessness of the human condition.

"I'm sorry," I said.

I dropped the remainder of the doughnut on a napkin on the desk. I had lost my appetite. I had known he had feelings for her and still I had . . . done what I had done.

"It's none of my business," he said, "but if you don't see a future, please don't start anything."

Unable to speak, I nodded.

His sadness made him look smaller somehow, as if his physical form was merely a projection of his true self.

Finishing up his doughnut and taking a big gulp of coffee, he wiped his hands and mouth.

"Tommy Boy drowned," he said. "No sign of foul play."

"Doesn't mean there wasn't any," I said.

"No."

"It's what we expected."

"Yeah," he said, "but I was hoping for something."

"What about Tammy?"

"Be a while before we get toxicology and DNA, but we've already got a ton of physical evidence against Father Thomas. His blood's under her nails, hers under his. No surprise there. He was covered in it."

"We knew he was," I said. "What about sexual assault? Sorry to have to ask."

He shook his head. "It's okay. She had definitely had intercourse recently, but it seems to have been consensual. No sign of . . ."

I nodded. "Have they determined cause of death yet?"

He frowned and shrugged. "Lot of injuries. Can't say which one of them actually killed her. Coroner called it multi-system trauma. She had a combination of ruptured abdominal organs, broken bones, and brain trauma.''

"What about blood loss?"

"She'd lost a lot—enough to be going into shock—but he's not sure if any one thing was enough to actually kill her. It was more the cumulative effect. If she had been taken to a hospital in time . . .''

I shook my head and thought about what he'd said. I also thought about him some more. I seemed to be finding it more difficult to talk about Tammy's death than he was. I knew what he was doing. I had done it myself. Containment. Everything was in a little compartment—including his feelings for Tammy, including considering her anything other than a homicide victim. He could close the lid on that box and think about his cousin as only a case. He could think of himself as only a cop, only a man with a job to do and a deadline in which to do it.

"I'm not sure he killed her anymore," he said, "and I think it's at least possible he's telling the truth about what happened."

"Because of the murder weapon?" I asked.

His eyes grew wide. "How'd you know?"

"What else is there?"

"He says for the majority of injuries, he can't determine what caused them. Says many of them seem more like rips and tears than cuts—what he'd expect to see from bites, but there's no teeth marks. Says he can't explain it."

"Does he know the circumstances of the case and what Father Thomas is claiming?"

He nodded. "You're saying he was predisposed, but I know this guy—he wouldn't let something like that cause him to contradict the evidence. And there's something else. I talked to Father Thomas's doctor. He confirmed what Sister Abigail told us. Says Father Thomas is too sick and too weak to be able to do what was done to her. Says he would testify to it in court, but won't have to because Father Thomas won't live long enough for there to be a trial."

"But—" I began, but stopped when we heard someone calling for Steve in the hall.

"CHIEF. CHIEF. YOU IN HERE?"

"IN HERE," Steve yelled.

Muscle-fat opened the door and looked inside.

"We got something," he said, and waited for Steve to ask what.

"Yeah?" Steve said after a moment.

"A boat," he said. "Not far from here. And it's got blood in it."

Chapter Thirty-five

We didn't have to go far to find the boat. It was tied to the end of a floating dock with a yellow nylon rope and part of a cement block at the upper corner of the abbey property in the Intracoastal. The dock—large blocks of Styrofoam encased by weathered wooden planks—was partially hidden by a boathouse and a thick stand of cypress trees.

Steve and I stood near the edge of the dock, looking around, Muscle-fat a few feet away calling FDLE to process the scene.

Up a small slope sat the dormitory opposite the one I was staying in, but the boathouse blocked most of it from our view. We turned and looked down toward the lake. We could only see maybe twenty yards before the hill started sloping downward. Neither the lake nor the cabins were visible, only the back of the dining hall.

"It's not like anyone could see what was going on at the cabins from here," Steve said.

"They could've already known," I said, "or seen from up at the abbey."

"How would they know to go to the clearing? Why not just run after them? The boat would take a lot longer."

I shrugged. "I'm not sure. The only reason I can think of for them to take the boat is to avoid being seen."

He shook his head. "I hate cases like this."

"No you don't."

"No. *You* don't. *I* do."

We stepped onto the dock, which sank down with our weight

and bounced up and down as we walked toward the end where the old green boat had been haphazardly moored.

"Sure this thing'll hold both of us?" Steve asked. "'Course you don't mind goin' in the water, do you?"

I thought about what I had done at the pier when Tommy's body was found and how long ago that seemed now.

The embattled boat was full of nicks and gashes, its hull splintering, its paint fading. Its back sank deeper in the water than its front and held several inches of water. A faded orange life jacket and two paddles were in the front. The middle seat and at least one of the paddles showed obvious traces of blood.

"Could be from someone fishing," I said. "Could've hooked or cut themselves."

"Hell, could be fish blood," he said.

"No other signs of fish—scales, slime, guts. We need to know who used this last."

He yelled for Muscle-fat to go and get Father Thomas or Sister Abigail. Sister Abigail arrived a few minutes later, stopping at the edge of the dock.

"It embarrasses me to admit it," she said, "but I have a real phobia of water. Would it be too much trouble for us to talk on land?"

Easing back down the dock, we joined her.

"Does this boat belong to the abbey?" Steve asked.

"Not technically," she said, "but it's been here many years. Some trespasser left it on the lake and we've had it ever since."

"Who all uses it?"

"Sometimes Kathryn paddles to the middle of the lake in it and writes, but it's been a while since she has. Keith carried it over here to try to catch some fish over a year ago and it's never made it back. I guess he's the only one who uses it, but I can't be certain. Why?"

"It has blood in it."

Her eyes grew wide. "Human?"

"We can't be sure, but it looks like it," he said.

"You think the killer used it? That would prove Tom really is innocent, right?"

"We won't know what to think until the lab looks at it," Steve said.

"Why would someone use the boat?" Doesn't make any sense, does it?"

"Not that we've been able to figure out," Steve said.

For a moment, none of us said anything, then Steve looked up at the back windows of her corner room in the dorm.

"You didn't see anyone down here the night of the murder, did you?"

She followed his gaze to her room, then looked back down at the boat and shook her head. "I'm sorry. I didn't. I went to bed early and any time I got up—for water or the bathroom—I didn't look out the window."

Steve looked at me. "Can you think of anything?"

"When's the last time you saw the boat down here?" I asked.

She shrugged. "I'm not sure exactly, but it hasn't been that long."

"But not the day before yesterday?"

Her face wrinkled up as she strained to remember. After a moment, she exhaled loudly and shook her head. "I'm just not sure. I may have, but I can't be certain."

"Whatta you thinkin'?" Steve asked.

"That the boat could've already been down by the clearing and the killer used it to get back to the abbey."

They both raised their eyebrows at the possibilities.

"It'd make a lot more sense than someone using it to get there from here," Sister Abigail said.

Just then Muscle-fat walked up with Keith Richie. "Here he is," he said, as if revealing something to us. "And I just got a call from Suzie. A rental place at Lake Grove Landing had one of their boats stolen."

"When?" I asked.

He ignored me.

"He asked you a question," Steve said.

"I didn't ask. But I'm sure it was the night of the murder. When else could it've been?"

"The two guys who stole Tammy's journal could've stolen it yesterday," I said.

Steve shook his head in disappointment at his officer. "Find out when it was stolen."

"Yes, sir," he said, pulling out his cell phone and walking a few steps away.

"Are you finished with me for the moment?" Sister Abigail asked.

Steve nodded. "Thanks."

"Sorry I couldn't be more help."

Steve looked at Richie.

"What?" Richie said like a man with a guilty conscience.

"When's the last time you used the abbey boat?" Steve asked.

"About a week ago," he said, "but that's not the abbey's boat."

"What?"

"That's not the abbey boat," he said again. "I moved it back over to the lake a week ago."

Chapter Thirty-six

Sister Abigail stopped walking and turned back toward us.

"You're sure?" Steve asked.

"Positive," Richie said. "I know our boat and that's not it."

"Then whose is it?"

Richie shrugged. "I've never seen it before."

I knew any minute Muscle-fat would state the obvious.

"It could be the one stolen from Lake Grove Landing," he said.

"Maybe you better show us the abbey boat," Steve said to Richie.

"Okay."

"And on the way you can tell me why you wouldn't answer John's questions this morning," he said. As we walked past Muscle-fat, Steve said, "Stay here and keep the scene secure until FDLE arrives."

"Yes, sir."

"I don't understand," Sister Abigail said when we reached her. "How can this not be our boat?"

"Lot of possibilities," Steve said. "We'll figure it out."

"Whatever the case," she said, "it's looking better and better for Tom all the time."

She then turned and walked back toward the dorm and the three of us continued down to the lake.

Like many cops, Steve had a hardness that enabled him to deal with the hardened, and though it was similar, it was not the same.

"I *want* you to refuse to answer *my* questions," he said to Richie. "Few things I enjoy more than kickin' the shit outta rapists."

Keith Richie was scared and it showed, but only if you were looking carefully for it. Not only was he walking differently—as if his joints had lost some of their flexibility—but the skin of his neck had become splotchy beneath tiny beads of sweat.

"I'm not the same man I used to be," he said. "I'm different. A new creature in Christ Jesus."

"You and every other convict I've ever talked to," he said. "World would be a better place if we could all just go to prison."

"You ask anybody here," Richie said. "I've never done anything that even looked wrong."

"Until now."

He stopped walking.

"What the hell you think you're doin'?" Steve asked.

"No sense investigating if you're just gonna pin it on me. You don't need to even look at the boat."

"All these little tactics to keep from answering our questions aren't gonna work," Steve said. "So just move your ass and your mouth or getting butt-fucked in the shower because you take the fall for Tammy's murder'll be the least painful thing that happens to you."

Richie started to protest, but before he had gotten out three words, Steve punched him in the chest. It caught him by surprise and shut him up, knocking him back a few steps and making him gasp, but he didn't fall down, and when he took a step toward Steve, which his whole life had programmed him to do, Steve slapped him across the face so hard his head whipped to the side.

Instinctively, Richie swung back, but the punch was a looping right hook that Steve easily blocked, then countered with a digging right uppercut into his gut. Richie fell to his knees, his mouth open as if trying to suck air that wasn't there.

By the time the brief exchange was over, Steve was out of breath, and I waited while both men took a moment to regain their composure.

After a couple of minutes of silence, Richie stood without speaking and began walking toward the lake again.

Steve and I followed.

"Were you involved with Tammy?" Steve asked.

"You don't have to rape a woman who's givin' it to you."

"Unless she stops," Steve said.

"She didn't. I was drunk when I supposedly raped that girl in Pensacola. She was too. I honestly don't know what really happened, but I haven't had a drink since that night."

"That may be true, but we're not dealing with a rape here. This is murder. And we know you've got one hell of a temper and rage control issues."

Steve waited, but Richie didn't say anything.

"What'd she do to make you so mad?"

"Tell me what my motive is," he said.

"It's internal," Steve said. "It's anger. It's rage. It's violence. It's not outwardly motivated. Oh, I'm sure she did something to set you off, but that's all you needed. She was just a trigger."

"You had more of a motive than I did," Richie said.

"Yeah, I did it," Steve said, his voice full of a mean sarcasm.

"Well, *I* didn't. That's all I'm saying. I swear to Christ, I didn't do it."

We passed near Kathryn's cabin, and I felt both excitement and guilt.

"See," Richie said as soon as the small boat became visible. "That's the abbey boat. It's been here at least a week."

The small wooden boat was tied to a stump and half hidden by the hay-colored underbrush. It looked nearly identical to the one we had just seen in the waterway.

"Why'd you move it over here?" Steve asked.

"I wasn't using it in the waterway and I figured Kathryn would use it if it was over here."

"Damn you're a nice guy," Steve said. "But from now on, I don't want you even saying her name. Understand? You better not come within twenty feet of her. If you do, rather than take a chance, I'll cut 'em off just to be safe."

"I've got to get lunch started," Richie said, beginning to turn. "You know where to find me."

"You better be there when I come looking for you."

Richie walked away.

For a moment we stood there in silence staring at the lake and the small boat.

After a while, Steve turned to me and said, "What the hell's goin' on here?"

I shrugged.

"You think that's Tammy's blood on the other boat?"

I nodded. "I do. Maybe some of her killer's too."

"Why the hell use the boat in the first place?"

I shook my head. "Don't know."

"Can't see the devil paddling away in it," he said.

I laughed.

"And where'd it come from?" he asked. "You think it's the stolen one?"

"I do."

"So it could've been someone from the outside," he said.

"Why not leave in the boat? Why just paddle back to the dock?"

He shook his head. "For a moment I thought we found something, but all we got is more questions."

Chapter Thirty-seven

"I understand you have evidence that proves my client's innocence," Ralph Reid said.

He and Father Thomas had come out of his cabin and joined us at the water's edge.

Steve shook his head. "We've got a little blood in a boat. Don't even know if it's related."

"But if it is—" Reid began.

"It could *belong* to Father Thomas," Steve said. "Could *prove* he did it."

"It doesn't," Father Thomas said, "and it won't."

"I'd really like to believe that, Father, but there's a lot of physical evidence against you."

"What happened wasn't physical. It can't be explained in physical terms. That's why your search for a killer is so vain. Human agency wasn't involved."

"That's not exactly true," I said. "Even if what you're saying is true, it's not purely physical or Tammy would still be alive. What happened to her ended her physical life."

"You're right, of course. All I meant was her killer's not flesh and blood, but spirit and darkness."

"And yet," I said, "we have a stolen diary, a stolen boat with blood in it, and a drowning."

He didn't say anything.

"How do you account for those things, Father?" Steve asked.

"I don't. I don't have to."

"Well, I do," Steve said. "And everything else that's happened."

"It may be your job, but it's arrogance to think there's an answer for everything."

"How did your skin get beneath her fingernails?" Steve asked.

"It had her scratch me," he said.

"It?"

"The demon."

"Did it also have you scratch her?"

"Of course not," he said. "I only tried to restrain her."

"Did the two of you have sex?"

Reid jumped in. "We've already been over all this. We've answered all your questions. Why, when you have evidence pointing in another direction, are you asking them again?"

"We have evidence now," Steve said to Father Thomas. "We'll be able to prove it if you lie. Did you have sex with her?"

For a moment Father Thomas hesitated. Finally, he shook his head. "No," he said so softly it was difficult to hear, "I did not."

"Well, somebody did not long before she was murdered, and we're gonna find out who."

"We're going now," Reid said, "but let me remind you that if you ignore the evidence of the boat and its implications, I'll clobber you with it in court."

Steve's eyes widened and I knew he was thinking the same thing I was. "Tell me you didn't plant it after the fact to establish reasonable doubt."

"I didn't," he said with a self-satisfied smile, "but I'm glad you agree it creates reasonable doubt."

Chapter Thirty-eight

I found Kathryn crying in her cabin.

"Was it that bad?" I asked, a small smile on my face.

She was wearing the same clothes as this morning, which were wrinkled and grass-stained in spots from our alleged picnic, and her hair was sticking up on one side from where she had been laying on it.

"It was wonderful," she said.

"What's wrong?"

"Nothing."

"You're crying," I said as if having Muscle-fat's gift for stating the obvious.

She nodded.

"What're you crying about?"

"Nothing," she said, "and everything."

There was nothing manipulative in her words or tears. She was just as genuine as she had been in all our previous encounters. I had merely interrupted her private experience of existential suffering.

"Is it a rainy-days-and-Mondays kind of thing?" I asked.

"Exactly," she said. "Just the noonday demon."

I nodded.

"You sound like you have some experience with it," she said.

"Hello darkness my old friend," I said.

"Mine's hormones," she said. "What's your excuse?"

I shrugged.

"I've learned there's nothing I can do about it," she said. "I just hang on, wait it out, try not to kill myself."

"How often does it happen?" I asked.

"Usually not more than a couple of times a month. Not counting my period, which is a different shade of blue."

"Anything I can do?" I asked.

"Just be gentle. I need a non-demanding, TLC-filled afternoon."

"So it's probably not a good time to ask you about the tape," I said.

She looked puzzled. "What tape?"

"The one you took from Father Thomas's camcorder night before last," I said. "The one that's supposed to exonerate him and implicate the devil."

"Oh, *that* tape," she said with a forced smile. "I really need to get out of this cabin. Tell you what, take me into town for an early dinner and I'll tell you all about it."

Chapter Thirty-nine

Bridgeport had changed.

Far from the fishing village I had visited as a kid, it was now a quaint touristy town of gift shops, art galleries, and eateries. A restored theater housed a local acting company and hosted traveling players, and a turn-of-the-century inn stayed booked year round.

As we strolled down the sidewalk past the toggery, kitchen shop, and bookstore, I gazed out at the great bay and the barrier island of Pine Key beyond. Shrimp, oyster, and sailboats bobbed beneath the midday sun, as cars slowly cruised the causeway.

We ate at a place on the corner I had eaten at as a kid, but only the good food remained the same. North Florida's filmmaker, Victor Nunez, had shot scenes for a couple of his movies here, and framed one-sheets from his films hung around the room.

"My depression doesn't scare you?" Kathryn asked after we had ordered.

I shook my head.

"You're not afraid I'm like this most of the time, that I'm unstable, maybe even dangerous?"

"Are you?"

"No," she said. "And I didn't kill Tammy."

I nodded. "But you did take the videotape from the room."

"How'd you know?"

"You knew it was in there and had time to get it when Steve came to get me."

"Father Thomas could've taken it," she said, "or the killer."

"That's true," I said, "but it was you. You offered to keep the camera in your cabin because you wanted to use it to see what was on the tape."

"I knew I couldn't hide the whole thing, so I just took the tape, but then I wanted to see exactly what was on it."

"You took it to protect Father Thomas," I said.

She nodded.

Our food came, and we ate in silence for a while, bits and pieces of the various conversations of the early evening crowd around us drifting over to our table.

The quality of Kathryn's beauty was more obvious now, sitting across from her in the unflattering light of the restaurant, than it had been at any other point I'd been around her. Her soft, delicate features, her pale, unadorned skin, her thick blond hair, and the deep brown of her eyes were just short of mesmerizing, her unselfconsciousness only adding to the effect.

"Whatta you gonna do?" she asked.

"Watch the tape."

"With or without Steve?"

"Without the first time."

"Then what?"

"Depends on what's on the tape."

"Just remember he's a good man," she said. "He's helped so many people over the years. He's been like a father to me. No matter what's on the tape, don't forget that."

"I won't."

"What about me?" she asked. "Whatta you gonna do about me?"

I knew what she meant, but to stall I said, "Whatta you mean?"

"Do you suspect me more now?"

I shrugged.

"What about what happened last night and this morning? It was so wonderful. I hope I haven't jeopardized anything we might have had."

I thought about it. I wasn't sure what we had, but so far she hadn't really done anything that would make me unwilling to explore it.

"Do we need to talk about that?" I asked.

"What?" she asked. "Our future?"

I nodded.

"You told me up front your heart belonged to Anna," she said. "We agreed to just let this be what it is and not try to make it into something it can't be."

"That's a lot easier to say than do."

"Especially for us girls."

"Perhaps," I said. "Though the reason we're even having this conversation is that I'm still hung up on my first love."

"So that could be me if our timing were better?" she asked.

"Absolutely."

She considered me for a moment. "There's nothing typical about you, is there?"

I could tell by the things she was saying and the way she was acting that it would be best if we slow down some, but could we? Would we? Would we be able to resist the urge to define and possess and want more?

"Maybe what I should have asked is if you think less of me," she said.

"For trying to protect Father Thomas?"

"You can't be sure that's all I was doing."

"True."

"But it was" she said. "I swear it. I'm not trying to hinder your investigation. Just the opposite in fact. And I can prove it."

"Oh yeah? How's that?"

"I'm the one who put Tammy's diary in your room."

Chapter Forty

We were getting into my truck when we saw them. They were walking toward a car across the street in front of the hardware store. I got Kathryn's attention and pointed to them.

Her eyes grew wide in alarm. "The two who attacked us?"

I nodded.

She ducked beneath the cab of the truck, though they weren't even looking in our direction.

"Get in," I said. "Let's see where they go."

We jumped in, Kathryn crouching down in her seat.

"You're gonna follow them?" she asked.

"Yeah," I said. "You wanna stay here?"

She hesitated a moment, seeming to think about it. "No, I guess I'll go, but can I call Steve?"

"Sure," I said. "I was gonna suggest it."

She opened her purse, withdrew her phone, and began tapping Steve's number.

The two men backed out of their parking place and drove in our direction. When they passed by, I let a couple of cars get between us, then pulled out and began to follow them.

They drove out of the downtown area and headed toward Highway 98, which ran along the coast between Pensacola and Carrabelle. Taking a right on 98, I followed three cars behind them as they drove back in the direction of St. Ann's.

Seeming to rise out of the bay, the empty shell of Gulf Coast Paper Mill loomed in front of us. In contrast to the abandoned mill, the new Bridgeport marina next to it was alive with activity—boats trolling into and out of the bay, fish being unloaded on the docks by sun-burned families and their charter guides, and people coming from and going to the Café on the Dock.

"Where is he?" Kathryn was saying.

I glanced over at her.

"Do you know when he'll be back?" she asked. After a pause, she added, "Can you reach him by phone or radio?"

The car directly in front of us turned, leaving only two between, and I slowed to increase the gap.

"Well, would you have him call Kathryn as soon as he can? It's very important. . . . What? . . . Oh yeah, hold on. What's your cell phone number?"

I told her, she repeated it into the phone, then reiterated how important is was that Steve return the call as soon as he could.

"Where is he?" I asked.

"They're not sure. Left the abbey about an hour ago, checked in, and told them he'd be ten-something for a while, which evidently means unable to be reached. They'll continue to try him, but said he would check back in as soon as he's able to. I wish he were here."

"I have a gun if that makes you feel any better."

"I probably shouldn't've come," she said.

"My previous performance what's inspiring all the confidence?"

"I can still feel the way he held me, still smell him, still feel his grip around me and the blade of the knife against my throat. At first it was cold, but then, when he pressed it harder into my skin it got so hot it seemed to burn."

"I'm sorry," I said. "I won't let anything happen to you. I won't put you in danger. Let me just see where they go so I'll know where to come back with Steve, okay?"

"Thanks. And sorry to be such a baby. You're certainly not seeing me at my best today. Found out I battle with depression, steal evidence, lie about it, and that I am just a big fraidy cat."

Perhaps I should take all these as signs, but I didn't—and didn't feel my objectivity had been so compromised that I was incapable of doing so.

"Yeah," I said, "if you weren't so good in bed . . ."

Nothing I could discover about her could detract from the

mystical experience I had with her earlier in the day. In fact, being exposed to her flawed humanity allowed me to resist the temptation to make an idol out of her, but instead enabled me to better focus on the true source of the encounter.

She smiled.

"Not too depressed or afraid if you can smile like that," I said.

"Both are reasonably mild."

The cars in front of us slowed and I could see that the two men we were following were turning.

"Aha," I said.

She looked over at me. "Aha?"

"That's what I say when I get a big clue."

"And you had the audacity to say something about *ransacked*?"

"But look," I said. "I think an 'aha' is warranted."

She looked back to see them turning, her eyes widening when it registered that they were turning into the paper mill.

"The mill? I thought it was closed. Aren't they blowing it up tomorrow?"

"Yeah," I said. "They've been using some of the front offices, but everything should be cleared out by now."

I continued up the bridge above the railroad tracks, pulled onto the shoulder, parked, and watched as the two men parked their car next to the two others present in the huge empty lot and walked inside the business office.

"You think they work for Ralph Reid?" she asked.

"I do," I said.

"Why would he get men like that to do what they did?"

"Think I'll go ask them," I said.

"But—" she began.

"You can sit inside the little café in the marina and keep trying Steve. You'll be safe."

I made a quick U-turn, eased back down the bridge, and took a right onto the road that led down to the marina. All along the road, new buildings were popping up in anticipation of the tourism boom being predicted to result from the Gulf Coast Company's developments. According to the signs, every new business was either a bank or a real estate agency.

When Kathryn didn't say anything, I looked over at her.

"That's okay, isn't it?"

She gave me a small shrug. "I guess. What would you do if I said it wasn't? You seem set on doing it."

I let out a long sigh. I was getting frustrated with her and I was beginning to let it show. "I can take you somewhere else. Just tell me where."

"Café on the Dock is fine. I'm sorry. I can't help that I'm scared."

"I know. I'm sorry. But you'll be safe and chances like these don't come along very often."

I pulled into the parking lot next to the green tin building used for a dry dock and in front of the marina gift shop. The entrance to the café in the back was down the breezeway.

She hesitated before getting out, and I turned and glanced out my back window toward the mill, but the view was blocked by the construction of a new strip mall.

"Keep trying Steve," I said. "I'll be back in a few minutes."

"And if you're not?"

"I will be," I said. "I'm just—"

"When I was little, a homeless man staying at the abbey held a gun to my head and led me into the woods."

"Oh, Kathryn. I'm so sorry."

I remembered reading a similar scenario in one of her novels.

"I'm not sure if he was going to rape and kill me or kidnap me. Father Thomas caught up to us and stopped him before he could do anything but scar me for life. It's why I freaked out in the clearing and why I'm not handling this as well as I should. I just wanted you to know."

I wondered how much her traumatic experience in childhood really had to do with her present day reactions. Maybe a lot. Maybe not. But that was her narrative, and the stories we tell ourselves to make sense of ourselves and the world are all-powerful. That was no less true of me and the person who killed Tammy than it was her or any other human on the planet. We are our stories. We are who we believe we are. Part of my reason for being at St. Ann's was to revise my stories.

"Come on," I said. "I'll take you back to the abbey."

"No, it's okay. I'll be fine. I need to face my fear."

"Are you sure?"

"Positive. I'll be fine. I know the owner. I'll sit and talk to him."

She opened the door and stepped out of the truck. "Now go. Be careful. And hurry back."

Chapter Forty-one

As I pulled out of the marina parking lot, instead of going back the way we had come, I took a left, driving toward the bay, then took a right onto a narrow oyster shell road that led to the back of the old mill site.

Driving around the mammoth marred-concrete and rusting-steel plant, I recalled the enormous stacks of pine logs, piles of pulp chips, and lines of loaded log trucks, where now there was only an empty lot. I imagined the fluffy white smoke, like cumulus clouds, billowing out of the smokestacks that now looked purposeless and out of place, and, most of all, I remembered the smell—that heavy, pungent stench that would cling to clothes and air currents alike, oppressive in its unrelentingness.

I pulled off the small road and parked among some tall stalks of sea oats, looked for the best place to get through the chain-link fence that surrounded the compound. Grabbing the small snub-nosed .38 from beneath my seat, I climbed out. Back toward Bridgeport, children played in a park next to the bay, while people stood on the retaining wall around the marina fishing with cane poles.

Like the structures and machinery of the dilapidated mill, the fence was in disrepair. Wired to its weathered links next to the faded and rusted signs warning not to trespass were bright new signs warning of explosive devices and the impending demolition of the remaining mill buildings, which according to the sign would take place in the morning.

Finding a place where the fence had been cut and poorly repaired, I pulled it apart and slid through, ripping my jacket on the jagged ends of the half-circles of aluminum as I did. Once inside, I checked to make sure my gun and phone were still in my pockets. Confirming they were, I moved through the maze of galvanized pipes, boilers, and buildings toward the offices in the front.

In preparation for demolition, the mill had been stripped of most of the machinery that was worth moving, but in testament to the sheer amount of materials required for a working mill to transform pulpwood into paper, an enormous amount remained.

A complex network of tubes and pipes of every size ran into and out of the ground and buildings, passing through shutoff valves with large, round handles like steering wheels. Glancing inside a couple of the buildings through broken panes of glass, I saw that the insides of the buildings looked similar to the outsides. Joining the pipes inside were enormous vats, extraordinarily long conveyor belts, and an elaborate system of metal-grate catwalks, beneath which the soiled concrete floor was littered with green barrels and drums, bleached and unbleached pulp, and rolled and unrolled paper.

As I neared the office building in the front, my phone rang. Answering it quickly, I looked around to see if anyone had heard it, but as far as I could tell, there was no one around to hear anything.

"Hello," I said in a whisper.

"John?" Kathryn asked. "Are you all right?"

"I'm fine. You okay?"

"Yeah. Still can't get Steve, but I'll keep trying. Just wanted to let you know I'm going back to the abbey, so take your time. Do what you need to do."

"How are you—"

"A friend of mine is eating here. I know she won't mind taking me. I'll see you back there tonight, and I'll call you if I get Steve."

"You sure?"

"Positive," she said, but it was unconvincing. "I'd rather be there and I don't want you worrying about me. Everything's fine. I promise."

When I ended the call, I set my phone to vibrate, slipped it back into my pocket, and continued toward the back door of the front office. I had taken maybe three steps when I felt the gun barrel touch me on the back of the head.

"Lift your hands very slowly," the voice behind me said.

I did.

Reaching into my pockets, he withdrew my gun, then my phone. After he did, I slowly looked over my shoulder to see who it was. As I suspected, it was the guy from the clearing who had taken Tammy's diary. Like before, he was alone, and I wondered where his partner was.

"You're trespassing in a very dangerous place," Ralph Reid said.

I turned to see him stepping out of one of the back doors of the building in front of me. He was wearing a hard hat.

"There are live explosives all over the place. What're you doing here?"

"You took Tammy's diary," I said.

"I was trying to help Father Thomas. I told them not to hurt anyone. Just get the book."

He was relaxed and comfortable, his words and manner demonstrating how untouchable he felt.

"They work for you or the paper company?" I asked.

"We all work for the company. They do the heavy lifting. We're here getting the last of our things. And we're not a paper company anymore."

No wonder he felt so confident. He had the weight of the monster behind him.

"What are you going to do with me?"

He looked surprised. "Escort you off this dangerous property and remind you that trespassing is a crime."

"That's it?"

"What'd you think I was going to do?"

"Don't know," I said, "but the guy pointing the gun at me gave me a few ideas."

"Oh, sorry," he said, as if it had slipped his mind. "Russ, put down the gun and give him his things back. John, I think you've been working in prison too long. Russ was just doing his job, securing the facility. We mean you no harm. I'm an officer of the court for God's sakes."

When I had my phone, I said, "Do you mind if I call your client?"

He made a sweeping gesture with his upturned hand. "Be my guest."

Russ walked around and stood by Reid, eyeing me cautiously as he did. At a minimum, Russ and his partner should be arrested for assault, but I'd have to wait for Steve for that.

Father Thomas was in his office. Sister Abigail was with him. He put me on speaker phone and I told them where I was and who I was with, then asked Father Thomas if he had anything to do with the theft of the diary.

"I most certainly did not," he said. "I would never—"

"He says he did it on your behalf."

"I never said any such thing," Reid said. "Don't put words in my mouth. I said I was trying to help my client. I had to know if what was in her diary could hurt us. And I had to get it before it became police evidence."

"Assault and theft are crimes whether or not it was in police custody yet."

"I realize that," he said. "I'm a good attorney. Sometimes I just get a little overzealous on behalf of my clients."

"Did you hear that?" I asked into the phone.

"Ask him how he can keep a straight face when saying such things," Sister Abigail said.

"You think I'm lying?" Reid asked with just a slight hint of outrage in his voice.

"If you expect me to believe that you risked disbarment because you were concerned about what Tammy's diary might say about Father Thomas."

"I told you," he said, "Father Thomas is the closest thing to a priest I've ever had."

I said into the phone, "Father, I think you need a new attorney."

"We all know good and well his primary if not only interest is in getting this land back for the paper company's new development," Sister Abigail said.

I repeated what she said.

Reid shook his head to himself and sighed heavily.

"Did you kill Tammy Taylor?" I asked.

"What?" he said in shock, his eyes wide and slightly wild. "No."

"Did you have your two, ah, heavy lifters do it?"

"No," he said. "I had nothing to do with it."

"Where is the diary?" I asked.

"Russ got overzealous and destroyed it," Reid said.

Russ smiled and said, "Sorry. I misunderstood."

"Why does the Gulf Coast Company want the abbey property so badly?" I asked.

"We don't," he said. "Not so badly. Certainly not enough to kill over it. We're just planning ahead. We have several developments in the works and we'd like to put one of them out there. If we can't, it's not the end of the world."

"Why do you continue to support St. Ann's if you want it closed?" I asked.

"Obviously we don't want it closed," he said. "We *would* like it relocated. That's it."

"Actually," Sister Abigail said, "they can't just stop their support. Floyd set up a trust for the abbey that will continue as long as the paper company does."

I repeated what she said.

"Unless—" Reid began to say, but stopped.

"Unless what?" I asked.

He shook his head. "Nothing."

Sister Abigail said, "Unless the board of directors has just cause to suspend support."

"Such as?" I said.

"Annual attendance drops below a certain number," she said. "We're convicted of a felony. The—"

"Who?"

"Father Thomas or myself or our successors."

"Aha," I said, but it wasn't the same without Kathryn there to appreciate it.

"What happens to the trust and land if St. Ann's closes?" I asked Reid.

He shrugged.

"The land wouldn't automatically go back to the paper company," Sister Abigail said.

I told him what she said.

"I'm not so sure about that," Reid said.

"So if Tammy's death gets the abbey shut down . . ."

"Then he gets what he wants," Sister Abigail said, "and that's the best motive I've heard so far."

Chapter Forty-two

"What happens if St. Ann's closes?" I asked.

"It depends," John David Dean, the abbey's attorney said.

I was sitting in his office in downtown Bridgeport. I had rushed over from the paper mill because when Sister Abigail called and asked if he would see me, he said now was the only time he had until after the first of the year.

"On what?" I asked.

"On when it closes."

John David Dean was a thin man in his early seventies with course salt-and-pepper hair that looked like a toupee, but wasn't. Though his movements were hesitant and his hands shaky, he was still suave, and I had no doubt he had been too smooth for his adversaries to know what had hit them as his younger self.

"Floyd never had much family," he continued. "He and his wife never had any kids together."

"That mean he had some without her?"

John David Dean smiled appreciatively. "It's more rumor than anything else, but if it's true, she would inherit the land, the buildings, *and* the trust money."

At one time, Dean's office had been elegant. Now, it was just old, the thick carpet and expensive furniture, though well-preserved, dated.

"*She?* He has a daughter?"

He shrugged. "I doubt he did. You know how small-town talk is."

Though his office and his clothes didn't smell of smoke, Dean's breath did, and even if it hadn't, his muffled, sandpaper voice said he had smoked a very long time.

"What would the Gulf Coast Company have to do to get St. Ann's land?" I asked.

He looked up and thought about it, rubbing his chin with shaky fingers as he did.

"Well, they could trade other land for it and relocate the abbey," he said. "If it closes, they could contest Floyd's will, take the heir or heirs to court, or they could try to buy it."

"So just getting the abbey closed is not enough."

"Which is why they haven't already done it," he said.

"They've got thousands and thousands of acres around here," I said. "How important is St. Ann's land to their developments?"

"From what I understand, vital, but that's just talk too. I'm not privy to their plans. I'll tell you this, they've got to figure out a way to convert their land into some cash pretty quickly or they'll go under."

"If Floyd doesn't have a daughter," I said, "who inherits St. Ann's?"

"According to his will, his niece and nephew would split the trust, while one got the land and the other the buildings, but if St. Ann's closes after they're dead, it—the land, the buildings, and the trust—automatically goes back to the paper company. I mean the Gulf Coast Company." He shook his head and frowned. "Can't get used to calling it that."

Knowing the answer, but wanting to hear him say it, I said, "Who's his niece?"

"Tammy was," he said.

"And the nephew?"

"Our distinguished chief of police," he said. "Steve Taylor."

Chapter Forty-three

The Bridgeport courthouse was obviously designed and built in a time when function was elevated above form. It was essentially a two-story square box made of that yellowish brick I associated with the 1970s.

Inside, I found the clerk of the court's office almost completely empty. There was nothing on the long counter than ran across the front, and two of the three desks behind it had no folders or stacks of papers on them. The room smelled of fried food and activator.

"Where is everybody?" I asked the large young black woman behind the counter.

Her skin was as dark and shiny as her shoulder-length hair, and she wore a formless black dress with white and yellow flowers on it, the front of which was covered in a light dusting of doughnut powder.

"The other two secretaries are already off for Christmas. The customers waiting to see what the paper company's gonna do," she said. "They do what they got planned and land value 'round here gonna skyrocket, but if they don't, no one want to be holding a buncha pine trees and sand spurs."

"I keep hearing about all these plans," I said. "I wanna see something."

"Honey, you've come to the right place," she said. "Step in here."

She held the small swinging door at the end of the counter

open for me and I followed her into the enormous vault. It was filled with oversized filing cabinets, computers, and wooden bookshelves, and smelled of old paper, dust, and an industrial air freshener that only made things worse. A framed color drawing of the proposed Gulf Sands Estates hung on the wall to the left of the door.

"Is that . . ." I began.

"The stuff dreams are made of," she said. "If they pull it off, this place'll never be the same again. We'll look like Orlando or Tampa and eventually Miami."

The detailed drawing showed a multi-stage development project of large-city proportions. It included golf courses, subdivisions, condominiums, restaurants, schools, a college, and even a theme park.

It was enormous in scale and scope, with the breadth and depth of an economic empire. The rumors were true. Florida's Forgotten Coast was about to be discovered, and like the original natives when Columbus landed, we would never be the same again.

I grew sick to my stomach, the rape of the land I loved so much sending me into a depression.

"Don't know nobody happy to see it coming," she said. "'Cept maybe the bankers and lawyers and real estate brokers."

"I'm surprised more people aren't protesting," I said.

"What good would that do?" she asked. "They gonna do what they want to. Hell, they already had a major highway moved so it would meet their new thoroughfare and give them more beachfront to sell."

I looked at the drawing more closely. I couldn't see how St. Ann's figured in. They really didn't need it. As beautiful as it was, it was too far from the Gulf and the rest of the development to even hold a golf course. I had to be missing something, but what was it?

Touching the spot where St. Ann's would be on the drawing, I asked, "Do you know what this tract of land has to do with the new development?"

She squinted at it. "That look like—I think that's—" she began, then broke off. "Hold on and let me check and see."

She withdrew a binder from a nearby bookcase and began to flip through it, nodding to herself as she did. "Mmm-hmm. That's where the new road's gonna go."

"New road?" I asked.

Closing the binder with a snap, she replaced it on the bookcase. "If this thing goes through, Highway 98 can't very well handle all the traffic. Plus, this new road will come directly from the new airport they tryin' to build in Panama City. And it'll connect to I-10. Rich bitches from all over the world can fly into Tallahassee or Panama City and be at their fancy resort in twenty or thirty minutes."

It was obvious that many of the challenges facing the Gulf Coast Company today were the same ones that faced Floyd Taylor and the Gulf Coast Paper Company when he first began assembling his great green empire—isolation, limited transportation linkages to areas outside northwest Florida, and the rampant poverty of our region. The very nature of the land, with its major river systems, numerous wetlands, and a geography that is on the way to nowhere accounted for much of our region's socioeconomic failings. It was this that made it possible for Floyd to accumulate so much land here in the first place.

"And the abbey is right in the middle of it," I said.

She looked at it again. "That's right," she said, "that *is* where St. Ann's is. Well, I guess they gonna have to move it."

I knew from recent media coverage of county commissioner meetings and state legislative sessions that the Gulf Coast Company was working on a plan that would use taxpayer money for the estimated ten million dollars per mile it takes to convert our existing two-lane highways to four lanes, and the several billion it would take to build the new regional airport in Bay County, but first they had to get St. Ann's back.

"Why can't they just put the road on either side of it?" I asked.

"Several reasons," she said, "but only one that really matters."

I waited as she paused for a moment.

"Wetlands," she said. "Both sides of that property's protected by wetlands. Can't even look at them the wrong way. If the road don't come through St. Ann's property, ain't no road coming through."

Wetlands are ecosystems typically found on the transition between terrestrial and aquatic systems. To be classified as a wetland, an area of land must have water on the ground's surface or in the root zone for at least a portion of the growing season.

Wetlands support a wide diversity of life. Many organisms depend on them completely for their survival, but even those who live in primarily aquatic or terrestrial habitats may rely on the ecotone border for a portion of the year, or for a portion of their life cycle.

Before scientists formally identified the values of wetland ecosystems, U.S. policies allowed the draining of wetlands. By the time these policies were overturned, more than half of the original wetlands in the landlocked states had already been drained.

National wetlands protection was set in motion when President Jimmy Carter issued two executive orders in 1977 that established wetland policies for all federal agencies.

The Clean Water Act requires a permit for most activities that would dredge or fill any of the nation's waters, including wetlands. Certain farming, ranching, and forestry activities that do not alter the use of land, as well as some construction and maintenance activities, are exempt from permit requirements. The Gulf Coast Company's plans for a new highway connecting the new airport they want built with their new development near Bridgeport would not qualify.

"'Course that probably won't even stop 'em either," she said. "They do what the hell they want to. It's their world. We just live here."

"But it's not," I said. "The earth belongs to all of us. They can't just do what they want. Not even with the land they own. Ownership isn't sovereignty. Not even the most radical right wing free-market fundamentalist believes that."

"Can if we all just keep letting them."

"I should've said we belong to the earth, not her to us. I just meant they can't—"

"Have so far. You have any idea how many promises they've made, just to break 'em? How many settlement agreements they've violated? How many clearing violations to conservation easements? The impact they having on wildlife habitats, aquatic preserves, and sea grass habitats? They say they gonna set aside such and such acres over here to mitigate the impact over there, but do they? They do what they want and the state and the DEP and the pathetic little county commissioners don't do a got damn thing. If anything they help them."

Chapter Forty-four

How's that for a motive? St. Ann's closes or a multibillion-dollar development deal doesn't happen.

I was in my truck driving back toward the abbey. I drove slowly, thinking about what I had just learned, adding it to what I already knew, and trying to figure out who killed Tammy.

Where the hell was Steve? How could he disappear in the middle of a murder investigation? How could I trust him when he's the one who benefits the most from St. Ann's closing?

Like the cottages on either side of it, the beachfront highway's traffic was light and sporadic, and I found it difficult to imagine it ever changing.

I thought about Ralph Reid and how he had acted like he was looking out for Father Thomas, working on his behalf, and all the while—

Seeing a sign up on the left for Gulf Sands Estates, I stomped on the break pedal and hit my blinker, the teenage girl in the car behind me laying on her horn.

I turned into the development to find that far more had been developed than I realized. This wasn't something that might happen, this was something that *was* happening already.

The lamppost-lined streets of Gulf Sands were black asphalt with a foot of white cement on either side and cobblestone sidewalks. To the right two golf carts were parked in front of a huge brick home that was being used as the sales office. It was the only finished building on the property, but a host of other homes were under construction.

Everything about the property looked exclusive and expensive, and it made me angry and nauseous at the same time.

Wonder how multicultural this neighborhood will be?

Planted palms joined the indigenous pines and plants that surrounded the marked-off lots, each with a pale green PVC pipe the color of scrubs coming out of the ground in front of it at an angle. Crews worked at tacking up Dupont Tyvek HomeWrap on the frame of two of the mansions.

It was going to be enormous, and it was only one small part of one phase.

The land was littered with little orange flags that snapped in the wind and pink ribbons that curled around the wooden stakes that held them.

I looked at the wooden boardwalks behind each lot that led to the beach and thought about the privileged few who would use them.

Greed would destroy something sacred—something we'd never get back again. Forget Father Thomas's exorcism of Tammy. Here was the real devil. True evil was the devastation and destruction, the death and extinction, the rape and pillaging of something far too fragile to be any match for the money motive.

Feeling sick, I pulled out of the development and back onto the highway. To fight off the dark mood descending, I made myself think about the case some more, starting with suspects and motives. Father Thomas still had to be considered a frontrunner. He was the only one we knew for sure was there, and all the physical evidence pointed to him.

Then there was Steve, who'd inherit big and who really didn't have an alibi if Kathryn was sleeping. Of course, even if he had been asleep when he says he was, he still could've done it. Before getting me—or even after—he could've come upon Father Thomas and Tammy alive in the woods. He could've knocked him unconscious and killed her.

Through the windows of my truck, the day looked deceptively warm. The sun inching toward the Gulf was bright and looked hot as it sparkled on the surface of the water, but the empty beach and the wind waving palm trees and sea oats told a different story.

Then there was Kathryn. If Steve really was asleep, then

she didn't have an alibi, and she could've stolen the tape to protect herself, not Father Thomas.

Blocking the cold breeze, but allowing the heat of the sun through, the cab of the truck grew too warm for the winter clothes I was wearing, and I reached over and turned on the air conditioner.

Then there were all the jealous lovers—including, but not limited to, Clyde, Tammy's dope-dealing boyfriend, Brad Harrison, the hellfire and brimstone handyman, and Keith Richie, the rageaholic rapist.

It could have been the drug suppliers she and Clyde owed money to. It could have been Russ and his partner. Reid could've hired them to do it—or he could've done it himself.

Then there was the demon she was supposedly possessed by. Maybe Father Thomas was telling the truth and what we were witnessing was a mystery that can't be solved.

When I got back to the abbey, Steve was standing in front of the chapel. He wore jeans, boots, and a leather jacket, very little of his tanned skinned showing. His blond hair was mostly hidden beneath a black baseball cap with BPD in white across the front. He started toward me the moment he spotted my truck and reached me by the time I was opening my door.

"Guess who stole the boat?" he asked.

I got out, closed the door.

"Guess who has the biggest money motive?" I said.

I could tell my posture and tone had him confused, but after a moment's hesitation and the dance of a question across his face, he said, "I asked first."

I glanced over at Kathryn's cabin. The porch light was off and very little illumination came from inside. Was that a message? Leave me alone. Don't come calling tonight. Was she upset with me for going to the mill, for leaving her? Maybe she was just resting and I was reading too much into the fact that she hadn't turned on the lights yet. After all, it was just now getting dark.

"I don't know," I said, "Clyde."

"Who told you?"

"No one."

"Then how the hell'd you know?"

"It was just a guess. He was most likely to try to sneak into St. Ann's."

The engine of my small, old truck ticked as it cooled down, and I could smell an unpleasant mixture of burning oil and antifreeze.

He continued to consider me. "Yeah, I guess he was."

"Do you know where he is?" I asked.

"My men are pickin' him up right now. Think he's our guy."

He didn't sound very certain—more like a man trying to convince himself that what he was saying was true—and I wondered if that were true or just my prejudiced perception.

"I'll let him sit in a cell overnight and interview him first thing in the morning," he said. "You wanna be there?"

I nodded, but didn't say anything.

He turned and I followed his gaze out toward the lake. I let my eyes wander over the yellowish-brown grass lying limply, on to the gently sloping hill, and down to the choppy grayish waters of the lake. The cold breeze blew the Spanish moss in the cypress trees and waved the straw-colored underbrush, and there was nothing appealing about what, in summer, would be a lush lakeside paradise.

I could tell I was looking at Steve differently now that I knew how much he stood to inherit, because I was acutely aware of just how expensive his ostrich boots, leather jacket, and aviator sunshades looked.

"What the hell's the matter?" Steve asked, turning back to face me. "I figured you'd jump up and down when I told you. It explains what the boat was doing here and it means Father Thomas is likely innocent."

I told him about spotting the two men who'd taken the diary, following them back to the mill site, and what Reid had said.

"I'll have them picked up and brought in for questioning," he said. "And to answer your question, the Gulf Coast Company has the biggest money motive."

"I meant which individual," I said.

He shrugged. "Reid?"

"You."

"*Me?*"

He seemed genuinely surprised.

"Only three people stand to inherit the land if St. Ann's closes," I said. "Floyd's daughter—if he even has one, Tammy—who's now dead, and you."

"That can't be right."

"You saying you didn't know?"

"*No*, I didn't *know*. Floyd has a daughter?"

"According to John David Dean."

"Was he sober when he said it?" he asked.

"How could you not know you stand to inherit?" I said. "Your uncle owned it—owned the paper company."

"I have nothing to do with it. Nothing. Not one single thing. Wouldn't if they wanted me to. I have no stock in it, no interests whatsoever, and I thought St. Ann's owned and would always own this land."

"It's a hell of a motive," I said.

"Yeah," he said, "I'm a greedy bastard. It's why I'm a cop."

The sun and the temperature were falling, and as the day came to an end, the buildings of St. Ann's increasingly became vague black objects.

"What'd Tammy say?" I asked.

"Huh? When?"

"When you went to see what she and Father Thomas were up to and ask her about being the last one seen with Tommy."

"Nothing. I couldn't find her."

"You couldn't *find* her?"

"You motherfucker. You really suspect me, don't you? I went to Father Thomas's but they weren't there. I was about to look around when I saw Kathryn. Went to her cabin instead. Wish to God I hadn't, but that's the gospel on what happened."

"Where've you been all day?" I asked.

"Working my investigation," he said. "I don't report to you."

"Why couldn't you be reached?"

"I was trying to get the lab to put a rush on things. I physically walked some of the evidence through. And then I worked on finding Clyde after the landing operator picked him out of a photo array."

I nodded.

"You really think I . . . I'm behind all this—for *money*?"

"Sometimes it seems it's behind everything," I said.

He raised his eyebrows, looked from me to Kathryn's cabin, then back to me, and said, "No, sometimes it's just sex. Both cloud the judgment."

Glancing down at the badge clipped to his belt, I said, "So does power."

He shook his head and rolled his eyes.

The door to the counseling center opened and Sister Abigail walked out of it. When she saw us, she headed in our direction.

"Speaking of power," I said, then told him about the wetlands around St. Ann's and their impact on the highway, the airport, and the development.

He looked all around us, a sick expression on his face. "They're going to close it down."

The certainty and uncharacteristic vulnerability of his statement coming from the chief law enforcement officer in the area was like an unseen punch—one that couldn't be slipped or blocked, but only felt fully and irrevocably.

"Good evening gentlemen," she said. "How goes the good fight?"

After we responded and shared and batted the breeze around a bit, she looked at me and asked, "Was John David Dean helpful?"

I nodded.

She said she was glad, but surprised me by not asking what he'd said.

"Kathryn already go to her cabin?" she asked.

"She should already be in it," I said. "Should have been back hours ago."

"I thought the two of you were together?" she said.

"Are you sure she's not in her cabin?" I asked, already starting to move in that direction.

"I've tried calling her several times."

As we rushed to Kathryn's cabin, I told them what had transpired earlier in the afternoon and what Kathryn had told me about getting a ride back here with a friend.

Within seconds we had discovered that Kathryn was not in her cabin, within minutes that she was not at the abbey, and within an hour that she had left Café on the Dock with someone who resembled Russ's partner.

Chapter Forty-five

"If anything happens to her . . ." Steve said.

His threat didn't bother me, but his implication did—this was my fault. I was responsible. I shouldn't have left her. He was right. If anything happened to her, it was on me.

"How could you have left her?" he asked.

I didn't answer. The circumstances didn't matter. It didn't matter that it was her choice, that she knew the manager, that I was nearby and we both had cell phones, that there had been no reason to believe she was in any danger there.

We were racing toward Ralph Reid's house in Panama City in Steve's Explorer, siren on, emergency lights flashing. Sister Abigail was back at the abbey calling Kathryn's cell in between calling her friends who would've been most likely to have been at Café on the Dock.

"Whatta you think he wants with her?" he asked. "If he's trying to use her for leverage, why hasn't he contacted us? I just can't see how taking her helps him. You think he's doing this on his own? Why aren't you saying anything?"

"Where is she?" Steve asked.

When Reid had opened his door, Steve shoved him back into the house and now had him pinned to the wall of his foyer. His hair was sticking up on one side, one of his cheeks was red, and he acted groggy. He was wearing the same dress shirt and slacks as when I had seen him early in the afternoon, but his tie and shoes were off and his shirt was half untucked and very wrinkled.

"What?" he asked. "Who?"

His house was surprisingly humble—an older ranch with simple furnishing. Obviously the home of a bachelor, there were no signs of feminine sensibility or recent improvements. Though tidy and cleanish looking, there was the unmistakable odor of animal, as if the dwelling were home to pets as well as Reid, but the smell was the only evidence in the foyer.

"Don't pretend like you were asleep," Steve said. "It's too early."

"I came home after work and fell asleep in my recliner. I'm not pretending any—"

"I will kill you," Steve said, dropping his right hand to the gun holstered on his hip. "I can do it. And I can get away with it."

Reid seemed to shrink in on himself, an undeniable fear creeping into his face, his usual confidence replaced by a sad, pathetic vulnerability.

"What are you talking about?" he asked, suddenly wide awake.

"Kathryn," I said. "Where is she?"

"Why are you asking me? How would I know where—"

His confusion seemed authentic, but he was a professional, practiced liar. Steve relaxed his hold on him slightly, but didn't let go.

"She's missing," I said. "This afternoon when I was with you and Russ, we think the other guy—what's his name?—"

"Cole?"

"—took Kathryn from the marina."

"Are you sure? I can't believe—"

"You saying you had nothing to do with it?" Steve asked.

"Of course not. I had no idea. Kathryn's like a daughter to me. I'd never be involved in anything that—"

"You had us assaulted and robbed," I said.

"I told you. I just asked them to get the diary," he said. "I specifically told them not to hurt anyone."

"This afternoon your guy was pointing a gun at me."

"He's not *my* guy. He works security for the Gulf Coast Company. You were trespassing. If you'll recall, I intervened on your behalf."

"Who do they work for if not you?" Steve asked.

"I really don't know. There's a lot of restructuring going on. I just asked for their help getting the diary because I knew they could."

"Why would they want her?" I asked.

He shrugged. "I have no idea."

"Where would they take her?" Steve asked.

"Do you realize how much property they own?" he asked. "Nearly a million acres. They could be anywhere."

"What are we going to do?" Steve asked me.

I thought about it. I really had no idea where to start.

"I need to get an APB out," he said. "Get my guys out of bed. Start a search."

"Can you call Russ or Cole?" I asked.

Reid shook his head. "I really am just a cog. I don't know—"

"What about—"

"Wait," Reid exclaimed. "There's an old isolated fish camp. I've heard them talk about it. They called it Hotel California. I thought they were kidding, but—"

"Why Hotel California?" Steve asked.

"They say people check out, but never leave."

"Where is it?" I asked.

"I can take you," he said.

Steve said, "You didn't think we were leaving you here, did you?"

The fish camp was a small, unremarkable house on a bend in the Chipola River that elevated function over form. Its purpose was practical, not aesthetic. It was at the end of a long dirt road off of an empty county highway, surrounded on three sides by pine woods thick with undergrowth and the river on the other.

As we neared it, Steve cut his lights. The car I had seen Russ and Cole get into in downtown Bridgeport earlier in the day, a champagne-colored Ford Taurus, was parked in front of the house.

"Listen to me," Reid whispered from the backseat, "don't hesitate. These men are dangerous. I'm not sure why they're doing this, but it's not on my orders. It probably doesn't have anything to do with the company either. Maybe one of these sociopaths has become obsessed with Kathryn."

As Steve brought the Explorer to a stop, we both turned and looked at Reid in disbelief.

"What?" he said. "I'm just saying. Be careful. Do what you've got to do to get Kathryn back."

Steve looked at me. "This bastard's already trying to distance himself and the company from the two dead men in the house."

"That's not—"

"Shut the fuck up," Steve said. "One more word from you and I'm gonna shoot you."

With Reid cuffed in Steve's backseat, the two of us slowly moved toward the house. As we had agreed, when we reached it I split off to take the back.

"Hey," he whispered. "Don't shoot me when we bust through the doors."

"Ditto," I said.

Though brittle, the weeds were high and made a swishing sound as I walked through them. The only light in the house seemed to be coming from the center, perhaps in the main room, the windows I was ducking beneath on the side dark.

When I reached the back of the house, I could see strips of light on the wooden slats of the porch. They were coming from the partially opened blinds of the sliding glass doors, which meant I would be able to see inside before breaking in.

Easing over to the side of the door, I leaned against the wall and risked peeking in. Though it shouldn't have, what I saw shocked me. I should have been prepared for anything, but I wasn't prepared for this.

I tried the handle of the glass door, but it was locked.

Jumping off the porch and running around to the front of the house, I tried to catch Steve before he broke in.

"STEVE," I yelled as I neared the front corner of the house. "IT'S ME. DON'T SHOOT."

"What the hell are you doing?" he asked when I reached him.

"Trying not to get shot," I said.

"What about—"

Before he could finish, I stepped around him and opened the door. He spun around, crouching in the doorway, gun drawn, in a shooter's stance.

His eyes grew wide and his gun came down a little when he saw what I had.

The large rustic living room had very little furniture, a couch and a chair on one wall, a recliner on another, and nothing in the middle of the floor—except the two dead bodies of Russ and Cole.

Each man was laying on his back, the old rug beneath him soaked with his blood. Both men's guns were on the floor next to them. Cole's hand was still on his.

"What the hell?" Steve said. "Where is Kathryn?"

"I don't know," I said, "but she's not here."

When I had looked in the back door, I could see that the house had only one great room and a small bathroom in the corner. The side windows I thought belonged to darkened rooms were actually just taped up so no light could escape. From the back door, I could see into the little bathroom in the front corner. It was empty. The two men were the only people in the house.

"She may never have been here," I said.

"You think they shot each other?" he asked.

"I think that's what we're supposed to think," I said, "but this thing's as staged as an amateur play—and about as well."

"What if we're wrong?" Steve asked.

We were standing in the front yard of the house watching as FDLE processed the crime scene, Reid still locked in the back of Steve's Explorer. It was late. We were tired.

"What if it's not him?" he said, nodding toward Reid.

"He led us straight here."

Beneath the huge halogen shop lights that lit up the entire area, the crime scene techs were processing the Taurus as well as scouring the yard. They wore protective coverings over their clothes and shoes to prevent contaminating the crime scene any more than absolutely necessary.

"I didn't mean this," he said. "He's definitely involved in this. I mean Kathryn. What if they didn't take her? If Reid or his boys didn't kill Tammy, then maybe whoever did has Kathryn."

"It's possible."

From the backseat of Steve's vehicle, Reid was motioning and yelling, but none of us gave any indication we saw or heard him.

"I've got to be here," he said. "And when we're done, I'm gonna go at Reid hard, but I'd feel a lot better if you were following up the other leads. There's nothing you can do here anyway. Divide and conquer. Go back to the abbey and break some balls, rattle some cages. The longer it goes, the less chance we have of finding Kathryn alive."

Chapter Forty-six

I ducked beneath the crime scene tape and stepped into the cabin Father Thomas and Tammy had used, its wet copper smell filling my nostrils, its reverberating vibes of violence echoing through me.

The room, like the night, was dark and cold and felt disjointed and dangerous. A howling wind haunted the woods, whistling through the trees, whipping around the old buildings of St. Ann's, whining like someone in pain. Nearby, a shutter banged against a building—slowly, incessantly, like a dreaded knock of someone delivering bad news or the weak heartbeat of a dying man.

I searched the cabin to make sure I was alone, my flashlight beam creeping eerily across the horrific images of blood splatter and bed restraints, of crimson smears on sheets and blackened drip trails on the floor, of arterial spray on the wall and ceiling, and a deep red handprint on the door jam.

There was no one in the cabin, but it didn't feel like I was alone.

A few minutes before, I had searched Kathryn's cabin and found the tape. It was difficult enough to find that it didn't surprise me that Steve's officers had missed it when they conducted their search, but it wasn't so difficult that it alleviated my concerns about their incompetence.

After they had processed the scene, Steve had the techs leave everything in place—including the video camera. It had the residue of fingerprint dust on it, but was otherwise ready to roll, and as

I powered it up and opened the tape transport, I realized anyone looking would know the camera had been used after it had been processed.

Gently dropping the tape into the transport, I closed the door and began to rewind it. As it rewound, I looked around the room again, wondering if I were about to see a sex tape, an exorcism, or something else.

Finding it difficult to concentrate on anything but the fact that Kathryn was missing and my responsibility in it, I willed myself to think about the case and what it had brought up in me. Over and over I had been asked and had been wondering what I believed. Did I believe in the devil? Did I believe in possession, in exorcism?

The truth was, I wasn't sure what I believed. There could be something beyond human evil, something in the supernatural realm. I believed in transcendent good, why not transcendent evil? I just didn't know. I believed in God, in grace, in love—in good more than evil, but I did believe in evil. I had seen it, experienced it, fought it. Ultimately, evil seemed no match for love, seemed more inconsequential than anything else when compared to God, to grace, to love.

Finally, the whir of the tape stopped.

Was Tammy possessed? Maybe she was. Maybe she had been the victim of early, systematic sexual and/or physical abuse, a heavy drug user. Maybe she had a dissociative disorder. Maybe she had been made to feel vulnerable by abuse or drugs and wasn't really completely present in her own mind and body. Maybe she really was what some people would refer to as possessed, but that doesn't mean it means exactly what they think it means. Maybe like most things it's far more mysterious than we realize, and giving it literal limits, definitions, causes, cures was to diminish it, to reduce it, to dismiss it in ways those who believed in literal possession never meant to do.

I'd know soon enough, I thought, as I pushed the Play button.

When the tape started playing, the small pop-out screen filled with Tammy strapped to the bed, her naked body shivering slightly. Almost immediately, Father Thomas approached her from the other side of the bed in a black cassock holding the Catholic ritual book and a bottle of holy water. Even when he walked into the frame, part of him was still cropped off.

I glanced over my shoulder and looked at the room again. There was a lot of the room that couldn't be seen on the tape because it was zoomed in so tight on the bed.

Looking back at the screen, I watched as Father Thomas began the rite.

For a long while, nothing eventful happened. Father Thomas knelt beside the bed and began to pray the Lord's Prayer, Tammy watching peacefully, though not offering to join him.

The first abnormal reaction Tammy had was when Father Thomas withdrew a small crucifix from his pocket and held it up toward her. Recoiling from it, her face contorted into something serpentine and she hissed at him, her breath suddenly visible as if the temperature in the room had dropped drastically.

Caught off guard, Father Thomas backed up, before he realized what he was doing and stopped. Crossing himself, he held the crucifix even closer to Tammy and said, "The Lord rebuke you."

Like hers, his breath came out in tiny puffs of mist, and even in the dim room his skin looked impossibly pale, his wispy hair impossibly white.

Tammy then said something in a language I didn't recognize and the crucifix flew out of his hand and into the far corner opposite us. I glanced over to see that it was still sticking into the wall.

I paused the camera and walked over to take a better look at the cross. As I neared it, I heard a serpentine hiss from behind me and a little girl whisper, "Leave now before it's too late." The crucifix then shot out of the wall and would have hit me in the face had I not whipped my head around at the exact moment I did. As it was, it still grazed my ear before it landed on the floor and slid until it came to rest upside down against the opposite wall.

Walking back over to the camera, I could hear the tormented moan of someone in severe agony, but choosing to ignore it as well as all the questions ricocheting off the walls of my mind, I took the tape off pause and began watching again.

Tammy's free hand had shot out and seized Father Thomas by the neck. Her grip must've been extremely powerful. No matter what he tried, he couldn't break free. Soon, he was turning blue, gasping for breath, still unable to get loose. Releasing her hand from his, he reached down, grabbed the holy water and drenched her with it.

She let go of his throat and he fell back, sucking in air as he did.

Writhing in pain, her skin began to split open, blood pouring from her wounds, steam rising from her skin, a litany of shrill screams and profanities spewing from her mouth.

Father Thomas slapped Tammy hard across the face.

As if a feral animal, Tammy's free hand clawed at Father Thomas, scraping skin from his face before he could back out of her reach.

Spreading her legs even further apart, Tammy put her free hand inside herself and said, "Come back. I like it rough." She then clinched her fist and began to hit herself.

Father Thomas grabbed her arm and attempted to restrain it, but she swatted him across the room. He hit the wall next to the door and fell to the floor in a crumpled heap.

For a long moment, Father Thomas didn't move, but when the bed began to bang around, he slowly looked up.

And then I saw something that changed everything. With Father Thomas still on the floor, the shadow of a person crossed over part of Tammy and the bed.

I stopped the tape and rewound it.

Replaying the section, and seeing the shadow again, I said aloud, "Someone else was in the room."

"I was," a demented little boy hissed behind me.

I turned, but there was no one there, and I regretted it the moment I did.

Reminding myself to ignore the voice and concentrate on what I was doing, I turned back around toward the camera. No matter what the voice was—real or imagined, in my mind or in the room—I knew the best thing to do was give it no place.

Had someone come in during the exorcism? Was it a person? Steve was the first to leave the table after Tammy. Why wouldn't Father Thomas have mentioned that someone else was in the room?

Maybe he didn't know. He was across the room and had yet to look in this direction. He seemed very shaken up. Maybe he'd never seen the person.

I restarted the tape, but there wasn't much left to see. In less than a minute, the tape was stopped, which only confirmed someone else was there, because Father Thomas was still across the room on the floor.

I stumbled outside the cabin and stood in the cold darkness.

I shook my head and confessed to God and the wondrous, mysterious universe she had given birth to, "I'm an arrogant and ignorant man. Quick to speak, slow to learn. I've spoken of things I don't understand. 'I place my hand over my mouth.'"

The last part was a line from the book of Job. I didn't literally cover my mouth.

I wasn't sure what I had just witnessed was demonic, but I had never before experienced anything like it, and I was tempted to try to figure it out, to use deductive reasoning and investigative techniques to solve the mystery, but quickly decided not to, not to apply logic to something so illogical, not to try to figure it out, not to investigate, not to respond in the same tired ways I always did.

Some mysteries can be solved. Others cannot. When it comes to the truly great mysteries of existence, what we deal with is not vague unknowns, but specific unknowables.

I realized how dismissive I had been. Being so sure I could figure it out if I just put my mind to it. Trusting too much rationality and deductive reasoning.

I had to talk to Father Thomas, even if it meant waking him up. There were things I had to say, things that wouldn't wait. There were also things I needed to ask him, such as what happened after the camera was turned off, why it was turned off, and who had done it.

Chapter Forty-seven

"I owe you an apology," I said to Father Thomas.

I had found him in his study, dozing in a high-back chair by the fireplace. He asked if there was any word of Kathryn and told me he wouldn't be able to sleep until he knew she was safely back in her bed.

"For what?"

"I've seen the tape," I said.

"So *now* you believe?"

His tone was harsh and condescending and I realized how difficult it was going to be to talk to him. I had hoped to have a conversation about what I had experienced, to exchange thoughts and ideas, but I realized that wasn't going to happen. He was responding out of ego, feeling vindicated. A good conversation, a true sharing of souls, requires openness and humility—something a defensive, no-room-for-doubt religious stance doesn't allow. It was a shame though, a real missed opportunity. To me, faith and devotion is far richer when mixed with a good dose of honest agnosticism— something people like Father Thomas seemed not to have.

"I shouldn't've taken it so lightly," I said. "Not even allowing for the possibility that what happened could be inexplicable. I'm sorry."

"Well, I can't judge. As I'm sure you saw, I was unprepared for what happened. It completely caught me by surprise. Not just that there was a manifestation, but that it happened so quickly."

"It did seem pretty fast."

"It was as if all the demon really wanted to do was destroy me," he said. "Like an ambush. It was just hiding. Waiting to pounce."

I nodded. "Maybe it was."

The night was nearly over. It would be morning soon, and through his window I could see that the moonlit lake was perfectly still, its smooth surface a mirror image of the sparsely star-sprinkled sky above it. Still in a state of awe and wonderment, I breathed in deeply, held it, then let it out very slowly.

"I was easy prey," he said. "Should've been ready. What I did was stupid and I should've known better."

"Well—"

"She'd be alive and free from her torment if I hadn't been so derelict in my duty. I cost her her life. There's no justification for my negligence. I can hardly live with it, but I absolutely cannot live with people thinking I raped and murdered that troubled little girl."

I nodded my understanding.

The dying fire popped, sparks flying out onto the red brick, its flickering flame sending pulsating light dancing on the spines of his colorful books.

"You think once Steve sees the tape, he'll clear me and the investigation will end?"

I shook my head.

"Why not?"

"The tape doesn't show everything," I said, "and it raises as many questions as it answers."

"I don't understand. I thought for sure it would clear up everything. What doesn't it show?"

"The tape is stopped right after Tammy knocks you into the wall. You're still on the floor when it's turned off."

His eyes grew wide in alarm and looked genuinely fearful. "*Turned off?*"

"Someone came in and turned it off," I said. "Who was it?"

He shook his head. "I have no idea."

"You don't know who came in? You didn't see anyone?"

He hesitated, seeming to calculate too much for someone telling the truth. "No one came in during the exorcism."

"You had to think about it a little too long."

"I wanted to be sure," he said.

"Normally when someone hesitates that much and sounds

the way you do, they're lying."

"You sayin' I'm lyin'?" he asked, trying hard to sound offended, but lacking conviction.

"I'm asking."

"Well, I'm *tellin'* you. No one came in during the ritual. At least not that I saw. But I was banged up pretty good and maybe I didn't see them."

It was possible. He was preoccupied and he had just been nearly knocked out, but something didn't feel right. Maybe he was just nervous or shaken up or naive or worried about Kathryn, but he seemed to be lying.

"Why would someone turn off the camcorder?" I asked.

Shaking his head, a perplexed look filling his face, he said, "I have no idea."

"How much longer were you in the cabin after she knocked you into the wall?"

He looked off into the distance, squinting to see something that wasn't there. "It's hard to say. It seems so timeless during it, but I'd say around half an hour or more."

I shook my head in frustration. "That's a lot we don't have."

"And every bit of it further confirmation that what I'm sayin' is true. Tammy was killed by demonic forces, and my greatest fear is that they're now inside someone else at St. Ann's waiting to hurt or kill another child of God."

The fire popped again, sending an explosion of embers into the air with the smoke rising up the chimney, which in turn set off an explosion in my mind.

Jumping up, I dug the phone out of my pocket.

"What is it?" Father Thomas said. "Where are you going?"

Chapter Forty-eight

"What time is the demolition of the mill?" I asked.

I was talking to Steve on my cell as I ran toward my truck.

"About an hour," he said. "Some of my guys are working crowd control. Why?"

"I could be way off on this, but I'd rather be wrong than—"

"What is it?"

"If they want to kill Kathryn, what better way to do it than in the destruction of the mill? They've already gotten rid of the only two guys connecting them to the criminal activity we know about. If they had Cole abduct her and tie her up at the mill, then killed him and Russ, they'd—"

"Wouldn't they just kill her?" he said. "Even if they were going to try to destroy the body during the explosion?"

I reached my truck and climbed inside as the first hint of false dawn illuminated the horizon.

"Maybe," I said, pressing the phone to my ear with my shoulder as I started the truck. "But what if they have Cole and Russ tie her up and she escapes or is discovered before the explosion, she points the finger at them, but they're already dead—supposedly killed each other."

"Why would they want to kill her?"

"I don't know yet," I said. "Why take her at all?"

"Well, if they do want her dead, what you're saying makes sense," he said. "We've got to search the mill before—"

"I'm on my way," I said.

Bouncing down the dirt road toward the highway without a seatbelt on, holding the phone between my shoulder and the side of my head while having to shift, I dropped the phone several times.

"John," he said, "I'm over an hour away. I'll never make it in time."

"Can you get the demolition delayed?"

"I can try. It'll be hard by phone. Plus, if you're right about what they're doing . . ."

"How many officers do you have at the site?" I asked.

When I reached the highway, I slowed just enough to make sure there was nothing coming, then floored it, slinging dirt onto the road, my tires screeching on the pavement.

"Not many," he said. "And they won't be much help. It's a crossing guard and school resource officer."

I thought about it, but didn't say anything.

"I'm gonna start making calls now," he said. "I'll try to get the demolition pushed back first. At certain spots on the way I'm not gonna have coverage. I'll get there as soon as I can, but it'll be too late. If she's there, you've got to find her."

A large crowd had gathered to see the last of the mill go the way of the paper market, imploding at the dawning of a new day. They lined both sides of the highway, the first of the sun cresting over the tree tops glinting off their cars.

I had hoped to drive down the road beside the marina like I had before and sneak into the back of the mill through the same hole in the fence, but I could tell immediately that wasn't going to be possible because of the crowd and the roadblocks.

Parking in the lot of a closed drugstore in town, I ran as fast as I could toward the site. By the time I reached the first roadblock, I was breathing heavily and my side was beginning to hurt. Still, I couldn't help smiling a little when I saw that the officer standing guard was the same one I had encountered at the entrance of the marina the morning Tommy's body was found.

He held his hands up the moment he saw me.

"I've got to get in there," I said, bending forward slightly and gasping for breath.

"Oh, no," he said. "I learned my lesson. Chief said if I ever did something like that again, I'd be doing this my entire career."

"He's the one who sent me. He was going to call you guys, but he must have lost reception on his way."

"Good one," he said. "That's good."

"I don't have time for this. We think someone might be inside one of the buildings. I'm going in, you go see if you can get them to delay the detonation."

He hesitated a moment, but shook his head. "If the chief's on his way, he can do it when he gets here."

"He won't make it in time."

He smiled and nodded as if that confirmed I was lying.

"Call him," I said.

He hesitated again, squinted as he considered me a moment, then lifted his radio. He asked if any of the other officers had heard from Steve. They hadn't. He then pulled his cell phone off the clip on his belt and punched in a number I assumed was Steve's.

While we waited, I glanced at my watch. We had less than half an hour.

"No answer," he said. "You're just gonna have to wait."

"Okay," I said, lifting my hands in a placating gesture.

He relaxed slightly, and as he did, I made my move.

Closing the distance between us in one big step, I came up with the little .38, which I pointed beneath his chin as I pinned him to the side of the car.

"Chief Taylor will straighten all this out once he gets here," I said, "but I can't wait that long to go in."

As I spoke, I reached down and unsnapped his holster and withdrew his gun.

"I'm not going to hurt you or anybody else. Just have a seat in your car until the chief gets here."

I opened the back door of his patrol car and shoved him inside, then pocketing both guns, ran down the road between the mill and the new marina, trying not to think about the ramifications of what I had just done or what I was about to do.

Chapter Forty-nine

The back of the mill was farther away than it looked, and by the time I reached it and crawled through the fence, I was gasping heavily, my side felt like it would split open, and I had a little less than twenty minutes left.

I felt like my heart might explode, but I kept running, my eyes scanning each area as I whipped my head around to search it. I figured that if she was here, it was far more likely that she was inside one of the buildings than out, but I still searched beneath the various networks of pipes as I ran between the buildings.

The first structure I entered was an old, rusted metal storage building with broken windowpanes and a missing door on one end. Except for a couple of huge rolls of paper, the building was empty. It was a waste of time, but I checked behind them anyway.

I entered the largest of the buildings next, running beside a row of large pipes, looking beneath the enormous vats and the long conveyor belts. It was huge, probably more than an acre, and I was again amazed at how much machinery had been left. It would be easy to miss a small area where she could be hidden.

I started calling her, yelling her name as loud as I could. It reverberated off the concrete and metal and got lost in the open space of the three-story building. After a few moments, I stopped and waited, but there was no response. Eventually, I climbed up onto the metal catwalk and looked down into the vats, barrels, and drums, and all along the soiled concrete floor.

From the high vantage point, I could see the massive

amounts of explosives running along the walls, wired to the support beams of the ceiling and to the larger pieces of equipment. It was at that moment I fully realized the situation I was in. This building or the entire plant could explode at any moment. I could be spending my very last minutes on earth looking for someone who probably wasn't even here.

When I came out of the building, light-headed from sleep deprivation and too much oxygen, I looked at my watch and realized there was no way I could do even a cursory search of the entire facility. I had less than ten minutes, and the business offices in the front would take longer than that.

I would have to narrow down my remaining search to the most likely places. I just had no idea what those were. For a moment, I was so at a loss, so overwhelmed by the sheer size of the facility, that I froze. Just stood there. Unable to think. Unable to move.

Was this how I was going to die? Standing still, waiting for the bang?

When the first sound and vibration came, I jumped. By the time the second one occurred, I realized it was my cell. Ripping it out of my pocket, I shouted into it.

"You find her?" Steve asked.

"No," I said. "You get them to delay the demolition?"

"I couldn't get through to the right person before," he said. "I just got service back. Where are you?"

I told him.

"You've got to get out of there," he said. "Hopefully she's not in there, but either way you've got to get out now."

"Okay," I said. "Tell your men not to shoot me. I had to assault one to get in."

I hung up with no intention of leaving and glanced at my watch. I had a little under five minutes, probably not even enough time to get out safely.

I had to go, but I couldn't. I just couldn't leave knowing she might be here—knowing it was my fault if she was and that I could do something about it.

I paused for a moment and prayed for help—something I rarely did during an investigation. I routinely prayed for the victims, occasionally for the perpetrators, often for wisdom and insight, but rarely for actual help. I guess I believed that God left these things largely up to us—if not, my time would be better spent locked away somewhere praying instead of investigating. Now, I was desperate, at the end of my abilities, and quickly running out of time. So I prayed.

And God answered.

I couldn't explain what happened. Didn't even begin to understand it. But I knew a spiritual impression when I had one. And I had one.

I quickly ran over to the large pipes rising out of the ground. Finding a door, I forced it and entered an underground service tunnel. It was dark and dank, and my shoes splashed water as I ran along the sidewalk, crouched beneath the pipes.

About ten feet down the tunnel, I found Kathryn cuffed to one of the pipes, her head hanging down, duct tape around her mouth. I couldn't tell if she was conscious or not, but she didn't lift her head as I ran toward her.

"Kathryn. Can you hear me?"

She looked up, seeming to wonder if I were real or imaginary.

"We've got to get out of here now. The mill's about to explode."

I yanked on the cuffs and examined the pipe. They weren't coming off.

"Kathryn," I said, my voice loud, "listen to me. I've got to shoot the cuffs to try to get you free. It's going to be loud. Hold your head down and don't move your hands."

I pulled my gun out, put the barrel next to one of the lengths in the cuffs, ducked my head behind my other arm, and fired.

The sound was even more deafening than I had thought it would be, and my ears rang as I checked the chain.

Nothing. The round had made no impact on the chain.

Wishing I had something more powerful than my .38, I pulled out the gun I had taken from Steve's officer. Thinking it was a .9mm, I was pleasantly surprised to find it was a .45.

"I'm going to try it again," I said. "Be very still and keep your head down."

Before I fired the first round from the .45, the first explosion sounded. It shook the ground and sounded like a jet breaking the sound barrier.

Realizing time was out, I jacked a round into the chamber and fired the .45 at the handcuff chain several times without pausing. The sound was even louder than the .38, but nothing compared to the explosion.

The shots lit up the tunnel, filled it with the acrid smell of burned gun powder, rained down spent casings, still burning hot, and broke the chain.

As Kathryn's hands fell to her sides, I removed the tape from her mouth, dropped the gun, snatched her up, and began to make my way out of the tunnel as best I could, hearing other explosions around us as I did.

When we surfaced, we stepped into a thick cloud of smoke, ash, dust, and debris that reminded me of footage I had seen from the streets of New York when the Twin Towers had come tumbling down. Unable to see, I lifted Kathryn across my shoulder and ran in what I thought was the direction I had come in. As the mind-rattling, ear-deafening explosions continued, I realized they were coming from up front. They must have started there and were headed toward the back where we were.

I knew we didn't have long.

We were close to the largest building in the plant and once it started exploding, we'd be dead.

Coughing and stumbling, head and heart aching, I ran as quickly as I could, nearly falling several times, but somehow able to stay on my feet.

When I reached the fence, I laid Kathryn on the ground, crawled through, then pulled her out.

Even when we were on the other side, I realized we were still too close to the largest building, and there was no time to get away from it. This was it—unless . . .

Hoisting Kathryn up again, I ran toward the retaining wall. When I reached it, without stopping, I tossed Kathryn into the bay and dove in after her.

In the water, Kathryn conscious now, we waited for the final series of explosions, but they never came.

Eventually, I heard Steve yelling my name, and I told him where we were.

When he looked over the wall and saw Kathryn, the relief on his face was indescribable.

"If I'd known y'all were just back here swimming, I wouldn't have interrupted the hard work of the demolition crew."

"Thank you," Steve said.

We were standing several feet away from the ambulance Kathryn was being treated in. A blanket was draped over my wet clothes, but did very little in the way of warmth, and I shivered in the cold breeze blowing in off the bay.

"If you hadn't found her," he added, letting it hang there between us.

It was obvious how much he cared for her—far more than I realized.

"Why'd he do it—or try to do it? We *are* thinking Reid was behind this, right?"

I nodded. "He has the two guys from the cabin do it, then takes them out. That's our best working theory right now."

"But why?"

"That's what we have to find out. Did she see something? Does she know something? She poses a threat to him or more likely the Gulf Coast Company in some way. Now that we know that, we can figure out what it is."

Chapter Fifty

Later that afternoon, following a few hours' sleep and a shower, I drove into Bridgeport to the courthouse. I felt groggy and disconnected, out of it, my mind a beat behind, my body a step slow. My head hurt, my ears were ringing, and I couldn't hear very well.

Kathryn was asleep in Sister Abigail's room, too frightened to be alone, too weary to do anything but sleep. Her homecoming had been difficult for me to watch. Father Thomas and Sister Abigail actually broke down. Still in shock, she didn't seem to know how to take it. Even allowing for her condition, things were different between us. There was a distance, a polite coolness that let me know she blamed me for what had happened and could never fully forgive me for leaving her.

Steve had questioned her, but it was obvious she didn't know why they had tried to kill her. He was now busy with the fish camp crime scene, though it wasn't in his jurisdiction, and the fallout from stopping the demolition. Reid was in custody waiting to be interviewed, which Steve had invited me to be in on. I was headed to the courthouse to gather more information in preparation for what was likely to be more interrogation than interview.

I found the same large African-American woman working alone in the clerk's office, an open bag of Double Stuf Oreos and a pint of milk on her desk.

"Where's everybody today?" I asked.

Her mouth was full of Oreos and she had to finish chewing before she could respond.

She said something, but I couldn't make it out. I explained about my hearing and asked her to repeat it.

"Lunch," she said. "I cover the office while they go eat."

She stood, reached down, grabbed the pint of milk, took a long pull on it, replaced it, wiped her mouth with her hand, and walked over to the counter.

"That doesn't seem fair," I said.

"Oh, I don't mind," she said, smacking as she used her tongue and lips to get cookie off her teeth. "I get to go early, which is good, 'cause I don't do good when I get hungry. My sugar gets messed up and I get bitchy. One time I passed out."

I wasn't sure what to say, so I tried to look interested in her story and concerned for her health at the same time, all the while nodding vigorously.

"What can I help you with today?" she asked.

"I wondered if you'd let me take a look at the deed for St. Ann's land?"

"Sure," she said.

That was easier than I thought.

"It's all a matter of public record," she said.

"How do I find it?"

"I'll help you," she said. "I know right where it is. Lots of people looking at it lately."

"Really?" I asked, my eyebrows shooting up. "Like who?"

She started walking toward the vault and I followed her.

"Gulf Coast Company people mostly. You know . . . lawyers and developers. Chief of police came in and looked at it, and a few folks I didn't recognize."

"When?" I asked.

"Over the last few months," she said.

"No. When did Steve Taylor come in?"

She shrugged. "It's been a while."

When she got to the entrance of the vault, she stopped. "Go on in," she said, "I'll be there in a minute."

I stepped around her and walked inside. She went back to her desk, shoved two cookies in her mouth and palmed a couple more, then joined me.

Inside the vault, she withdrew a large book—awkwardly because of the cookies in her hand—laid it on a table, and opened it to a marked page. "This is the log book," she said, swallowing the remainder of Oreos in her mouth. "It's where we log in the information from the deed—date, time, who recorded it."

She ran her finger down the first column until she found what she was looking for.

"How many deeds related to this property you wanna see?" she asked.

"How many are there?"

She said something, but I couldn't hear it, and I had to ask her to repeat it.

"Three most recently," she said.

"Three?"

"Yeah," she said, "all recorded on the same day."

Every time she talked louder, she spoke more slowly and condescendingly, as if my impairment were mental not physical.

"I'd like to see all three if I can."

"Piece a cake, baby," she said, popping the other two cookies into her mouth, then talking around them before chewing. "They all in the same spot. Two of them's recorded within minutes of each other."

"Really? That's unusual, isn't it?" I asked.

I waited as she chewed up and swallowed the two cookies.

"Not necessarily. We'll know in a minute."

While she pulled the deeds, I wondered how there could be three deeds registered in one day within a few minutes of each other. The abbey's land meant millions to whoever owned it and billions to the Gulf Coast Company, and I found it difficult to believe it wasn't somehow connected to all that was going on.

A moment later, she returned carrying several legal-size papers stapled together in three packets.

"Everything looks in order," she said. "I don't understand why she did what she did, but there's nothing illegal or inaccurate about the recordings."

She handed me the packet on top.

"This one's the oldest," she said. "It's from when Floyd Taylor bought it the first time."

Beneath "Articles of Agreement" centered at the top and written in Old English, the normal legalese included dates, descriptions, signatures, seals, and witnesses. At various places on the document, small white stickers with typing on them revealed the fees, date and time it was recorded, and by whom.

As I scanned the deed, I noticed her periodically looking longingly at her desk. I wasn't a mind reader, but I was pretty sure it wasn't that she was anxious to get back to work.

"So Floyd and not the paper company owned this?" I asked.

Her face contorted and she shrugged. "Way back then there wasn't really any difference. Sometime Mr. Floyd would put it in his name and sometime in the paper company's, but it was all the same in those days."

"What are these numbers?" I asked, pointing to one of the stickers.

"This the certificate number. This the book and page number of the log I showed you."

"And there's nothing odd about his deed?"

She shook her head. "Only thing it shows is what a good businessman Mr. Floyd was. This land's already worth a hundred times what he paid for it and soon it'll be a thousand."

"*If* they get the road through."

She cut her eyes at me and shook her head. "Oh, they'll get the road through. Monster this size can eat a lot of people and it just be an appetizer."

I wondered if all her metaphors involved food, concluded it was a safe bet they did, and, when she snuck another peek at her desk, I figured that subconsciously the devourer who had inspired her use of figurative language was most likely the Cookie Monster.

"Here's the next one," she said as she handed it to me. "This the one where Mr. Floyd deeded his land to this woman, ah, Grace Taylor."

"Who is she?"

She shrugged. "A relative, I guess. Don't really know."

"Do you know if he had any children?"

"No idea, but I can tell you who can tell you."

"Who?"

"Miss Jane Willow White," she said. "She was Mr. Floyd's secretary when she was young."

"Do you know where I can find her?"

"Back of the courthouse most any time," she said. "She works in the driver's license office, but most any time you look for her, you can find her out back taking a smoking break."

I glanced over the next deed. It looked much like the first one, only with different names, numbers, dates, fees, and witnesses. When I saw the two witnesses, I blinked and looked at it again to make sure I had seen what I thought I had. Looking again confirmed it. Father Thomas and Sister Abigail had been the witnesses when Floyd Taylor deeded what was now the abbey property to Grace Taylor.

Handing me the last one, she said, "Now, this is where it gets a little unusual—though it ain't illegal or nothin'. This is a quit claim deed and it's registered just a matter of minutes after the other one."

I looked at it, comparing it with the previous one. Much was the same, including the two witnesses.

"So just a few minutes after getting the land from Floyd, Grace just gives it to St. Ann's Abbey?"

"Uh huh."

"Why would she do that?" I asked.

"You'd have to ask her."

"Why wouldn't he just deed it directly to the abbey?"

She shrugged, her enormous lips turning up. "I got no idea."

"It doesn't make sense," I said.

"No, it don't."

"Have you ever seen this done before?"

"No, not like this," she said.

"And you can't think of any reason to do it this way instead of giving it directly to—" An idea stopped me in mid-sentence.

"What is it?"

"Can I borrow your phone book?"

"Sure," she said. "Who you callin'?"

"John David Dean," I said.

"No need to look him up," she said. "He's in the speed dial."

We walked back into the outer office and within a minute she had him on the line. The moment she handed me the receiver, she was back in the cookies, trying unsuccessfully not to rattle the bag too loudly.

Without preamble I said, "What happens to the land if the abbey closes?"

"What?" he said. "Who is this?"

"John Jordan. It's very important. You set it up, you have to know. If St. Ann's closes, what happens to the land?"

He hesitated. "Didn't we already discuss this? Well, they told me to cooperate with you, and it's not a big secret anyway. It'd go to the paper company. It's in the articles of incorporation. They told me that's what they wanted it to say."

"Who did?"

"Father Thomas and Sister Abigail."

"Listen," I said, "this makes a world of difference. Does it specify the paper company or does it say previous owner?"

"Previous owner," he said, "but it's the same thing."

"Actually, it's not," I said, and hung up.

Chapter Fifty-one

Miss Jane Willow White was right where I was told she'd be.

She was an older woman with the look of a lifelong smoker, her skin wrinkled and leathery, her voice gurgley and hoarse as if filed with an Emory board and filled with phlegm. She had short, white back-combed hair that didn't budge—even in the strong breeze.

She sat on a wooden picnic table next to an ashtray, sucking on a cigarette as if it were the world's only source of true happiness. The ashtray next to her was full of rainwater, gum wrappers, and cigarette butts.

"Jane White?" I asked.

"Who are *you*?" she said, her manner and voice gruff and challenging.

I told her who I was, what I wanted, and about my hearing.

"Cheap bastard," she said.

"You don't even know me," I said, smiling.

Without smiling back she said, "Floyd."

The back of the courthouse and the front of the sheriff's station were less than twenty feet apart, their walls forming a wind tunnel. We would have had to raise our voices over the sound of the wind regardless, but with the ringing in my ears, she had to practically yell.

"Really?"

"I worked for him for nearly twenty years . . . and you know what he left me? Shit. Nada. Zip. Zilch. A big fat nothing. I gotta spend my golden years working for the damn DMV. He could've given me a million and not missed it, but what's he do? Leaves it all to the paper company—as if they need it."

"Not that you're bitter," I said.

Not only was the wind around us cold, but it blew Jane White's cigarette smoke into my face, and I wasn't sure which was stinging my eyes more.

"So whatta you wanna know about the son of a bitch?"

"Did he have many women?"

"What's many? He had a few. None for very long. He always managed to maneuver away from them before they sunk their claws in too deep."

"Have any children with any of them?"

She smiled for the first time. "How'd you know?"

I didn't think she was really asking, so I didn't answer.

"He did have a kid. A girl. Not that he was a father to her or anything. He was just the donor. If you know what I mean?"

"I do," I said.

Finishing her cigarette, she flicked it toward but not into the ashtray, pulled another from her pack, tossed it in her mouth with the acumen of a veteran, dug in her Polyester pantsuit and came out with a lighter, cupped her hands, and lit it.

I asked, "Did he have any kind of relationship with her at all?"

"None I know of—and I'd know. I arranged everything for him—including most of his women."

"What ever happened to her?"

She shrugged. "Haven't the foggiest. She was put up for adoption. Floyd probably paid the mother off to do it. There's probably some Little Miss Heiress running around somewhere without a pot to piss in or a window to throw it out of and she's worth millions. Well, she would've been."

"He didn't leave her anything in his will?"

"Same as me. Not a nickel. No one. Not either of his sisters or their kids. Just that blasted paper company."

"So even if she found out she was Floyd's daughter . . ."

"Wouldn't do her any good."

"If he was so stingy, why'd he give so much to St. Ann's?"

She let out a mean, smoke-filled laugh and gave me an elaborate shrug. "Exactly. Doesn't that beat all?"

"You have no idea?"

"None. Well, that's not true, exactly. I know without really knowing, you know? It's obvious they had something on him."

"Who?"

"Someone from the abbey."

"Blackmailed him for the land and the trust?"

She nodded.

"With what?"

"Don't know, but it had to be like one of them cookies they got over in the mall. Not just a doozie, but a double doozie."

Chapter Fifty-two

"We made a deal with the devil," Sister Abigail said.

"And now we're reaping what we've sown," Father Thomas said.

We were standing in front of the chapel, the midafternoon sun providing just enough heat to make it bearable. I had confronted them with what I had learned at the courthouse and they seemed not just willing, but eager to unburden themselves.

"Are you saying you blackmailed Floyd into giving you the land and the trust for the abbey?" I asked.

"It wasn't blackmail. It was . . . an agreement."

"It was us agreeing to his terms," Father Thomas said. "If anything, it was him bribing us."

They both seemed older now—especially Father Thomas, whose already weakened physical state seemed now also an outward manifestation of his psychological and emotional fragility. They had been through a lot over the past few days and the cumulative effect on them was palpable.

"The land and the trust was hush money?" I asked.

They both seemed to consider that for a moment, before nodding. "I've never thought of it that way," Sister Abigail said, "but that's exactly what it was." She shook her head. "Funny how you can justify things."

"Rationalize," he said.

"It wouldn't hurt anyone," Sister Abigail said. "A lot of people would be helped. He wasn't doing anything better with the land."

"We were giving the selfish, bitter old bastard a chance to do something good for once," Father Thomas added.

I considered him. He was angry, his face contorting in disgust, and I wondered if it were directed toward himself or Taylor.

"It wasn't that hard for us, but the truth is, you can rationalize anything," Sister Abigail said.

A cold gust of wind blew in, puffing out Sister's habit and tossing our hair, but neither of them offered to step inside, and I wondered if on some level they wanted to avoid the chapel, as if their confession would profane it somehow.

"What exactly were the terms he wanted you to agree to?" I asked.

Sister Abigail considered me intently. "I'm sure you know," she said.

"I have some ideas."

"Well, let's hear them," she said. "I'll tell you if you're right."

"Why won't you just tell me?"

"I'd rather you say it," she said. "It's difficult for me."

"Is that it or are you just wanting to find out what I know?"

She smiled a wry smile.

"He wanted you to take in his daughter," I said. "Raise her for him and her mother."

She nodded. "In a way, he was giving the money to her. She'd have a place to live—a family. She could get a good education, go to college, live here again if she wanted, and if the abbey ever closed, the land would go back to her. No one would ever know he had a daughter."

So Kathryn was Floyd Taylor's daughter. They had confirmed it. No wonder Reid and whoever he was working for in the Gulf Coast Company had tried to kill her.

"Why go to such lengths to conceal the fact he had a daughter?"

"He was pretty old by then. It was embarrassing to him—especially considering who the mother was."

"A young slightly mentally handicapped girl who worked in one of the fish houses," Father Thomas said.

"He didn't like kids anyway," Sister Abigail said. "Never wanted any. And the thought that this young piece of white trash, as he called her, would get his money just about killed him. He said he'd rather die than have anyone know."

"We thought if we didn't accept his offer," Father Thomas said, "he might kill her."

"The baby or the mother?" I asked.

"Both. Though the mother didn't live long after she gave her baby to us. I think it broke her heart."

Sister Abigail shook her head and frowned at him. "She was killed by a drunk driver."

"I still think she stepped in front of him on purpose," Father Thomas said.

There was something unconvincing about their words and the way they said them—especially Father Thomas. It was as if they were a little too eager to tell me, and though I couldn't quite believe they were lying, it felt as if the story I was hearing had been rehearsed.

"Anyway, we know the fact that he might have killed them was just a rationalization, but as rationalizations go, it's not a bad one."

"We're talking about Grace Taylor, right?" I asked.

They nodded.

"When did she change her name to Kathryn Kennedy?"

Their eyes grew wide and they froze like children caught in an elaborate lie. First, they looked at each other, then at me, then back at each other, all the while not saying a word.

After a long moment, I started to say something, but Sister Abigail cleared her throat.

"Actually, *she* didn't," Sister said. "*We* did it when she was a toddler."

"Does she know who her parents were?"

They shook their heads. "No idea."

I nodded and thought about it.

"I'm gonna get Steve to get a copy of Floyd's medical records. We'll be able to prove she's his daughter. That way, if St. Ann's ever does close, or the paper company pressures you to relocate, there will be no question who gets the land."

Their faces simultaneously grew alarmed.

"You're not going to tell her, are you?" Sister Abigail asked.

"I'm not sure yet," I said. "May not have a choice."

"Don't do that to her," Father Thomas pleaded. "Her whole

identity would—"

He broke off as the first of the screams started.

Chapter Fifty-three

Leaving them behind, I ran toward the screams, which increased in frequency and intensity. Running toward the girl's dorm, I paused to try to pinpoint exactly where they were coming from. The best I could tell, they were originating from behind the dorm by the Intracoastal Waterway where we had discovered the boat with blood in it.

As I ran in that direction, the screams, which were now joined by sirens in the distance, seemed to be moving toward me. When I rounded the back corner of the dorm, I collided with Sister Chris, the force of our collision nearly knocking her down. I grabbed her arms and held her up. She continued to scream all the while.

"What is it?" I asked, holding her at arm's length. "What happened?"

She tried to speak, but couldn't. She had, however, stopped screaming for the moment. Beginning to shake uncontrollably, she crossed herself and fainted, collapsing in my arms.

By the time I had her lowered to the ground, Kathryn had come up. "Stay with her," I said.

"What is it?"

"I don't know, but she doesn't seem to have any injuries. It must be something she saw. I'm gonna check it out."

"Be careful."

As I ran down toward the waterway, I caught a glimpse of several others, including Father Thomas and Sister Abigail, nearing Kathryn and Chris. I hoped they would stay with them, but doubted they would.

I didn't have to run far to see what had elicited such horror-filled screams from the young nun.

Down near the water's edge, on a gray cypress tree with a weathered board nailed up for a crossbeam, a young white guy had been crucified.

He had long hair and a scraggly beard, and his head hung down like the Spanish moss above him. Pale and extremely thin, his nude body looked unkempt and undernourished. As if a re-creation of the crucifixion of Jesus, his hands and feet had been nailed in place and he had wounds on his face, head, knees, and side.

Coming up behind me, the trinity of St. Ann's, Father Thomas, Sister Abigail, and Kathryn all reacted in horror.

"Oh my dear Lord," Sister Abigail said, and crossed herself.

Father Thomas turned away, falling to the ground and throwing up, his frail body lurching forward as he did. Sister Abigail immediately knelt beside him and began to minister to him.

Beside me, Kathryn stared up in stunned silence, seeming unable to look away.

"You okay?" I asked.

She shook her head. "Who would do such a—"

"Do you recognize him?" I asked.

She shook her head.

"You need to look away."

She slung herself around and buried her face in my chest. I put my arm around her and held her tightly.

Looking down at Father and Sister, who were getting to their feet, I said, "Do either of you recognize him?"

Without looking at him again, Father Thomas shook his head. Sister Abigail glanced quickly again, then shook her head.

Looking back at the corner of the dorm, I saw that everyone with the exception of Keith Richie had gathered around Sister Chris, who, conscious again, was being helped up by the others.

"Why don't you guys join the others?" I said. "Have someone call Steve. I'll wait for him here."

The two women got on either side of the aging, sickly priest and led him away, but before they reached the others, Steve passed them on his way to me.

He didn't say anything to them or me, just stopped beside me, looked up and said, "*Jesus Christ.*"

I understood why he said it. Not only was what he saw as shocking as anything he had ever seen, it, in fact, brought Jesus to mind—but it still bothered me to hear Jesus Christ said that way.

"What the hell's goin' on here?" he asked.

"I don't know."

"Hard to imagine anybody here doin' something like that."

"'Cept maybe Harrison or Richie," I said.

"I thought Harrison was all religious?"

"Whatta you call that?" I asked, nodding toward the young man nailed to the tree.

His eyebrows shot up. "Good point."

"What about Tammy's boyfriend? Could've been him."

"Clyde? Know for sure he didn't do it."

"Oh yeah? How's that?"

"Because," he said, nodding toward the life-size crucifix again, "that's him on the cross."

Chapter Fifty-four

The nails holding Clyde to the cross were not spikes and would not hold for long. Though there was very little blood, his numerous wounds looked to have been made with both sides of a hammer. That was just a guess, but there was a bluntness, a lack of precision and crude violence to the wounds that made it at least a possibility.

The horrific pose exaggerated his naked, emaciated body, making him look puny and pathetic, and I was saddened—not just for him, for no matter what any of us do or become, in the end we're all stripped in one way or another, exposed for what in some sense we are—dust of the earth.

"I thought you had him in custody?" I said.

"We almost did," Steve said, "but he got away. We found out where he was, but by the time we got there, he was gone."

All around us, Steve's men were securing the crime scene, waiting for FDLE to arrive to process it. Though the midafternoon sun was bright, the air cold, a strong breeze made the world around us seem to dance, and something about the way it rustled Clyde's hair made him seem alive.

"Look at him," Steve said. "He hasn't been dead for very long. You know what that means?"

I nodded.

"Our prime suspect was in custody when this happened," he continued.

He was talking about Reid, and he was right. Did this clear

Reid or was it unrelated to Tammy's death and the attempt on Kathryn?

"I didn't see this one coming," he said. "What the hell's he even doin' here?"

I looked from Clyde to the little boat at the end of the dock. "Looks like he stole another boat."

"But why come here?"

I shrugged. "Unfinished business, someone lured him, or maybe he was searching for sanctuary."

"I figured him for Tommy Boy and Tammy's killer if Reid didn't do it."

"Still could be."

"Then who the fuck did this?" he asked.

"Could be retribution. Someone avenging her death."

"I guess it could," he said. "But who here's capable of something like this?"

"We already said Richie and Harrison," I said. "Could be others—maybe a badass cousin with a badge."

His eyes intensified, squinting into slits. "So which is it? I killed *her* or I killed him because *he* killed her?"

"How about killed her *and* him?"

He shook his head. "You got any other scenarios or is your heart set on me?"

"We're pretty sure he was here the night she was killed," I said. "What if he saw something and the killer's covering his tracks?"

He nodded. "Could be. Or the devil could've gotten them both."

"I think it's something we've at least got to consider."

"What?" he asked in shock. "You serious?"

"We found the tape," I said. "Watch it and see what you think, but I think she may have been possessed, whatever that means."

"You watched it?"

I nodded.

"Police evidence?"

I nodded again.

He shook his head. "And you think she was possessed?"

"She was something I can't explain," I said.

"Does it show her death?"

I shook my head.

"Could it be an edited copy?"

"Sure," I said with a shrug, "but it doesn't seem to be."

"Where'd you find it?"

"That's privileged information," I said.

"You a lawyer now?"

"Confessor," I said. "Counselor. Priest."

"You can add son of a bitch to the list too."

"Confessor, counselor, priest, son of a bitch. Someone came in during the exorcism and turned off the tape. Someone was in the room with them."

He looked up at the cross. "Clyde?"

"Maybe."

I followed his gaze up to the surreal image. What little blood there was around Clyde's wounds was dry and dark. He seemed to be leaning more forward now, as if the nails were giving and any minute he would come tumbling down.

"Why is he on a tree?" he asked.

"A lot of crucifixions have been. There's a whole tradition that says Jesus was crucified on a living tree. If the killer was aware of it, then it's significant, and would tend to point to one of the more knowledgeable members of staff, but . . ."

"But what?"

"It may just be because the tree was the easiest to get to, and hidden enough, and the most accessible option."

"It wouldn't have been easy to get him up there," he said.

"Hard to see a woman doing it," I said.

"Unless she had supernatural demon strength," he said, and laughed.

I didn't say anything.

"Any other possibilities?" he asked.

"Two people? It'd be difficult even for a man by himself."

"But who?"

"They both could've been killed by the drug dealers they owed money to," I said.

"Wouldn't that be nice. I'd really rather it not be someone around here."

"How do you think he was killed?"

Muscle-fat stopped what he was doing, turned to me in disdain, and said, "You don't have to throw him in the Gulf, he was crucified."

I shook my head at him and laughed. "The crucifixion didn't kill him."

"Get the fuck outta here."

"See how little blood there is?" I said. "How his wounds don't have much blood coming out of them? His heart wasn't beating when he was nailed up there. He was already dead."

Muscle-fat looked up at Clyde again.

"Get back to work," Steve said, "and remember—it's better to be *thought* a fool than to open your mouth and remove all doubt."

He huffed off.

"How do *you* think he died?" Steve asked.

"There's no signs of violence on the body except the postmortem ones, and he's young. Best bet is a drug overdose. Although he looks emaciated enough to be malnourished or have AIDS."

He nodded. "I'm thinkin' OD. I'll try to rush up tox. But if he did die from a drug overdose, why nail him up?"

"There's a reason," I said. "We've just got to—"

Just then, the nails made a high-pitched squeaking sound as they pulled out of the board and tree, and Clyde's body pitched forward and fell to the ground in a loud, flat thump.

My stomach lurched, and I swallowed hard.

"*Goddamn,*" Steve said, looking down at the crumpled, naked body.

I knew how he felt. It was disturbing—both to see and to hear.

We took a few steps farther away from the body and stood in silence for a long moment, all sound but the wind in our ears receding as the cops strained to see Clyde's new position.

"Shit. With all this I almost forgot," he said, shaking his head. "The blood in the boat is human. Same type as Tammy. *And . . .* whoever had sex with her before she was killed is a secretor. I've got his blood type too."

"How long before you'll have DNA?" I asked.

"A while still," he said, "but I already have a match."

I nodded. I knew who he was talking about. There was only one other person whose blood he already had.

Chapter Fifty-five

"I never touched her," Father Thomas said.

"Evidence says otherwise," Steve said.

"I mean sexually," he said wearily. "Whatever was inside her made her offer often, but I never took her up on it. I never did anything inappropriate."

We had found Father Thomas sipping black coffee in the dining hall, trying to recover from what he had seen. Since no one had an appetite any longer, only he and Sister Abigail had been inside. She agreed to leave him alone with us after we promised to take it easy on him.

"Father, I'm not saying you killed her," Steve said in his most sympathetic tone. "Just that she was impossible to resist."

"Sounds like you might know what you're talking about, Steve," Father Thomas said.

I smiled. The old priest made a good point.

"No, we weren't kissing cousins," he said flatly, "but that doesn't mean I wasn't tempted. She was hot. I know you're a priest, but you're a man too, and I personally wouldn't think any less of you if you had done this most natural of things."

"Well, that's comforting, Steve. You'd make a compassionate priest, but I didn't. I swear."

"Father," Steve said, "the semen inside her is your blood type."

He shrugged. "Surely I'm not the only one here with B positive. It's not rare."

"Perhaps, but it'd be a pretty big coincidence if the blood type of the person she had sex with right before she was killed just happened to be the same as yours."

"Then it's a pretty big coincidence," he said, "because it wasn't me."

The dining room was cold and drafty, and though a fire was burning in the fireplace on the far wall, it was a small fire—of pine mainly, having lots of snap and pop and flame, but providing very little heat.

"You realize the time to deal is now," Steve said. "Change your story later and it'll be too late."

"I won't be changing my story. It's the truth today and it'll be the truth tomorrow."

"Okay," Steve said. "We can't help you if you won't let us.

Father Thomas shook his head. "I still can't believe you refuse to acknowledge the presence of the evil one among us."

"Father, we can't—"

"Think about what was done to that poor young man down by the dock," Father Thomas said. "Who could do such a thing? A mere man? You two can't really believe that? Who wants to mock Christ and profane this place more than our enemy? We're engaged in spiritual warfare here, and you two are trying to fight the forces of darkness with the arm of the flesh."

Without looking at us, Keith Richie walked out of the kitchen and over to the fireplace carrying an armload of oak logs. He dumped the oak onto the pine and walked back out of the room, carefully avoiding us as he did.

"We're open to all possibilities, Father," I said, "especially after viewing the tape of the exorcism, but we've got to investigate *all* possibilities. And looking into one doesn't mean we're excluding another. We're just doing what we can on every front. A murder investigation is almost always like this—stumbling around in the dark, feeling for clues."

"That *sounds* good," he said, "but the reality is a demonic force is picking people off one by one and nothing's being done to stop it."

The oak logs had smothered most of the flames, and they hissed as gray smoke rose from beneath them and up through the chimney.

"If that's true," Steve said, "that's your department, not mine. I can't fight the devil. So if you believe what you say, why aren't you fightin' the good fight?"

"I am," he said, "and I will continue, but I could use some help."

"Well, get some," Steve said. "Call in reinforcements from the Vatican if you want. Maybe John here can help, but I can't. I'm no priest."

Father Thomas started to respond, but before he could, a couple of members of the crime scene team came through the door. They were wearing white lab coats and carrying large hard plastic medical cases that looked like oversized tackle boxes.

"We're ready to start," the one in front said. He was an average man, except for a protruding belly, with very little hair that stood about an inch off his head.

"Set up over there," Steve said, indicating an empty table in the far corner. "You can start with us."

"Start what with us doing what?" Father Thomas asked.

"Not you, Father," Steve said. "Me and John. We've already got yours."

"My what?"

"Blood," Steve said. "We're gonna get a blood sample from everyone at St. Ann's. It's voluntary of course, but anyone who refuses can come down to the station and explain why."

Father Thomas nodded. "I'm glad you're at least open to the possibility it could be someone besides me."

Steve smiled. "We're wide open. And we're looking at everyone, but you're not doing much to help yourself."

"What am I—"

"You've kept things from us from the very beginning. And you're still not being completely honest with us now."

"How can you say—"

"Who came into the room when you were performing the exorcism, Father?" I asked.

"I told you, I don't know. I was knocked unconscious. I didn't even know the tape had stopped recording."

"Why did Clyde's death upset you so much?" I asked.

"Who?"

"Tammy's boyfriend," I said, nodding in the direction of the crucifixion. "The guy who was—"

"That was Tammy's boyfriend?" he asked, the little color that was left draining from his face.

"And seeing him upset you more than anyone else here," Steve added. "Even Kathryn and Sister Abigail."

"I'm very sensitive—unlike some people. I don't have long to live and I find death extremely upsetting these days. Sorry, but if compassion, sensitivity, and heightened awareness of mortality makes me guilty, then I'm your man. Cuff me and take me in."

"See," I said. "Like that. That wasn't helpful—not to your cause or our case. Why are you acting this way? What are you trying to cover up?"

"I'm telling the truth, John. I thought you realized that after you watched the tape."

"I believe you are—about that, but not about most of these other things."

"Like what?"

"Like why Clyde's death upset you so much."

"I told you. I'm dying. All death gets to me more than it once did."

"Not Tammy's. You got more upset about someone you say you didn't know."

Chapter Fifty-six

"I'm not sure I can do this," Sister Abigail said, rubbing her forehead with her fingers. She was obviously still shaken up from seeing Clyde.

It was time for my counseling session. I had come to her office to tell her I just couldn't do it right now, there was too much happening with the case, but she needed to talk, so I sat down, intending to just stay a few minutes.

Her bottom lip quivered. "I just can't get over what was done to that poor boy. He was . . . It was so . . ." She squeezed her eyes closed tightly and shook her head. "I just keep seeing him hanging up there like that."

Nodding, I said, "I know."

"I don't think I'll ever look at a crucifix again without remembering."

"It'll fade in time. I know it doesn't seem like it now, but it will."

"No wonder you have such a hard time dealing with all this. I had no idea it was so—"

"It's usually not that bad."

"Still," she said. "To see so much violence, to deal with so much death. It's no wonder you showed up here in need of help."

"It can get to you after a while."

"How are *you* handling things?" she asked.

"You tell me. I've seen you watching me pretty closely."

"You look like you're doing quite well," she said, "but I'm not talking about things that can be seen."

"I feel like I'm doing pretty well. A lot's happened in a little time, so it may be different if it drags on for a lot longer, but so far, I feel good. I haven't even thought about drinking. I'm still managing to get in a little time for meditation and reflection. Feel pretty centered."

"Centered or distracted?"

I thought about it. The truth was, working a case did center me—and it did distract me. As soon as it was over, as soon as my mind didn't have it to play with, I'd realize how lonely I still was, how unhappy, how nothing had changed.

"Both," I said.

She nodded. "I was thinking about something the other day I wanted to share with you. It comes from the Tao Te Ching. It says that the master does his work then steps back."

I thought about it. "I like it."

"It's related to the Eastern philosophy of non-attachment, which is something I think could really help you. In this case what I mean is practicing non-attachment to outcome. It's what I have to do with my work. I can't control the outcome of my patients. And if I try then I stay discouraged and depressed. But if I do my work and step back, letting go of the outcome, then I have peace. I know the same would work for you. Let go of your attachment to the outcome. Accept what is. 'Cause there is nothing else. Can you do that?"

I thought about it.

"Can you do your best work and accept the outcome even if it's an unsolved case? Can you do your best work and accept if the killer isn't punished in this lifetime? Can you create some space between you and what you do by practicing non-attachment and letting go of outcome?"

"I've studied non-attachment before, but I've never quite seen it this way—related to outcome. It's something I'd like to explore more."

"All I can ask," she said, a slight twinkle in her eye.

"'Cause anything else would not be practicing non-attachment to outcome?"

She smiled.

There was a comforting sameness to our sessions, she in her recliner, hands folded in her lap, me on the love seat in front of her.

It was as if rather than many different sessions, we were having one long continuous one, with occasional interruptions.

I started to say something, but she moved—the first time I could recall seeing her do so during one of our sessions—and it stopped me.

She rubbed her left upper arm with her right hand.

"What's wrong?" I asked.

"That damn nurse that drew my blood. Felt like she used an ice pick."

"I'm surprised Steve's having the women tested," I said.

"I told them I was A negative and had records to prove it, but they insisted on sticking me."

"It's your clothes. Make you look very suspicious."

She smiled. "I'm sorry," she said. "What were we saying?"

"I can't begin again until you fold your hands in your lap," I said, and smiled.

She did as I had asked, and a new scent of hand cream wafted over my way. Like the room, it smelled of gardenia, and I doubted it was a coincidence. She probably had entire sets of matching fragrances—scented candles, potpourri, hand cream, perfume. Her office was a garden of olfactory delights.

"Okay," she said. "So you were saying?"

I laughed. "I can't remember."

"Why don't you tell me who you suspect and why?" she said.

"You wouldn't like the list."

"Try me."

"Father Thomas is still the frontrunner. Regardless of his health or the validity of his claims about Tammy's condition. Then there's Reid and the monster he works for. I don't think there's any question but that he was involved in Kathryn's abduction and attempted murder, and Tammy certainly was in the way of his plans—plus he seemed to be obsessed with her sexually and she taunted him with it—but we're pretty sure his boys were already dead and he was in custody when Clyde was killed. Doesn't mean he couldn't have it done, but . . ."

She nodded slowly as she listened, but didn't say anything.

"Then there's Clyde, Brad, and Keith. All of or some of whom could be involved in a drug deal gone bad or just good old-fashioned jealousy. Clyde could have been killed because of something he saw the night Tammy was killed or he could have killed her and somebody killed him because of it. We're pretty sure he was here."

I paused for a moment, but she didn't say anything, so I continued.

"Then there's the inexplicable," I said.

"The what?"

"What Father Thomas is calling demons or the devil," I said. "What others call the supernatural or the unexplained."

"You believe—"

"That there are things I can't explain? Yes."

I told her about the tape.

"Tom said you'd seen it. So you're open to the possibility that—what?"

"See previous answer," I said. "There are things I can't explain. That's all I can say for sure. Then there's Floyd's daughter or nephew. They both stand to gain an enormous amount of money."

"Kathryn doesn't even know she's—"

"I'm pretty sure Tammy told her," I said. "But even if she didn't, Kathryn could have easily figured it out by now. She may have even figured out you're her mother."

Chapter Fifty-seven

She sat there in stunned silence for a long moment. Eventually, she said, "How'd you know?"

"Floyd wouldn't give you all this land just to take his daughter. There had to be more to it than that. And let's just say I didn't find the story you and Father Thomas told to be very convincing."

"Please don't judge me too harshly."

"I'm not judging you at all," I said.

"I've been a mom to her in every way but name."

"I know."

"Everything I did, I did so I could keep my vows and be a mother to my child."

I considered her, wondering if it was so important to her to keep her vows, how she got pregnant in the first place. "How'd you and Floyd get together?"

"He and my oldest brother were friends. We grew up around each other. I thought he was such a big deal back then. He always had a shiny new car, the coolest clothes, and plenty of folding money. He was a good bit older than me, but he always seemed to pay attention to me, carry a torch for me. Anyway, when I came back here, he began to pursue me—even though I had already taken my vows. The first thing he did was lease us the land and an old schoolhouse to start St. Ann's for next to nothing. Then he continued to be so generous, helping us when we needed it. He used to come out and eat here at least once a week. Anyway, at a time when I was lonely and desperate, I gave in and we made Kathryn Grace. It was just the one time. It was nothing special, but it sure produced something that was. He must not have enjoyed it either. He never asked again. Anyway, when he found out it was his, he knew I wanted to keep it as much a secret as he did, so he suggested he give us the land, a few buildings, and a trust for St. Ann's. I went away for awhile, came back later with a little girl the abbey would adopt. He deeded the land to her, then she—well, we on her behalf—donated it to the abbey, and we set it up so that if anything ever happens to it, everything will go back to her."

"Who all knows?"

"The whole story? Just you and me," she said. "Tom has figured out a little over the years, but not nearly all of it. If you're right, Kathryn may know more than I thought, but she can't know very much. Are you going to tell her?"

"I'm afraid it's gonna come out one way or another. You may want to go ahead and tell her yourself."

She was silent a long moment.

"Would you be there when I do?"

We found Kathryn in her cabin working on her novel. She was seated in a recliner by the fire, a laptop on her outstretched legs. Beside her on the hearth, burning candles flickered, and soft instrumental music played from an unseen source.

When we had knocked on the door, she told us to come in, but didn't stop typing. Without saying anything, we walked over and quietly stood in front of the fire.

"Let me just get to a stopping point," she said, typing faster now, not looking up.

"Take your time," Sister said.

While we waited, I looked around the room. It was pretty sparse for an heiress. She had quite a few books, including several copies of her own, but no really nice ones, and many were paperbacks. Her computer and printer were nice, but not extravagant. There was very little furniture, and none of it matched. It made me think of the dilapidated little trailer I lived in, and made me respect her even more.

"Is something wrong?" she asked when she stopped typing.

"Nothing at all," Sister Abigail said. "Something important. Something wonderful. Nothing wrong."

Kathryn's eyes glistened and she turned and looked at the fire. "You know how you can know something without knowing it?" she asked.

We waited.

Finally she looked away from the fire and up at us.

"You've told me things over the years," she said to Sister Abigail. "Little things—answering *my* questions mainly. Sometimes very vague. Others, quite revealing. Nearly every time telling me more than you meant to."

"So you know?" I asked.

"Not everything, but more than I'm supposed to."

"I'm sorry I didn't tell you sooner," Sister said. "Sometimes I wanted to so badly it hurt, but I don't know... I guess I'm a coward. I'm sorry. Are you angry with me? You have every right to be."

Kathryn shook her head. "I'm still in shock. Should be dead. I'm not feeling much of anything."

"I'm so sorry to do this now. You've been through so much. It's not fair. But we just felt that it was going to come out soon because of the investigation and I wanted you to hear it from me."

"So you're only telling me now because you're being forced to," she said.

Sister Abigail frowned, then nodded. "I guess so. I'm sorry. Told you I was a coward."

Kathryn shrugged. "It's okay. I'm glad you're my mother. It's better than that retard story circulating around town. I knew you couldn't just come out and say it, but you made sure I knew. Knew I was wanted. Knew I was loved. Knew I belonged."

It made much more sense now. What Floyd had done was for Abigail as much as Kathryn. No wonder St. Ann's had taken in Kathryn. They had never taken in any other children over the years. Of course, they hadn't actually taken her in. She belonged here more than anyone.

Chapter Fifty-eight

Unlike the previous mornings, Steve didn't appear sharp or crisp. His uniform was wrinkled, his face pale and hollow, large, dark purplish-blue circles hung in the loose skin beneath his eyes, and he talked more slowly than he had. I wondered if it was the case, Tammy's death, Clyde's crucifixion, Kathryn's close call. It was a lot to process, and it was obviously taking a toll.

"We caught Keith Richie trying to leave town last night with all his worldly possessions," he said.

"He say why?"

"Said when God tells you to go, you have to go," he said, shaking his head. "You religious people crack me up."

"Yeah, we're a real riot. And all just the same. Where is he now?"

"Station. I'm detaining him for questioning. His parole officer and the cop that busted him are supposed to call me this afternoon. I figure we'll go at him after we've talked to them."

I thought about it.

"How do you like him for it?" he asked.

I shrugged. "Less than some, more than others."

"Running sure makes him look guilty."

"Heat gets turned up. He runs. Might just be in his nature. Or maybe he really is guilty—but of something else."

"Or maybe he's our guy."

"Maybe."

"He's got the right blood for it. Oh, speaking of which…"

He withdrew a piece of paper from his pocket and handed it to me. "Medical center called me to verify you were working for me. Said you had requested this on my behalf."

I took it and looked at it. It was a faint photocopy from Floyd Taylor's medical records.

"I meant to tell you about it," I said, "but with all that's happened, I forgot."

"What'd you want with Uncle Floyd's medical records? You don't think he did it, do you?"

"Thought we might need his blood type if the Gulf Coast Company tries to take St. Ann's and his daughter comes out of the woodwork," I said as nonchalantly as I could.

"You could've just asked me. He was O negative, but you're getting way ahead of things. I'm not gonna let them get St. Ann's."

I glanced at the paper to confirm the blood type, and wondered if I should tell him all I knew—about the road and the wetlands, about the deeds and Grace Taylor being Kathryn Kennedy, but just couldn't bring myself to trust him that much. He still had one of the strongest motives of anyone, and he probably already knew most of it anyway—especially after going to the clerk's office.

"Who knows their uncle's blood type?" I asked.

"A nephew he got blood from when he had an operation," he said. "Suspicious son of a bitch, aren't you? Come on."

He led me past the counseling center and kitchen, and around B-dorm. I followed him, letting him set the pace—of the walk and the conversation. The morning was cool and damp, the only light a difussed grayish glow. Though not really necessary, he held a long black metal flashlight in his hand.

"We were right," he said. "Clyde died from an overdose."

I nodded and thought about it.

"So why crucify a man who's already dead?" he said.

"To conceal the real reason he died?" I said. "Send a message to someone? Bring more embarrassment and shame to St. Ann's? I don't know."

He nodded and seemed to think about what I'd said.

We ducked beneath the perimeter of yellow crime scene tape flapping in the wind, and stopped in front of the cypress tree that had held Clyde.

Pulling another folded piece of paper out of his pocket, he

said, "Here's a list of the blood types of everyone who was here the night Tammy was murdered. Father Thomas was right, he's not the only guy with B positive."

I took the list and read over it.

Kathryn AB+
Brad Harrison B+
Keith Richie B-
Sister Abigail A-
Father Thomas B+
Sister Chris King O+
Ralph Reid B+
John Jordan AB+

"It took some nerve to carry out the crucifixion," I said.

He snapped on the flashlight and moved its beam along the cypress tree.

"A fair amount of time too," he said. "You think we're dealing with two different killers?"

I shrugged.

"Be a lot easier if Reid hadn't been in custody and his boys dead at the time," he said.

"If someone killed Tammy in the landing right beneath Father Thomas's nose, that was pretty daring."

"*If*?"

"He could've done it," I said. "She could've done it. Or—"

"*She*?"

"Tammy."

"I knew who you meant," he said. "You think we could be dealing with suicide now?"

"I meant she could've been driven to do it," I said. "Or whatever was inside her could've done it. Have you watched the tape yet?"

"Freaked the fuck out of me," he said, shuddering. "I had to stop it, wait awhile and come back to it. I couldn't believe it was Tammy. I wouldn't've recognized her if I didn't know it was her."

"I should've said something," I said. "It was insensitive of me. I'm sure it was very difficult to watch."

"And it wasn't just that it was scary. Had all that sexual shit too."

"Do you think she was faking?" I asked.

"Don't see how something like that can be faked."

"But you don't think it could've killed her?" I asked. "Or made her do it? Whatever it is—mental condition or . . ."

"Drug trip. I guess it could. Hell, I guess that means it could've nailed Clyde up too. What if we got a demon jumping from body to body and killing people? First the killer's Father Thomas or Clyde, then it's Richie or Harrison or Reid. How would we ever stop it?"

I couldn't tell if he was serious.

"I can't arrest a spirit," he said.

We grew silent a moment.

Focusing the light where the crossbeam had been nailed, he said, "How the hell did he get him up there?"

I studied the spot again, though there was nothing new to see.

"What if—" he began, his voice filling with excitement, then breaking off.

"What?" I asked, looking at the branches.

"What if this was just what it looked like?" he asked. "An execution. What if the people here believed Clyde killed Tammy and they decided to do something about it?"

I shrugged. "It's possible, but they seemed genuinely shaken up."

"Maybe that's why."

"Look at that," I said.

"What?"

I pointed toward one of the branches above where the crucifixion had taken place. A couple of smaller branches growing off it were bent, and in one spot the Spanish moss and a narrow band of bark were missing.

"Yeah?"

"Did FDLE process that?" I asked.

"What?" he asked.

I took the flashlight and showed him.

"If they did, they didn't mention it to me. Why?"

"Look at it," I said. "It looks like a rope or a chain has cut into the wood. Could be how the body was raised into place."

"You mean—"

"Like a pulley or just a rope around the branch," I said. "Which doesn't rule out it being a mob or a couple of killers, but it does let us know how one person could've done it."

He took a minute to process it, nodding his head, studying the branch. "I'll get FDLE back on it, but if it is the work of just one person, who you thinkin' it could be?"

"Only one person on our list is a carpenter-handyman type *and* has B positive blood."

Chapter Fifty-nine

"It's cold out here," Harrison said. "Why don't we talk inside?"

"Something about this place bother you, Brad?" Steve asked.

Brad looked at him in disbelief. "*Yeah*," he said, "a man was murdered in a way that mocks the way my savior was killed. It doesn't bother you?"

As if his uniform, Brad was wearing the same faded, paint-speckled jeans and camouflage jacket, and though his boots still looked newer than anything else he wore, they were now spotted with dirt and grime and flecked with paint.

"We can talk about me some other time," Steve said.

"It's just that there are evil spirits at work here," he said. "Now, I'm not scared of the devil. That lyin', thievin' serpent's under my feet. But I respect my adversary, and I know not everybody stays as prayed up as I do, so they can be vessels of wickedness without even realizing it. And the thing they want to do is destroy the light."

Steve gave him a perplexed look.

Brad rubbed the whiskers on his angular face with his thumbnail, tracing his jawline from beneath his ear to the cleft in his chin, sighing heavily as he did.

"People like me," he said. "Bearers of the light. Satan wants to destroy us. We know how to bind and loose and—"

"If that's all it takes, why don't you bind the forces of darkness at work here?" I asked.

"Why don't *you?*" he asked. "You're supposed to be some

hotshot prison preacher. Don't you know how to conduct spiritual warfare?"

"Did you rape and kill Tammy?" Steve asked.

"*What?*" he asked in shock. "*No.* I'm a sinner and I hate to admit it, but I didn't have to *rape* Tammy."

"But you slept with her shortly before you killed her?"

"I didn't *kill* her."

"We've matched your blood type," Steve said. "We know you did."

His eyes grew wide, fear entering his face. "No. You're not settin' me up for this, I can tell you that. You hear me? I did not kill her. I did not rape her. I——"

"You slept with her on the day she died," I offered.

He shrugged. "I might have, I can't remember. We did it a lot. It all runs together, you know? But *if* I did, it was because she seduced me and I was led astray. I'm weak, but I didn't kill her."

"Did you kill Clyde?" Steve asked. "Nail him up to this tree?"

Steve moved the beam of his light up to the spot where Clyde had hung.

"*No,*" he said, squinting up at the tree. "Of course not. I'm a man of God."

"A man of God with feet of clay who commits sins of the flesh," I said, using his own words against him.

"You're also a handyman. You're about the only one around here who could've done it."

"Well, I didn't," he said. "And anyone who knows me'll tell you I couldn't have."

"Oh, yeah," Steve said. "Why's that?"

"First of all, I would never do anything that mocked my Jesus. I love him too much. And second, if I'd've nailed him up to that tree," he would have never fallen down."

Chapter Sixty

As Steve and I were leaving the abbey to go interview Reid and Richie, Sister Chris stopped us and asked to talk to me. Steve said he'd go talk to Richie's parole officer and get things ready and I could meet him at the station.

When he left, Chris and I stepped into one of the classrooms.

Actually sitting face to face with Sister Chris, I noticed she was much rounder and heavier than she first appeared, and I realized her habit hid her weight well, especially how round and full her pale face was. We were seated in two desks that faced each other.

Before she said anything, I said, "I read about you in Tammy's journal."

I just wanted to see how she responded and what she might say.

"I wondered if she wrote about us," she said, adding with a sheepish wince, "I looked through your room when I heard you had it. I'm sorry. Someone had already been there, because it was a mess."

I nodded.

Unlike the other classrooms, this one had been remodeled, and was now a smart classroom with built-in audio-visual equipment, carpet, new desks, handicap access, and a marker board, the sharp alcohol smell of erasable ink replacing the dull, dusty smell of chalk.

"I'm relieved you know," she said. "I've been tiptoeing around here waiting for this. Now, I'm just glad it's over. Well, not over, but hopefully it's the beginning of the end."

Wondering what she was relieved I knew, I said, "Tell me."

"It wasn't a relationship really. Just sex—especially for her. I wanted more, but she had no interest in me as a person. I was just what was around when Kathryn turned her down."

I nodded, encouraging her to continue.

"I realize it's breaking my vows in a way. It's just . . . I don't think it's a sin. I'm not sure what kind of minister you are, or what you believe, but I don't take the Bible literally. The fact that lesbianism isn't even addressed in scripture gives us some insight into the bias of the writers and their male-dominated worldview. The few times where homosexuality is mentioned, I think it's either an example of what the writer considers wrong or it's talking about things that would be wrong in heterosexual relationships too. Anyway, since I don't see it as sin, I don't think abstinence should be one of our vows. I'm certain I'm called to be a bride of Christ, so since my choice was between following my vocation without keeping all of my vows or not making any vows but not following my vocation, I chose the former."

I nodded my understanding.

"It's not like I've had a string of lovers, but God made me a sexual being just as much as he made me an intellectual and spiritual one, so I've never been completely abstinent either. I knew Tammy was troubled and I shouldn't get involved with her, but she was so . . . anyway, I found it very difficult to resist. Also, and I know how lame this sounds, I thought I might be able to help her."

"I've been guilty of thinking the same thing before," I said.

She smiled, her pale, full-moon face seeming to grow even larger. "Of course, Kathryn doesn't need helping, does she?"

My face must've registered my surprise, because she quickly added, "Everybody knows you two have hit it off."

"You're right," I said, "she certainly doesn't need rescuing or saving."

"It feels so good to be able to talk to someone about this," she said. "Especially someone so understanding. I've been so sad and had to keep it bottled up so tightly."

"I was wondering why you were being so open and honest with me."

"I've been so preoccupied with it that I haven't been myself. There's something I've been needing to tell someone, but just haven't been able to muster up the strength."

"What is it?"

"I heard you guys have Ralph Reid in custody."

I nodded. "Steve does. I don't have anybody in anything."

"Do you think he killed Tammy?"

"Why do you ask?"

"I didn't have anything to do with it. I loved her. I couldn't hurt her. I actually hoped once she was free we might actually have a real relationship."

"You knew about the exorcism?" I asked.

She nodded. "I was one of Father Thomas's prayer warriors. I was shut up in my room praying while she was being killed."

"So you didn't see anyone out and about that night?"

She shook her head.

We were silent a moment.

"I wish I would've believed her. She just always had some drama going and told so many lies. I don't know. I just didn't believe her."

"About what?"

"Not long ago she thought someone raped her," she said.

"*Thought?*"

She nodded. "She was unconscious at the time. That was the other thing that made it even harder for me to believe. She couldn't say for certain, but she knew. I mean, there was no way she could prove it, but she was convinced. She was certain who did it too."

"Reid?"

"He drugged her. Talked her into meeting him for a drink, said he had some family business to discuss with her. Told her he could make her a very rich woman. She met him, had one drink, and the next thing she could remember was waking up in her bed the next morning. She was fully dressed—even had her shoes on, but he missed a button, and he was rough with her. She felt it. And she could smell him on her."

No wonder he had taken such extreme measures to get Tammy's journal. If she wrote in it about what he had done, he would not only be implicated in her rape, but become the prime suspect in her murder.

"Did she report it?"

"Who would believe *her*? She had a reputation, you know? And it was well deserved. *I* even had a hard time believing her. But spreading your legs because you want to and having someone spread them when you can't stop them are two very different things."

Chapter Sixty-one

"I think Reid may have raped your cousin," I said.

Eyes narrowing, teeth clenching, jaw flexing, Steve's face flushed with anger. "If he did, he's a dead motherfucker."

I knew how he felt. There was something about rape that seemed even worse than murder.

I told him what Chris had told me.

"Son of a bitch," he said. "Why didn't she come to me?"

It was a good question, and one I'd have asked if she were my cousin, but now was not the time, and there would never be an adequate answer.

"She wasn't in a good way," I said. "I don't think she had been for a long time."

He nodded. "Thanks."

I patted him on the shoulder. "You okay?"

"I will be. A little time alone with Reid should start me in the right direction."

The first thing Steve did when he walked into the cell was take out his gun.

Pulling the slide back and jacking a round into the chamber, he pressed the pistol into Reid's forehead as he pushed him to the back of the cell.

Cowering in the corner, Reid's face was contorted in fear, and he looked like he was about to cry.

"Different rules today, Ralph. You lie to me today, you die. It's just that simple. Understand?"

Reid nodded slightly and slowly, unable to move much because of the barrel pinning him to the wall.

The holding cell we were in was large and the only one in this part of the building. No one could see us. No one could hear us. No matter what happened, there would be no witnesses.

"I'm gonna start out with an easy one, one that you shouldn't mind answering truthfully, okay?"

"Okay," he said, his voice soft and squeaky.

"Have you ever had sex with my cousin?"

Reid seemed to relax a little, his eyes squinting a little less, his shoulders dropping a fraction.

Nodding the best he could, he said, "Yes. Yes I have."

"Was she conscious at the time?"

I could see it in his face. He knew he was a dead man.

For a long moment, he didn't say anything.

"Ralph," Steve said, "was she conscious? Did she consent?"

He didn't say anything. Didn't move a single muscle, unless his heart was still beating, but I couldn't be certain of that.

"Refusing to answer is the same as lying, Ralph," Steve said. "And both result in the same thing. Your death. Do you under—"

"Please don't kill me, Steve," he said in the pathetic voice of a bully and a coward who knows he can't escape the fate he created for himself.

"Last chance," Steve said. "Did she consent? Was she conscious?"

"No," he said so softly it was nearly inaudible. "Steve, I swear to God, it was just the one time. I never touched her again. I didn't go anywhere near her the night she was killed."

"Well, DNA'll tell us soon enough."

"I swear it's the truth."

"But so is the fact that you raped her," he said.

"Oh, God, Steve, I'm so sorry. I was out of my mind. She was torturing me. Sleeping with everybody *but* me. She knew what she was doing. I just went crazy. I'm sorry. Please don't . . ."

"'Please don't' . . . that's what Tammy would've said if she had been able to, but you made sure she wasn't."

"I know what I did was wrong and I deeply regret it, but she was a very sick person. I read her diary before it was destroyed and let me tell you . . . You don't want the world to know what she did, what kind of person she was."

"Listen to me you piece of shit—"

"Steve, she killed Tommy. She drowned him at the marina. Held him down until he was dead. I think Father Thomas was right. She was possessed. She had super human strength. She killed him. She did it for fun. She said so in her diary. I tore the page out before the goons destroyed it. But the world never has to know. Do you understand what I'm saying? I can prove she was a murderer, but I won't."

"You're trying to blackmail me?"

"No. Of course not. I'm just saying no one has to know. Please."

"What'd you use on her? GHB?"

"Please, Steve," Reid pleaded. "Please don't."

"Don't what?" Steve asked.

"You know," he said.

"Say it."

"Please don't kill me."

"Did you kill her because she figured out what you had done to her?" Steve asked. "Because you knew what I'd do to you when I found out?"

"I didn't kill her. I swear to God."

"But you were going to kill Kathryn."

He started to say something but stopped.

"You had her tied up at the mill. You were going to let her explode into a million pieces, you psycho son of a bitch."

"I had nothing to do with that. I swear it."

"Lie to me again and see if I don't cover that wall with your diseased brain."

"I—"

He stopped as one of Steve's officers came to the cell door and called to him.

"Go away," Steve said. "Whatever it is, it can wait."

"No it can't, sir," he said. "I wouldn't interrupt you if it could."

Steve let out a mean laugh and shook his head. Easing the hammer down and holstering his gun, he said to Reid, "He just bought you a few more minutes of life. Use it wisely. Make peace with your maker."

After Steve had gone and Reid and I were alone in the cell, he said, "You gonna let him kill me?"

"What can I do?" I asked. "I'm just one guy."

"Whatta you—"

"That's what one of the girls in town was saying about stopping the way in which the Gulf Coast Company is gonna rape our land."

"What does that have to do with—"

"You corporate rapists are so used to doing whatever the hell you want and having the government and everyone else just wink and hold out their hands, that you think you can do anything anytime. And most of the time you're right. But not this time. Try offering Steve some of your precious money to forget about the fact that you raped his cousin."

His eyes grew wide as he heard Steve's footsteps coming down the stairs.

When Steve entered the room, he motioned me over to him. Walking out of the cell and closing the door, I joined him over at the bottom of the stairs.

"Come on," he said.

"What?" I asked. "Where?"

"Father Thomas just confessed."

Chapter Sixty-two

"I would've confessed sooner, but I didn't realize what I'd done," Father Thomas said.

"What do you mean?" I asked.

We were in Steve's office. Steve was seated behind his desk. I was leaning on a filing cabinet in the corner behind him. Father Thomas was seated in one of the two chairs in front of the desk. Two walls of Steve's office were mostly glass, but the blinds were down. So were the blinds on the door, and it was closed.

"Until I was delivered, I was deceived," he said. "It had me blinded, my memory blacked out."

"I don't understand," I said.

"The exorcism worked after all," he said.

Most of what was in Steve's office looked to have been chosen by an amateur decorator—probably a girlfriend. The black-and-gray furniture was modern and sleek and comfortable, but didn't seem to reflect Steve's personality or sensibilities. A laptop on his desk was closed and held a light covering of dust. Everything around it was neat, orderly, and symmetrical.

"It came out of her," Father Thomas continued. "I just didn't realize it until today."

"Realize what?" I asked.

"When the demon left Tammy, it came into me. In the clearing—I wasn't knocked unconscious, I was possessed. The wickedness flew right out of her and right into me. Knocked me down. And when she came over to check on me, I grabbed her and I killed her—well, the ancient evil that was in me did, but I'm still responsible. I did it. I killed her. Steve, I'm so sorry. Please just believe I didn't know what I was doing."

"Do you remember killing her, Father?" Steve asked. "I mean, actually remember doing it, how you did it? Everything?"

He thought about it, rubbing his beard with his thumb and forefinger as he did. Finally, he nodded. "I wish to God I didn't, but I do. I didn't—not until I was delivered. Now that the demon's gone I can remember everything."

Looking away from Father Thomas, I studied the only thing in the office that spoke of Steve. To my right, a large trophy case covered most of one wall. It was filled with pictures and plaques from Steve's career in law enforcement and several marksmen trophies from shooting competitions he had dominated.

When I looked back at Father Thomas, I saw a pale, frail man whose life was being measured in days instead of decades, whose time was spent in moments and memories rather than hope and plans.

"What about Clyde?" I said. "There's no way you could've lifted him up, let alone held him and nailed him into place."

"No, but the demonic presence *inside* me could have," he said. "I had superhuman strength. Don't you see? I was just the vessel, the incarnated. I was possessed, and in that condition, under that power, I had the strength of ten men."

"Father, are you sure about this?" Steve asked. "You can't take it back later."

"I'm sure," he said. "I'm a killer and I deserve to be punished. I just want to make sure my actions are seen as entirely my own and don't reflect badly on the Christian faith, the Catholic church, or St. Ann's."

"But you're saying your actions weren't your own," I said. "If the demon made you do it, that's the same as not guilty by reason of insanity."

"It's not a defense. I don't plan to offer any. Before a judge and jury I'll confess my guilt, but I wanted you two to know, especially you, Steve, what really happened. Not as an excuse, but an explanation."

"Still sounds like to me you're saying you're not responsible," Steve said.

"I'm saying I am. If there hadn't been room in me, the demon could've never come in. No, I'm as guilty as sin. Why do you think all the evidence points to me?"

Steve tilted his head and looked up at me. His expression said the priest had a point.

"Hold that thought a minute," I said. "We need to confirm something. We'll be right back."

"Sure," Father Thomas said, "take your time."

I started out of the room and Steve followed.

"And Steve," Father Thomas said as he reached the door, "I'm so, so sorry. I wish I could take it back."

In the squad room outside his office, Steve said, "What is it?"

"I want us to talk to Richie before we go any further with Father Thomas."

The squad room was empty except for a uniformed officer pecking on a typewriter at a desk in the back. He was a large man with wiry gray hair and a brown mustache. Though he was obviously not very fast with his two fingers to begin with, I could tell he slowed the pace of his pecking in an attempt to overhear us.

"Everything okay, Chief?" he asked.

"Fine, Wade."

"Need anything?"

Steve shook his head, then lowering his voice, asked, "Whatta you think of Father Tom's confession?"

I shrugged. "Don't know. I'm finding it hard to swallow."

He frowned and shook his head, then narrowing his gaze at me, said, "Could it be because you'd rather it be someone else? Or you wanted to uncover more evidence, make more amazing deductions, that kind of thing?"

"Could be. I don't know. But I'm having more trouble believing he crucified Clyde than he killed Tammy."

"I mean, all the evidence says he did it," he said. "Now we have a nice corroborating confession."

I shrugged and shook my head.

"What about what Reid said? You believe Tammy killed Tommy?"

I shrugged again. "I think it's possible."

"But?"

"No but, just . . . I don't think we'll ever know for sure. And

it's not just the nature of drownings. It's this case. I'm afraid there's
so much we'll never know."

"Do you believe he had nothing to do with the attempt on
Kathryn?"

"No. Though he may not have been involved directly. Order
probably came from higher up in the company. He really does just
seem like a drone."

"Why? Why try to kill her?"

I told him.

He looked weak and pale when I finished, his pallor pasty and
green-tinged.

"Goddamn," he said. "Kathryn's my fuckin' cousin? You
sure? Fuck."

We were quiet a long moment.

"Somehow Reid or someone from the Gulf Coast Company
found out—maybe it was in Tammy's diary. One of the signs of
possession is having knowledge you shouldn't have. Or maybe she
found out the old fashion way. Or maybe Reid or the company did."

"How long you known?"

"Not long."

"You wait to tell me 'cause you still suspect me?"

I didn't respond right away and we were silent a moment.

"You okay?" I asked.

"Will be."

"You sure?"

He nodded. "Wade," he said, turning toward him, "keep an
eye on Father Thomas for me."

"Sure thing, boss."

We walked through the squad room and down the hallway to
the interrogation room. When we reached it, he held out his hand as
if ushering me in. We walked inside, and the uniform who had been
watching Richie walked out and closed the door.

Chapter Sixty-three

I held up my phone as I walked in the room.

"We got a witness," I said. "Any minute the cop interviewing her is gonna call, and then you're done."

"I want a lawyer," Richie said.

Steve let out a low, mean laugh. "I want a world without rapists and murderers and thieves. Looks like neither of us are gonna get what we want today."

"But I have a constitutional right—"

"John here warned me this case was too personal for me, but I didn't listen. I knew I could maintain objectivity and professionalism. Truth is, I have until now. But it's not working so well and I'm havin' a little bit of a meltdown, so you know what I say? I say fuck it. If you cocksuckers aren't gonna play by the rules, how can I hope to catch you if I do?"

By the time Steve had finished his rant, Richie had grown very still and very quiet, and his eyes were full of fear.

"You ready to answer some questions?" Steve asked.

He nodded his head very slowly.

"Why were you running away from the abbey?"

"I got scared," he said. "I figured before it was all over y'all'd blame all this shit on me."

"You got scared."

It was a statement not a question, and Richie went with his right to remain silent.

"I knew we'd find a connection between you and Clyde,"

Steve said, tapping the file folder on the table in front of him.

Richie seemed to implode, sinking in on himself with nothing inside any longer to hold him up. As if actually shrinking, he didn't seem nearly as tall as he had before.

"We know you two were arrested together a couple of times. Used to have a lucrative drug business, but you had a falling out."

"They say if you can't stand the heat, get out of the kitchen," Richie said, seeming to regain some of his fight. "That's what I was doing. That's *all* I was doing. It had nothing to do with Clyde—'cept somebody killed him and I didn't want the same thing to happen to me. That, or you'd find the connection and jump to conclusions—just like you're doing."

"And you weren't running before we got evidence back from the lab?"

His eyes widened ever so slightly, but he recovered well, and I wondered if Steve had noticed it.

Steve shook his head in frustration.

Beneath the table, I reached into my pocket and pushed a button on my cell phone that made it ring. I then pulled it out and pretended to answer it.

"Really?" I asked, looking at Richie. "Are you serious? Yeah. We'll be right there."

Richie's expression let me know he was curious.

"What is it?" Steve asked.

"Come on," I said.

We stood and started to leave the room.

"What is it?" Richie asked.

"Witness is righteous," I said. "Says she saw what you did. We'll be back as soon as we get and verify her statement."

We turned to leave again, this time taking a step or two.

"Wait," he said.

We continued to walk.

"Wait," he said. "Wait. Give me a chance to explain. I can tell you exactly what happened."

"We know what happened," I said.

"But let me explain," he said. "You don't understand why I—"

We walked out and closed the door.

Outside in the hallway, Steve's expression asked the question.

I shook my head.

"Nice," Steve said. "You're a very convincing liar."

"Comes from years of practice."

Chapter Sixty-four

"We have an eyewitness who saw you crucifying Clyde," I lied.

The color drained from Richie's face.

"Shit, man, I was afraid of that," he said. "Listen, you gotta believe me. I didn't kill him. I swear to God. I didn't kill him."

His words rushed out as if escaping from prison. His movements were jerky, his hands jittery.

"You saying you didn't nail him to that tree?" I said.

"No," he said, "I'm saying he was already dead when I did. He OD'd, man, I swear. On his own. I had nothing to do with it. He came to see if I'd handle his action while he was away. Said he had to get out of town, but I told him I couldn't. I wasn't goin' to prison again. I think his plan was to get me high and convince me. We went down to the boathouse and hung out. I did some shit, you know, just to be sociable, but he got all serious with it. Broke down about Tammy, said she was the best thing that ever happened to him. She was going to be rich—his one shot at a decent life. Anyway, he kept on pumping shit into his arm and sucking it down his mouth and snorting it up his nose until he just fell over. I swear that's the truth and I'll take a lie detector test to prove it. Strap it on me. Give me a drug charge. Violate me back to prison, but don't charge me with murder. I didn't kill nobody. I swear."

I wanted to tell him to settle down, to relax, but that's not what we needed, and I wondered, not for the first time, at how often my two vocations conflicted with each other. Richie needed pastoring, but we needed the truth.

"So why crucify him?" Steve asked.

"With all the spooky shit goin' on, I figured everybody'd buy it—at least for a while. Distract everyone long enough for me to get away."

"It was just a *diversion?*" Steve asked.

He nodded.

"Did you have help?" I asked.

He shook his head.

"Then how the hell'd you do it?"

"With a pulley. Threw a rope with a pulley on it over a branch and hoisted him up. I had already nailed him to the board. Wasn't hard at all. Hell, if I'd been a little less shit-faced I couldda done it a lot quicker."

I nodded. I was satisfied. I looked at Steve. He seemed to be too. We both stood at the same time and headed out of the room.

"It's the truth," Richie said. "I swear it. Strap me to the machine and I'll prove it."

Before I stepped out of the room, I turned and said, "Since you're telling the whole truth and nothing but these days, tell me this: Did you have sex with Tammy the night she died?"

He glanced at Steve, then back at me and nodded. "We had a go right before dinner—but only because she wanted to. I didn't force her. And I didn't kill her. I swear."

Chapter Sixty-five

"Father, we know you didn't kill Clyde," I said.

His eyes narrowed and his forehead furrowed. He started to say something, but stopped and shook his head. "Are you sure?"

I nodded.

"I thought for sure I did," he said. "After I killed Tammy I knew I was capable of it, and I knew there was nothing the demon would like more than mocking Christ."

I was half sitting on the front edge of Steve's desk, directly across from Father Thomas. Steve was standing to my right close to his trophies.

"Maybe you didn't kill Tammy either," I said. "I think you need to reconsider your confession. Wait until we can finish our investigation."

"I wasn't sure about Clyde, but I am about Tammy. I'm certain I killed her. There's no doubt in my mind whatsoever." He looked up at Steve. "I'm so sorry. I didn't mean to—I mean, it was the demon. I know I'm still responsible, but I just wanted you to know, I never would have otherwise. I'm just so sorry for what I've done, not only to her, but to your whole family."

Steve nodded and patted him on the back. "It's okay, Father. I understand."

"I'm just not convinced you did it," I said.

"Well, I don't know what I can do to convince you," he said. "Is there anything to say I didn't?"

He looked from Steve to me and back to Steve. We both

shook our heads.

"I know you don't want to believe it about me," he said, "but it's the truth. I just wanted to explain why. I won't offer any explanation to anyone else, just an apology and plea for forgiveness."

He stood, turned, and Steve began to cuff him.

"But Father—"

"John," Steve said. "He's our man. We would've had to arrest him sooner or later anyway—on the physical evidence alone. Think about it. Come on now, let it go. Don't make this any more difficult than it has to be."

Chapter Sixty-six

That night Father Thomas died in one of Steve's jail cells.

The ME ruled it death from natural causes—though he noted in the strictest sense of the word there was nothing natural about cancer—but I would always wonder.

Three days later, Father Thomas was lowered into the ground in a small ceremony before a small crowd. Like most of us, he had lived a little life in obscurity—something that was made manifest nowhere more than in the smallness of the final farewell being bid him.

Sister Abigail had asked me to say a prayer, and I stumbled through it the best I could.

Afterward, she was crying so hard when I hugged her that she couldn't say anything but "Thank you, John."

Kathryn, though just as upset, was less demonstrative.

"I'm sorry," I said as I hugged her.

The graveside was cold and windy, and as our faces touched they were too numb to feel.

"Because he died or because you helped arrest him?" she asked.

Stunned, I remained silent.

"That was a cheap shot, I know," she said, "but it's the way I'm feeling right now."

I nodded.

"He didn't deserve to die the way he did," she said. "He was a good man who spent his entire life helping people. He was noble and honorable and" —she began to cry— "so very, very kind."

Too cold to linger, most of the attendees had dispersed by now. Only Steve and Sister Abigail remained, but they weren't speaking.

Without saying anything else, she turned and joined Sister Abigail, and the two of them walked with their arms around each other back to Kathryn's car and drove away, leaving me to catch a ride with Steve.

Chapter Sixty-seven

"So you're closing the case?" I asked.

Steve nodded.

He was driving faster than he should have, and I wondered if he was trying to put as much distance between himself and death as he possibly could.

"Too much physical evidence not to," he said. "And with his confession, it's ironclad."

I shook my head.

"Give me one thing. One shred of evidence that says he didn't do it, and I'll keep it open."

The early afternoon sun made the Explorer hot, especially in our coats, but he didn't turn on the air conditioner. The sky was clear, the air clean and crisp, the woods on either side of the road quiet and peaceful.

"You gonna be able to make a case against Reid?"

He nodded.

"Think you'll be able to show any Gulf Coast Company involvement?"

He shook his head. "But they're not gonna get the abbey. That's something."

"Yes it is."

We rode along in silence for a few moments.

"You know what?" he said. "I believed Father Tom's confession. I think it *was* him. Now I still don't know about all this demon shit, but I *do* know the truth when I hear it from a witness or a suspect *and* can see it in the evidence."

I shook my head. "He dies the night he confesses."

"Maybe that's why he confessed. Knew his time was almost up. He wanted to make things right before he died. I shouldn't have to tell you something like that."

I shrugged. "It's possible. I guess—I don't know. Can I see the autopsy report?"

"Of course. What? You think I'm lying? You think I killed him to cover up something?" He shook his head. "I'm not hiding anything, John. Father Tom was our doer."

"What about Tommy?" I asked. "You believe Reid?"

"Says he's gonna produce the diary page for me, but I'm ruling it an accidental drowning. There's nothing to suggest anything else. We've carried the case as far as we can. Now it's time to let it go."

"You seem anxious to do that with all the cases."

"Fuck you, John," he said.

"I'm just saying."

"So am I," he said. "Fuck you."

"Sort of touchy about it, aren't you?"

"You've been accusing me in one way or another since this thing started and I'm sick of it."

He turned off the highway into the entrance of St. Ann's, passing beneath the sensor lights Brad Harrison had installed on the gates. Everything was quiet and serene, as if the abbey had never witnessed a single act of violence.

"You would've done the same thing if our positions were reversed," I said.

He took a deep breath and sighed, softening a bit as he did.

"This is good for you," he said. "A valuable life lesson. Everything can't be wrapped up in a nice, neat little package. This kind of thing forces you to face your limitations. Be a man about it. Quit pouting. Learn your lesson. Move on."

He pulled up near the dining hall where everyone had gathered to eat and celebrate the life of a man they all loved and respected.

"Yes, sir," I said, and saluted him.

He saluted back, but when he brought his hand down he gave me the finger.

I looked at the dining hall. Through the glass door I could see the small group awkwardly gathered around a large picture of Father Thomas, their nervous body language betraying their relaxed, supportive expressions. Not only were they in shock and filled with grief, but they were left with many unanswered questions.

"You going in?" I asked.

He shook his head.

"It'll be far more comfortable for them if I don't," he said.

"You sure have been understanding, even sympathetic to the memory of the man you say killed your cousin."

"What's that supposed to mean?" he asked, his anger flaring up again.

I shook my head at him. "Just that you're as welcome in there as anyone."

"Oh," he said. "Well, I just can't."

We were quiet a moment, and I looked down at the lake. Its windswept surface rippled like a miniature ocean seen from high above.

"Like you, I'll keep my eyes open," he said. "The case is officially closed, but that doesn't mean I won't still poke around in it for a long time to come. All this ain't over. The Gulf Coast Company's not gonna give up on this land without a lot more fight. And if Uncle Floyd had a daughter, I'd like to find her."

That's when it hit me. That's why Father Thomas had confessed. He had done it to protect Kathryn, to save the abbey.

As I got out of the Explorer, Kathryn came to the door and waved us in.

"Come on in and get some food," she said.

"No thanks," Steve said. "I've got to get back to the station."

We shook hands, I closed the door, and he pulled away.

"John?" she asked.

I shook my head.

"I'm sorry for how I acted," she said. "I was just upset."

I waved off her apology.

"What is it?" she asked. "What's wrong?"

Chapter Sixty-eight

"So this is our last session together?" Sister Abigail said.

"I'm leaving," I said, "but I'll be back."

"Not exactly what I asked, was it?"

"Yes," I said, "this will be our last."

"I'll miss them. I haven't felt the need to keep the clinical distance with you I normally do, and I've come to care very deeply for you."

"Same here."

"We've been through it these last few days," she said.

"You've helped me," I said. "A lot."

"I'm glad," she said. "But I seriously doubt I've done much. So what shall be the subject of our final session?"

"Truth," I said.

"Have you not been completely truthful with me, John?" she asked.

"Yes, to the best of my ability, I have," I said. "But you, on the other hand, haven't been completely truthful with me."

She looked surprised. "I haven't really said much. This is about you, not me, but I honestly don't think I've been dishonest."

"You know what I'm talking about, Sister. You're far too clever not to."

"You're the one who's too clever. You've completely lost me."

I leaned to the side, stretched my leg out, and withdrew the photocopy of Floyd's medical information from my pocket. "I think this is why Father Thomas went ahead and confessed."

She looked perplexed. "What's this?"

I handed it to her. She took it and gave it a cursory glance.

"Floyd's blood type is O negative," I said.

She shrugged. "Is it?"

I nodded. "Yours is A negative."

She nodded, attempting but failing to pull off nonchalance. Her movements were stiff, her expression plastered into place.

"Kathryn's is AB positive."

"Is it?" she asked, her voice tight, her face pinched.

"It is," I said, "which means there's no way he's Kathryn's father. Father Thomas on the other hand is B positive."

"Is he?"

"Kathryn was his child," I said.

Tears began to stream down her face. "I still can't believe he's dead."

"You haven't just been a mother and a father to Kathryn," I said, "you've been husband and wife to each other. You really have been a family—naturally as well as spiritually. Someone said it was rumored you two used to be an item and I watched the way you took care of him when he heard about Tommy. You're the only one who called him Tom and of course you fought like an old married couple."

She smiled, wiping her tears and sniffling. "I guess we did," she said, her voice softer now. "In a way, we've had it all here. It's why we love it so much."

I nodded. "And why you've gone to such lengths to protect it."

She nodded her agreement. "Tom's confession protected both Kathryn and the abbey," she said. "It was something he felt he had to do. If the investigation continued, everyone would know about us, about Kathryn, and about Floyd not being her father. Not only would the abbey close, but she would lose everything."

I thought about what she had said.

"Are you going to tell her?"

"Who?" I asked.

"Kathryn," she said.

"About what?"

"Tom being her father."

"I told you this was about truth. I think no matter how

painful it is, knowing the truth is better than not knowing it, but I'm gonna let you tell her."

"What if I—"

"Tell me about Floyd," I said.

She hesitated. "I can't imagine what you must think of me. It's just like I told you, except when we had our one night together, I was already pregnant with Kathryn."

"I'm surprised he didn't demand a paternity test."

She choked up again. "He trusted me," she said, her voice trembling. She then let out a harsh, ironic laugh. "That's what makes it a double sin. He just wanted it to go away."

I waited while she pulled herself together.

"It's painful to be confronted with what you're capable of," she said. "I feel so bad about what I did. It was horrible. Unforgivable. But if I had to, I know I'd probably do it again. I now know what I'm capable of. Of course, the truth is, what I was asking for and what he gave wasn't much—to him I mean. At the time, the land, though beautiful, was some of the least valuable he had, and he had money to burn. The trust was basically some of the interest he was earning on just some of his money."

When I didn't say anything, she glanced at her watch. "Our time is almost over and I've done most of the talking today."

"Still haven't told the whole truth yet."

She looked surprised and offended in equal parts. "What do you mean?"

"I'm talking about Tammy," I said.

"You've lost me again."

"Oh, I don't think so, but we can go through the same routine as before. She was here to shut you down. She knew what this land was worth and she came to figure out a way to get it."

"I don't doubt that."

"And you killed her."

"*What?*" she asked in shock.

"The truth," I said. "What you're capable of. What lengths you'll go to, to protect Father Thomas, Kathryn, and St. Ann's."

"Tom already told y'all," she said. "The demon did it."

"He was far too experienced an exorcist to try to perform one alone. Even if he suspected she might be faking, he wouldn't really know until he began the ritual. Every exorcist I read about in the books he gave me said they always use a team. Father Thomas did too. He had people praying—Sister Chris and Brad Harrison that I know of—and he had you in the room with him."

She started to say something, but couldn't get it out. She began to shake.

"When I saw the tape, I thought someone came in during the exorcism and turned off the camera," I said. "But later I realized, when it came on, Father Thomas was on the other side of the room. You turned it on for him too. You were there the entire time, assisting with the ritual."

I paused, but she didn't say anything. Tears were streaming down her cheeks again, tremors running through her body.

"Of course, I can't know what happened after you turned off the tape, but I bet she began to reveal her plans for St. Ann's, began telling you all she'd discovered."

She sighed heavily, seeming to begin to slow her implosion. As if finally surrendering, her guard came down, her face registering her resolve. "She really was possessed. One of the signs is revealing hidden things. She revealed it all. Knew everything—and it wasn't the result of research. She knew things no one did, things we'd said, things we'd done, things I hadn't thought of in decades."

I nodded, but didn't say anything.

"Tom didn't even know I killed her. Though, I think he began to suspect. I know it's a big part of why he confessed. It happened like he said. She broke free and ran down the path. He followed her. I was much slower than them. I started for help, but thought she might say some of the things she had said to us in front of them, so I stopped and went after them. When I got to the clearing, Tom was unconscious and Tammy was lying across the way bleeding to death. I could tell she was dying. It was only in that moment that I knew I'd let her."

"What'd you do?"

"Nothing at first. I was just going to do nothing, commit a sin of omission. Wait and let her die, but then I panicked when I heard noises at the cabins. My maternal instinct kicked in like you can't imagine. Don't ever underestimate what a mother's capable of. I knelt down beside her, cupped one hand over her mouth and pinched her nose with my other one. She was gone within minutes."

Sister Abigail's voice had become flat, almost robotic,

as if she were recounting a story she had heard many times and memorized, something that had nothing to do with her.

"When I heard voices on the path, I went to hide down by the waterway, but when I got down there and saw the boat, I got in it and paddled back up to the dock and ran to my room. I got in just before Kathryn came to my door."

I nodded, thinking about the ways her story differed from what I had imagined.

"She would've died anyway. You can't imagine what that thing had done to her. All I did was rush it along a little. That doesn't make it any less wrong. I'm truly sorry for what I did. I am, but she would have died either way."

"Neither you or Father Thomas caused any of her injuries?" I asked.

She shook her head. "Tom may have inadvertently, trying to restrain her, but no, we didn't hurt her."

I wasn't sure I believed her, but I'd never know for sure. It was like Tommy's death and the whole question of possession. There were many mysteries I would never solve, and learning to live with that was part of the lesson I was meant to learn and it was humbling.

"It feels so good to tell someone," she said. "The past few days have been the worst of my entire life. Whatta you gonna do?"

"Let you tell Kathryn, then Steve."

"What if I can't?"

"You can."

"How do you know?"

I smiled. "I know your strength. I know what you're capable of."

Chapter Sixty-nine

Later that afternoon, I found Kathryn down by the lake. She now knew the truth. Any innocence she'd had left was long gone. Sister Abigail had told her everything, just before confessing to Steve.

I stood beside her for a long time without speaking. I didn't know what to say.

After a while, I said, "I'm sorry."

"It's a lot to take in," she said.

"I know."

I was having difficulty taking in certain things myself.

I guess I'd never know exactly what happened to Tammy. I had seen and I had heard—video footage and confessions—but neither had helped a whole lot. Something profoundly mysterious had happened, and it wasn't as simple as who killed whom—of course no mystery ever is. There's always the why. Even when we know the who and the what, we rarely know the why—not really, not fully—not even the murderer knows that. We know why they and psychiatry and religion and philosophy say they did it, but all fall short of giving us true understanding and insight into the deep, dark mystery of a murderous heart.

"I'm not sure how to feel," she said. "The truth is, I don't feel much of anything."

"Your mind's just protecting your heart—the way it does your body when it's in severe pain. It's actually a grace. You'll feel again. And whenever you do and whatever you feel will be fine. Right now, you're just numbed a little by shock."

"When I think about how much they both love me—" she began, but broke off and let it hang in the air. "But when I think about what she did . . ."

I wasn't present when Sister Abigail had told her what she did, but if it was anything like what she shared with me, I had no doubt she would understand in time.

"She didn't come out and say it," she said, "but I know she did what she did for me."

I nodded, but didn't say anything.

"I get sick just thinking about that."

"Our motivations for mundane things are complex, but for something like this, they're unimaginable. It wasn't just for you."

"I thought I knew her," she said. "I thought . . . Now I wonder if I know anything at all. It's just so . . ."

"I know."

I thought about how little I knew about what had really happened. I had no way of knowing if Tommy's death was anything other than what it was officially believed to be, though I thought it likely Tammy did kill him. I knew far less about the mystery of possession and exorcism than when I had arrived. I didn't know what would happen to Sister Abigail or St. Ann's. The one thing I did know was that I didn't know, that the universe was a profoundly mysterious place, far beyond anything I had ever thought or imagined.

She turned to me and touched my face. "I'm sorry for the way I've treated you."

I thought about all we had shared, the way in which the Mystery had revealed herself to me through this lovely woman. She had been the conduit for an intense sexual-spiritual encounter, but like all graces God uses in our lives, she was the vessel, the sign pointing me beyond her to the boundless beyond. As grateful as I was to her, I wasn't about to make an idol out of her. She was a gift—one I was thankful for, but my most focused attention and adoration was reserved for the giver.

"You don't have anything to apologize for. I'm sorry. Sorry that I left you. I truly thought you were safe there. Sorry for what you went through at the mill. Sorry for all you've found out about your family—and I'm very sorry you lost your father."

"I can't even think about us right now."

"I know."

"But when I've had time to process all this—"

I nodded, but didn't say anything, just let it be there between us, pregnant with possibility.

Dropping her hand from my face, she shook her head and let out a long sigh. "I just found them and I've already lost my dad. Now, I'll be losing my mom soon."

She began to cry.

I put my arms around her and held her.

After a long moment, she looked up at me and asked, "What's going to happen?"

I smiled and shook my head. "I have no idea, but anything's possible. I'm convinced of that now more than ever before."

After Kathryn had gone, I stood staring at the lake for a long time, preparing to depart, ready to get away, but in some ways not wanting to leave.

In homicide investigations, as in religion—or life for that matter—we know so little compared to what we think we do, and we understand even less. There's a reason why they're called mysteries. And just because we happen to discover who committed the crime doesn't mean we really understand much about it. This was nowhere more true than in Tammy's case.

I had watched and heard as Tammy displayed superhuman strength, revealed things she couldn't possibly have known, spoke in languages she didn't know. What did it mean? Were they signs of demonic possession? Or was there some other more scientific explanation? Was what was revealed the presence of unseen spirits or the unlocked potential of a dark, mostly unused part of the human mind? Not only did I not know, I seriously doubted I ever would.

Could I live with that? What other choice did I have? It wasn't likely to change, but then, neither was I. I'd continue to investigate and continue to be baffled and humbled and surprised and in awe of life and the Great Mystery who created it, who sustains it, who *is* it. What else could I do? I had a strong suspicion that's what she created me for. And perhaps I could learn to do it with more peace. Perhaps I could do my work and step back as Sister had suggested, letting go of my attachment to the outcome and the angst that goes with it.

I wasn't sure how long I had been there like that when Steve walked up.

"I've finished my official report," he said. "Wanted to run it past you to make sure you don't have any problems with it. I don't want FDLE knocking on my door one day soon because you tell them you have questions about my investigation."

I shook my head. "They won't."

"I don't want to, but I don't have a choice. I'm charging Father Thomas with Tammy's death."

I turned and looked at him in surprise.

"You got a problem with that?"

"Yeah. I do. We don't get to decide what to do with the guilty."

"We?"

"Investigators. We don't get to punish or exonerate. Only investigate. We'd have too much power otherwise."

"I know that, but . . . just this one time."

"You know how many times I've wanted to—how many times I told myself I would just do it the one time?"

"Have you ever . . ."

I nodded. "Stone Cold Killer case in Atlanta. It's one of the reasons I quit the cops."

We were quiet a long moment.

And, as usual, I recalled the recurring nightmare.

In it, I'm running up Stone Mountain, my heart slamming against my breast bone from exertion and the fear of what I'd find when I reached the top. I'm weary and unsteady, a mixed drink of bone-tired fatigue, mental exhaustion, and vodka coursing through my veins. Still I run as fast as I can, but I'm too late. When I reach the top, he releases her, and her body slides down the cold solid granite, following its contours like a tear in the crevices of a wrinkled face.

"I killed a serial killer," I said finally. "A very, very long time ago now. And not a day goes by I don't regret it."

"I'm not charging her mom," he said. "What're you going to do?"

"Stand back."

"Huh?"

"I told you I wouldn't contact FDLE. You know what I think you should do. You know why. What you do is up to you."

"There's been enough lives lost," he said.

"That mean Ralph Reid's safe?"

"I'm talking about human life," he said.

I shot him a look.

"I'm not gonna take him out. I'm not."

I nodded.

"So . . . you can reverse your collar and let what Sister Abigail told you be a sealed confession."

I was conflicted about his decision, wishing there was a solution that would allow for both justice and mercy, but I could let it go. At least I was pretty sure I could.

I nodded again.

"I figure if I save her mom's life and her abbey, I might just win her over."

"You deserve her," I said. "I wish you luck. I really do."

"I'm just glad she's not my cousin."

We were quiet a few moments, the cold breeze blowing off the lake stinging our eyes.

"Well," he said, "whatta you waitin' on? The case is over. It's time for you to go home and get on with your life."

"It certainly is," I said. "It most certainly is."

Michael Lister

A native Floridian, award-winning novelist Michael Lister grew up in North Florida near the Gulf of Mexico and the Apalachicola River where most of his books are set.

In the early 90s, Lister became the youngest chaplain within the Florida Department of Corrections—a unique experience that led to his critically acclaimed mystery series featuring prison chaplain John Jordan: POWER IN THE BLOOD, BLOOD OF THE LAMB, FLESH AND BLOOD, THE BODY AND THE BLOOD, and BLOOD SACRIFICE.

Michael won a Florida Book Award for his literary thriller DOUBLE EXPOSURE, a book, according to the *Panama City News Herald*, that "is lyrical and literary, written in a sparse but evocative prose reminiscent of Cormac McCarthy." His other novels include THUNDER BEACH, THE BIG GOODBYE, BUNRT OFFERINGS, SEPARATION ANXIETY, and THE BIG BEYOND.

Michael's "Meaning" books are meditations on how to have the best life possible and include THE MEANING OF LIFE IN MOVIES, THE MEANING OF JESUS, and MEANING EVERY MOMENT.

www.MichaelLister.com

You buy a book.

We plant a tree.

CPSIA information can be obtained at www.ICGtesting.com
Printed in the USA
BVOW07s2146190913

331696BV00001B/31/P